DEATH CHILL

THE JACKIE IN THE BOX MURDERS

DAVID JEWELL

A Wild Wolf Publication

Published by Wild Wolf Publishing in 2024
Copyright © 2024 David Jewell

ISBN: 978-1-907954-87-0
Also available as an E-Book

Cover Photograph: Phil Punton Photography
Additional Graphics: Joseph Punton & Phil Punton

www.wildwolfpublishing.com

Also by the author:

Death Rattle

To Chris and Des Wood… always in my thoughts.

With thanks to all my family and friends too numerous to name, who have constantly been there backing, supporting and putting up with me throughout the long process of writing.

My thanks to the acclaimed crime author Mari Hannah and her partner Mo for their encouragement and support.

Thanks to the acclaimed screenwriters Michael Wilcox and Elliott Kerrigan for their constant encouragement and faith in me.

Thanks to Proof Readers Marion Jewell and Barbara Gorman for their invaluable assistance.

Thanks to Gillian Thomson for her advice concerning up to date H.O.L.M.E.S. procedures.

Thanks to Alistair McNaughton and my former colleagues Paul Brunton, Michael Robinson, Barry Worthen and Steve Maitland for allowing me to borrow their names for characters in this work of fiction.

A special thanks to my good friend Philip of 'Phil Punton Photography' and his son Joseph whose skill and professionalism brought my cover images to life.

A very special thanks to Brenda Blethyn, aka 'Vera' for all her encouragement, support and frequent promotion of my previous work. You are right Brenda… you should have been my agent.

Death Chill or Algor Mortis (from Latin) is the third stage of death. It refers to the steady decline in body temperature Post Mortem, until the ambient temperature is matched.

It is used by forensic scientists and pathologists to give an approximate time of death.

Death Chill is not accurate if the body has been exposed to extreme environmental temperatures... such as having been frozen.

Chapter 1

The pungent stench of the river mud assailed his nostrils with each step of his black wellington boots as they sank into the sludge.

Joe Sample had always been a bit of a scavenger. He wasn't ashamed of it. On the contrary he was quite proud of the fact; telling anyone who would listen that he was doing his bit for recycling. The truth was that there was nothing that Joe loved more than mooching about with a metal detector on a beach or, as now, on the mud flats of a river after the tide had receded.

Whilst many found the smell of the river repugnant, for Joe it conjured up childhood excitement watching the tide ebb back to expose the cloying black mire and whatever secret treasures that might be concealed below.

Glancing up he could see in the distance the outline of the Scotswood bridge spanning the River Tyne and could hear the steady hum of the early morning traffic crossing over the dark waters below.

The River Tyne was his river; he had lived within sight of it since his birth and it had been his constant companion throughout his youth.

Growing up overlooking the banks, the Tyne had been his adventure playground as he enthusiastically explored its length. As a young child he would often pedal his rusty bike along the Tyne Valley, passing the narrow road bridge at Newburn and along the wooded tracks, sometimes as far as Wylam.

There, where the pretty village spanned both sides of the river, he would stop and tuck into a jam sandwich, escaping into his fantasy world of treasure seeking.

Now almost fifty years later the river still held a special thrill for him. What had once been his childhood playground was now his adult hobby. The river would draw him eagerly to its muddy banks, armed with a spade and metal detector; never knowing what each turn of the oozing sludge might reveal.

He had come to love the fast-flowing river. With each ebb and flow the dark waters could churn up a plethora of objects from beneath the disturbed sediment, depositing them on the riverbed, exposed by the outgoing tide.

Even when not uncovering hidden treasures Joe loved to just stare down into the dark waters, watching the opposing currents forming little black whirlpools, swirling and dragging in pieces of small twigs. The hidden current of the river depths fascinated him, but he was well aware from the frequent drownings over the years, that they could be treacherous if not treated with respect.

Joe hadn't always confined his treasure hunting to the riverside. Back in the nineties he used to do his scavenging on some allotments in the West End of the city. During the war, garden allotments had been positioned on the site of an old Victorian era rubbish dump and decades later, by digging down only a few feet, a scavenger could recover old bottles, still intact, and worth a pretty penny at the local antique fairs. If you were lucky enough to uncover one of the cobalt blue stoppered bottles, embossed with the manufacturer's name and with the right type of pontil mark, it could fetch hundreds from the right collector.

Unfortunately, the allotment holders became increasingly irate at having their prize vegetables dug up during the process. After several complaints to the local police, a number of the 'bottle diggers' were arrested on charges of criminal damage. After a while the word was passed around, with many deciding that a night in the cells and a hefty fine or even a prison sentence, wasn't worth the hassle. They gradually, if reluctantly, moved on to pastures new.

One night when the 'polis' had come down, several bottle diggers that Joe knew were nicked. He considered himself very lucky not to have gone down there on that particular night... but then Joe always considered himself a bit of a lucky man.

In his forages over the years, he'd uncovered numerous discarded coins and several pieces of lost jewellery. One time he found a heavy solid gold snake ring with diamonds for eyes. When he took it to a jeweller to get it valued, he was offered two hundred quid on the spot. Because the man behind the counter had been so quick to offer that much, Joe didn't trust him. He was sure that he should have held out for more. It was probably worth two or three times what he had been offered, but Joe took the two hundred just the same. A bird in the hand...

When he told old Fred down the pub of his find, the old man muttered that he should have handed it in to the police. If it was so valuable it might have great sentimental worth to someone.

Silly old bugger. Like that was ever going to happen.

"Finder's keepers" had always been Joe's motto.

Gripping the battered spade that he used for digging, Joe used it as a makeshift walking stick, as he fought his way through the reeking black mud several feet from the riverbank. His boots were sinking a little deeper with every step, until they were covered well past the ankles and each extraction from the cloying muck became an effort.

It was as he was freeing himself and trying not to lose his balance that he first spotted the box.

It was a dirty brown colour and almost submerged in the muck. Just the corner was sticking out of the black river bed to betray its presence.

Almost losing one of his boots with the effort, Joe dragged himself laboriously through the mud and water, carefully checking for any hidden voids, until he eventually reached his goal. Using the spade, he cleared away the surrounding muck and began the task of levering the box from the cloying grip of the Tyne. Finally, the sludge reluctantly released its hold on the box, and with a final wrench Joe was able to haul it out and make a closer examination of his prize.

The box was made of metal, rusty in parts and coated in black slime. As he lifted it up it felt very heavy, and clearly contained something substantial. Tipping it onto one side, a small amount of putrid water gushed from the keyhole at the front. Rinsing off some of the mud with river water, Joe peered more closely at his discovery.

It was a cube of just over eighteen inches, and despite a little surface rust didn't seem to have been in the river very long. Even after the majority of the water had drained from inside, it still felt very heavy. Joe couldn't help giving a sly smile, displaying a row of nicotine-stained teeth; monuments to five decades of poor dentistry.

Joe my boy, it looks like you've struck lucky again.

He considered trying to force it open there and then using the spade but thought better of it. There was a much more suitable small jemmy in the kitchen cupboard at home. Besides it wouldn't do for some passing nosey sod to see him inspecting the contents, especially if, as he hoped, it contained something valuable.

Perhaps silver… or from the heavyweight, maybe even gold.

Placing his prize into the beige canvas haversack that he always took with him on his scavenger hunts, he made his way out of the foul-smelling water and headed home.

The walk only took a few minutes and, on the way, Joe fantasized about what his latest find might contain. Perhaps jewellery or maybe the proceeds of some crime, dumped by a burglar who was getting rid of evidence, intending to return and retrieve it at some later date.

Either way it's mine now.

Joe refused to entertain the notion that it could just be rubbish, offering a prayer up to the God that he had never believed in, to keep his luck good.

Lucky Joe Sample would strike again.

Ten minutes later he was back at his small brick built terraced house, the kettle was on and the brown tea-stained mug stood waiting for a celebratory drink.

He glanced down at the metal box resting on the kitchen table; now sitting on some old newspapers to soak up the foul-smelling dark fluid that was still oozing out.

If anything, it smelled worse than when he had first pulled it from the river.

Fetching his jemmy from the box of tools in the cupboard beneath the sink, he looked for a suitable leverage point to force it open and snap the lock.

After a short struggle, he managed to make a small gap below the lid sufficient to force the lever in and allow it to get a decent hold. Then putting all his weight into it he prised open the box.

Crack!

With a noise like a gunshot the lock gave way and the box tipped onto its side spilling brown water along with the contents, out onto the table.

Joe felt himself gagging and turned away to vomit.

The reaction was not just from the smell of the river water, or even the fetid stench of decaying flesh.

It was from the vision of the dismembered head that angrily glared up at him from sightless eyes.

Chapter 2

Detective Inspector Jack Slade stood in the dirty kitchen of the small council house and tried not to breathe in too deeply. During his years on the force, he had always been able to cope with the spectacle of most things; witnessing many scenes that would turn most men's stomachs.

Images of dead or dismembered bodies had become just a part of his job and held no fears for the experienced detective. At the time cops just get on and deal with whatever confronts them. It's only later when they return home that the images flash through their minds. For Jack at a crime scene, sights could be endured with little effect… but the smells… they were something else. The odour of decomposing flesh could invade his nostrils and grip him at the back of his throat; making him struggle to keep from retching.

The filthy room itself had a prevailing smell of rotten vegetables and several unwashed plates were stacked untidily in the sink, with the remnants of a takeaway lying on the side bench. It crossed his mind that under normal circumstances the occupant was probably 'nose blind' to the usual aromas from the grimy, squalid kitchen.

Nothing, however, could prepare anyone for the stench coming off the decomposing head staring up from the table.

Despite the cold wind outside, Slade had insisted on the outside door to the kitchen being left open in a vain attempt to allow some of the disgusting smell to escape.

Glancing down at his watch he noted that it was just past eight o'clock, and he inwardly cursed that he hadn't even finished his first cup of coffee before he had taken the call and been forced to hurriedly leave the office.

At six-foot two Jack Slade presented an imposing figure. Regular exercise ensured that his weight rarely fluctuated from an acceptable eighty-five kilo; not a gram of which was excess fat. His lean body was more often than not packaged in a smart suit, and his style of always wearing a tie fastened in a double Windsor, had gained him a reputation amongst his colleagues as a sharp dresser.

Slade's thick dark brown hair and pale blue eyes did not go unnoticed amongst the women at the nick, but he had learnt from other cops' mistakes and had adopted a golden rule never to date other police officers or office staff.

Jack's suits weren't an expression of vanity; such thoughts would never occur to him and he was oblivious to the covert glances from the

5

admiring female staff. He dressed as he did, because his father had always ingrained in him that dressing smartly afforded him a subconscious edge over those he had dealings with. Whichever side of the law they were on.

His father, Charlie Slade had been a police officer working the same force back in the eighties and was still remembered by many of the older cops, despite having retired more than ten years ago.

Growing up in the tough West End meant that one or two of Jack's school friends had not always stuck strictly to the law, but he had always been very careful to avoid any occasions that might lead to him ending up in a police station.

Meeting his dad in those circumstances was a scenario too terrifying for the teenage Jack to even contemplate.

When he had first joined the police force his father was still serving in the City Centre C.I.D. and Jack had found it hard living in his shadow. It still irked him that even to this day many of the older cops referred to him as "Charlie's young lad".

In a strange way that annoyance had spurred him on to climb the ranks further than his father, but it had taken Slade senior's retirement and several years of hard work by Jack to finally emerge as his own man.

Despite this, he knew that he owed a lot to his father. Early in his service Jack had learnt a lot from him about police work and the skills of being a good detective… including the advantages of always dressing the part.

This morning however, the smart modern navy-blue suit was concealed under a white forensic coverall, with blue plastic coverings over his shoes and blue gloves to complete the ensemble.

Looking down at the surreal sight of the severed head lying on a kitchen table next to a dark brown teapot and mug, he slipped another of the extra strong mints into his mouth to suppress the smell, and moved in to get a closer look at the remains.

The head was that of a female with long hair that looked at one time to have been blonde, but was now stained with black sludge. She appeared to be late teens or early twenties. The face showed no evident signs of injury, but the features seemed odd, the skin shrunken as if pulled and stretched back.

Determined not to gag, Jack forced himself to lean in closer. Although still streaked with mud from the dirty river water the colour of the skin seemed tinged reddish brown. Not what Slade had expected.

6

As he stared down, he became aware of Detective Sergeant Dave Armstrong appearing at his side. Armstrong shot a glance around the kitchen before turning back to Jack. 'I guess today must be the cleaner's day off.'

Jack passed over the packet of mints.

A couple of years younger than Slade and a couple of inches shorter, Dave Armstrong was clean shaven with thick dark hair cut short. Although he had been in the force as long as Jack, he still had the look of an overgrown student, rather than the grizzled features of a hardened detective. Like Slade, he made a point of maintaining a level of fitness, but where Jack did so by running and swimming, Dave preferred the weights and the warm interior of the local gym.

Armstrong had always wanted to be a detective; right from first joining the force aged nineteen he had never harboured any desire for traffic or any of the many other departments within the police force. He was hardly out of his probation when he was accepted into C.I.D. as a temporary detective, and other than a brief time on promotion to uniform sergeant he viewed himself as a 'tec' through and through.

Whilst in C.I.D. he had built up an enviable reputation as a 'good thief taker' and despite his youthful looks, when it came to crime investigation Dave Armstrong had a mind as sharp as a cut-throat razor, and could hold his own against any other career detective.

Armstrong and Slade had first met as young cops at the Police Training College at Durham and, sharing the same sense of humour, had immediately hit it off, quickly becoming good friends. Several years later when the chance of working alongside his friend came up Armstrong snatched it with both hands, transferring into H.MET; the acronym for the Homicide and Major Enquiry Team.

Dave peered over Slade's shoulder at the remains lying face up on the table.

'She looks a bit odd to me.'

'You don't say Dave. You have noticed that she's missing her torso and limbs?'

'You know what I mean. There's something that's not right here.'

'I know. The skin just doesn't look normal,' said Jack leaning even closer to the gruesome object, careful not to breathe in as he did so. 'It could be from immersion in the river but I'm not sure.'

There was a clatter from the doorway as Ged Kirkby the Scenes of Crime Officer lumbered in carrying two silver coloured metal boxes. Short and ruddy faced with an untidy mop of ginger hair that was starting to go grey, Kirkby had been with the department for as long as

Jack could remember. Although nearing retirement he seemed to have slipped through the net when most of the C.S.I. Department had been civilianised over the recent years. No-one knew the secret of his longevity but some older cops joked that like the ravens in The Tower, the forensic department would crumble and fall if Kirkby ever left fortress C.S.I.

Slade glanced up as the Ged spoke. 'If you're after a cause of death there's one that springs to mind,' he muttered looking around the room. 'I don't suppose you know where the rest of her is?'

Jack was used to the gallows humour of cops which for many of them was a coping exercise to suppress their real emotions.

'This is all we've got … for the moment. If the rest of her turns up I'll keep your number on speed dial.'

'You're all heart Jack.' Kirkby replied, pulling a forensic mask across his mouth and nose, before opening one of the silver cases and extracting a digital camera.

Slade moved aside to allow him to get better access.

'Well Jack, from what I can see there's no obvious signs of injuries to the facial area. I'll get the usual shots in situ but before I package her up I'll photograph the back of the head to check for any wounds beneath the hairline.'

Slade and Armstrong stepped back and waited whilst the forensic officer took several photographs from different angles. Then reaching out a gloved hand he moved her head onto the side so that he could take some more of the back of the head. The room was eerily silent except for the steady click, click, click as the digital camera recorded the macabre scene.

With no visible injuries apparent Kirkby gave a sigh.

'Nothing obvious, and clearly without the rest of her to examine a cause of death is obviously impossible to ascertain at this time. Fingers crossed the pathologist will have better luck.'

Jack was staring intently at the face and frowned.

There was definitely something not right.

Kirkby cut into his thoughts.

'I know what you're thinking. The skin looks leathery and she's a funny shade, isn't she?'

Slade glanced at him before nodding back towards the grisly body part.

'So, what do you make of it, Ged?'

'Not sure Jack. I've seen a few 'dead uns' in my time but there's definitely something odd about the look of this one. The head's pretty well preserved so I don't think she's been in the river long. If she hadn't been in the box the small fish would have had the eyes out before now. I wouldn't like to guess at that skin discolouration. It's all a bit above my pay scale. We're going to have to wait until Paul Clifford has had a look.'

Paul Clifford was the Home Office Pathologist and would ultimately be responsible for carrying out a post mortem and attempting to establish a cause of death for the coroner. In his time as a murder squad detective Jack had frequent contact with Clifford and over the years had built up a great respect for his methodical examinations of murder victims.

Having recorded all he required, Kirkby placed his camera back into a grey foam lined case, walked over to his stack of equipment and reappeared moments later with a large circular plastic forensic box which he placed next to the severed head.

'The pathologist's not got a lot to go on here,' Armstrong said, keeping well back to allow Kirkby to carefully pick up the head and place it into the large plastic receptacle.

'Aye,' Kirkby muttered in reply, 'It's just as well he doesn't get paid by weight. There's poor pickings to be had on this one.'

'Is that you about finished here Ged?' asked Slade quietly.

'There's not much to do. This obviously isn't the primary location of the murder. That could be anywhere. I'll take swabs of the fluid on the table but we all know that it's going to be river water from the Tyne. I'll package the metal box that the head came in separately for the lab.'

'The finder used a jemmy to break the box open,' said Armstrong.

'Right. I'll need to seize that as well for the Exhibits Officer. The lab rats can cross match the tool marks with the damage caused to the box when it was forced.'

'That'll help corroborate what the finder told the first cops on the scene. I think we're going to find that his story fits the evidence.'

'What's his name, and how did he come to find it?' asked Kirkby.

Armstrong glanced down at a note that he had made. 'The name's Joseph Sample. He was foraging down by the banks of the Tyne. It's apparently a hobby of his. People call it 'Mudlarking'. They scavenge in rivers for whatever they can find. Personally, I can think of better ways to spend my leisure time.'

'So, have we no way of establishing any primary scene?' Kirby asked as he screwed tightly the lid of the forensic box.

'Not really. We have a possible deposition site just off the river bank. The uniform cops took him down to the scene earlier and got him to point out where he had found the box, but obviously that doesn't tell us where the actual murder happened. The area's taped off and a couple of uniforms are securing the scene as a precaution, but from what they've said I don't think there's a lot to see. It's just the muddy bed of the river left when the tide went out.'

'Where's Sample now?' asked Kirkby.

'Uniform cops have taken him to Etal Lane nick. He's had a bit of a shock,' replied Jack.

'I suppose it's not every day you find a severed head in a box. After today, if I was him, I'd be looking for another hobby.'

The head sealed in the large translucent casing appeared surreal as it stared out through the plastic, and Jack turned away from the bizarre sight.

'Dave, come with me to the location where the metal box was found. I'd like to see the lie of the land before we speak to Sample. Can you also get on to the Control room and tee up an ASG team to head down there as soon as possible for a fingertip search?'

The A.S.G. or Area Support Group were all officers who were P.O.L.S.A. or Police Search trained and were often called upon to use their skills in cases of murder and other serious crimes.

'I want to check out exactly where he discovered the box and then we'll leave it to the ASG for the search of the bank... let's say a hundred yards either side of the deposition site just for now. We can expand the search later if need be.'

'OK Jack.'

'Can you also see if they can manage to get across to where the box was actually lying. Just in case there are other bits of our victim partly submerged in the mud.'

'Aye. Well, they'd best get a move on Jack,' Kirkby chirped up. 'The tide will be coming in shortly.'

When they left the terraced house Armstrong took in deep breaths of fresh air.

'Thanks for the mints Jack. It was a bit ripe in that kitchen.'

'Calling it a kitchen is being too kind. It was more like a fifteen foot square petri dish.'

'On a more positive note... at least it will make the Tyne mudflats smell like roses.'

The drive down to the scene took about five minutes. Slade had been given directions but it wasn't hard to locate. A large area of the river bank had been cordoned off with blue and white police tape. Two bored looking policemen were standing beside it chatting to three curious locals.

Jack knew the area well. When he had been a young detective he had been called down to what started out as a possible crime scene, but was ultimately referenced off as a death by natural causes.

It had been a cold January morning almost a decade earlier when a dog walker had discovered the decomposed body of an adult male under bushes down by the Tyne. Covered by a dark blue tarpaulin the fully clothed skeletal remains looked like they had been lying for some time and although there had been no bone damage to suggest violence, the secluded riverside location meant that foul play had initially been suspected.

When eventually identified the body turned out to be that of a well-known local vagrant who had often been seen sleeping rough in the area.

With no visible injuries, the investigation concluded that he had probably been seeking shelter and made camp amongst the thick foliage, where he had died and was subsequently discovered. Perhaps he had expired from some illness or perhaps had just succumbed to the cold and hypothermia, but when the December snows came, he had been covered up and had lain undisturbed for weeks.

By the time he was eventually found the river rats and local foxes had ensured that little remained from which to establish a definite cause of death.

The investigation was closed off as natural causes; just another statistic of the lost and unloved homeless in a modern 'care in the community society'.

The gaffers will be hard pressed to write off a head in a box so easily.

The two police officers guarding the crime scene straightened up quickly on spotting Jack's blue BMW, slowly bumping down the rutted mud track to where they stood. Slade and Armstrong climbed out of the vehicle and made their way across to the police cordon.

Both of the uniformed cops looked very young. It was obvious to the detectives that the two most junior officers on the shift had been given the tedious task of standing by the potential crime scene.

Routine sudden deaths, crime scene preservation and making the tea were the rites of passage for probationer constables. It hadn't changed much from Slade's father's early days on the force.

As Jack approached he thought one of the cops, who was clutching a black clipboard and looking nervous, appeared more like a sixth former on a school field trip than a copper.

Armstrong saw Slade's look and as usual could read his friend's mind.

'You know what they say Jack… you must be getting old pal.'

The detectives gave their names to 'baby face' who dutifully recorded them on the crime scene log, along with their time of arrival. Then, donning yet another fresh pair of plastic shoe coverings and gloves, the two detectives ducked under the police tape and walked purposefully down to the river bank.

Plastic tread boards had been strategically placed to allow officers access to the scene without contaminating any of the route. This would preserve the muddy ground for C.S.I. to record any footprints or other evidential markings.

Standing by the river's edge, Jack could see several indentations in the black muck where Sample had previously trudged through it. The footprints had almost filled in as the moist earth began to close back around them, but further out he could clearly make out a larger patch of disturbed riverbed about ten feet from the bank. He felt sure that it marked the spot where Sample had dug out the box.

The Tyne was wide at this point and he guessed that whoever had dumped the body part had thrown it in as far as they could, maybe without realising that it would be exposed by the ebbing tide.

Why not dump it from a bridge and into the middle of the river?

Had he been disturbed?

Chapter 3

That had been close. Too close!

Just thinking of it started his heart racing again and he took another large swig of whisky from the glass. If he hadn't heard the dog bark then that nosey old bugger might have walked right into him. It would have taken a bit of explaining if he'd been caught with the box. As it was, there was hardly time to throw it in the river before the dog appeared, and he knew that the mutt's owner wouldn't have been too far behind.

He sat alone, going over in his mind the events of the previous night. The only light came from the one dusty fluorescent tube above him, casting a harsh illumination across the cluttered basement room.

Thankfully he had managed to get away before he was spotted, but the panic was still fresh in his mind. It was a lesson learned. The next time he would have to make sure that he picked a more secluded place as a dumping ground.

When he had first thought about disposing of the body parts, his initial idea had been to take a long drive up to Kielder Forest, way up in the middle of Northumberland. In the two hundred and fifty square mile wide rugged landscape of lake and woodland, a corpse might lie undiscovered forever. However, to do so would have necessitated a hundred and twenty mile round trip of at least three or four hours during which he would have been transporting a dismembered body in the boot. Not the best of plans.

Even if he did get to the forest without being stopped, he would then have to locate a suitable burial site. That would mean leaving the van for some time and a parked vehicle in a remote area attracts unwanted attention. There was also the problem of digging the hole. How far down do you have to excavate to ensure it was deep enough to prevent some wild animal burrowing down and dragging it right back up again? The prospect of trying to dig six feet down through the rough wooded terrain held no appeal for him.

At one point he had considered boiling the head up, crushing the skull and flushing the boiled flesh away into the sewer. However, he'd read in one of his true crime mags, that doing so had proved serial killer Dennis Nilsen's undoing back in the eighties. Besides, the nauseous smell of boiling flesh was bound to alert the neighbours.

No! He had decided that it would have to be the river. One piece at a time.

The Scotswood Bridge had been his first choice, but there were far too many vehicles passing by, and the chances of being seen by a witness in the middle of the bridge as he dumped the head was just too much of a risk. In the end, he found what he thought would be the ideal spot down by the river bank. It had appeared isolated enough to be safe. With hindsight he wasn't so sure.

Putting down his empty whisky glass, he got up from his chair and moved across to the two large chest freezers at the back of the cluttered cellar.

Lifting the lid of one he peered inside at the contents.

There was still a lot to get rid of.

Chapter 4

Half an hour after leaving the chill of the riverbank, Jack Slade was sitting in the warm office of Detective Superintendent Thomas Charles Parker.

In his mid-fifties, overweight and with a half-moon of grey hair surrounding a bald pate, Parker gave the impression of Friar Tuck in an ill-fitting suit. Gruff and humourless, Parker was not well liked by those who had the misfortune to work for him. A fact that didn't appear to concern him.

Jack had experienced several previous run-ins with Parker, and had not warmed to the man. He was well aware that the feeling was mutual.

Slade was not alone in his opinion.

On one occasion, someone as a joke had pinned an advert around the police station purporting to be from Parker.

Books For Sale.

1. *The Man Management Handbook*
2. *Leadership Role and Responsibility*
3. *How to Win Friends and Influence People.*
All Unread and still in wrappers.
Unwanted gifts.
Best offers.
Contact Detective Superintendent T.C.Parker.

It turned out that Parker was not amused and was rumoured to have ordered forensic tests on the paper in an attempt to trace the culprit. They proved unsuccessful.

Ged Kirkby from C.S.I. had managed to keep a straight face when telling Parker that 'in his opinion' it was likely that the offender 'had some degree of forensic training.'

Most probably in the C.I.D.

With more than thirty years police service Parker could retire at any time on a full pension but had chosen to stay on. Many cops claimed that, having achieved such a dizzying rank, his ego would not allow him to give up being called 'Sir' and revert to being plain Mister Parker.

One time he had called at the desk of one of the rural police stations to be met by an old-time 'polis' with only months to retirement. He did not recognise the senior officer.

His pleasant greeting of 'Hello sir, how can I help you,' had not gone down well with the sour-faced Detective Superintendent who had glared at him and demanded loudly, 'Don't you know who I am?'

Undaunted and quick as a flash the old 'bobby' had called back over his shoulder, 'Hey Sarge! There's some bloke out here who doesn't know who he is!'

When the old cop finally retired a few months later he did so as a legend.

On his frequent memos to the junior ranks Parker would always sign himself T.C.P. which were the initials of his full name Thomas Charles Parker.

To those that were on the receiving end of his multitudinous memos it stood for "That Cunt Parker."

It would be fair to say that most cops disliked him.

It was also said by many in the Northumbria force that any cop who didn't dislike him… just hadn't met him yet.

'So Jack…' Parker barked, 'Are we anywhere near identifying the body?'

'Bit early at this time boss. Forensics have taken the remains, such as they are, to the mortuary and the Home Office pathologist Paul Clifford is attending shortly to do the post mortem. I've got D.C. Henderson checking through the current missing persons, but at this stage there's nothing to suggest whether or not she's local or even how long she might have been missing. After the P.M. we'll take the usual samples and start checking the DNA database to see if we can get a positive match.'

'Dental records?'

'I've asked for impressions to be taken along with the other samples. We'll circulate the results initially to all dentists in the force area. We can expand the search if necessary. As soon as we have any result I'll let you know.'

'Not a lot to go on just yet then,' grumbled Parker.

'As regards the standard "Motive, Means and Opportunity" we have absolutely nothing to go on. We're counting on a positive identification to give us a kick start and point us in the right direction.'

'Well Jack, I want you to prepare some kind of brief for the Press Office. No doubt the local media will be sniffing around shortly. All the activity down by the riverside will not have gone unnoticed by the locals.'

'The A.S.G. are on their way down there now to see what they can do before the tide comes back in.'

'Just bear in mind with the publicity this sort of incident attracts I expect Command Block will also be expressing an interest.'

'Command Block' was the term used by the cops to describe the suite of offices occupied by the Chief Constable and his assistants. It was a throwback to the days at the old Ponteland Police Headquarters when the senior command had been located in a separate building from other departments.

'Alright. Keep me informed,' snapped Parker signaling the end of the conversation.

Jack left his boss' office, heading up to the first floor, through a door marked H.MET, and into a large office containing several desks placed back to back.

The Homicide & Major Enquiry Team was a hub of activity with officers sifting through paperwork or talking away on the telephones. A long acrylic coated whiteboard dominated the room and served as the murder wall, but so far there was very little information displayed on it.

Black marker pen recorded details of the location, time and date of the discovery of the dismembered head, and next to it was a photograph of the finder Joseph Sample.

Jack noted that the face on the image showed a scowling Sample and had obviously been obtained from police records. This indicated that he had an arrest record which would be worth having a detailed check through.

In a corner of the office Jack spotted Detective Constable Jim Jackson typing away at a computer keyboard. Jackson had over twenty-five years in the job, eighteen of which were C.I.D and for his sins had been allocated the unenviable task of Exhibits Officer. This gave him responsibility for logging in any piece of evidence and subsequently documenting and tracking where it was stored or sent to.

It played a vital role in any major investigation; requiring meticulous records to be maintained. Should any exhibit go astray it could result in evidence being ruled inadmissible, and in the worst scenario a case being thrown out by the court. Jackson had performed the role on numerous occasions and had built up a reputation of being a safe pair of hands.

'Not much in the way of exhibits as yet Jim?' Jack enquired glancing down at the almost empty exhibits log.

'Plenty of time yet boss. There's bound to be a sackload of stuff found down by the river, though how much will be of any use God only knows. Sergeant Armstrong is going to head down to the interview room to speak to the guy Sample who found the body…. or rather the head. There's a post mortem booked for one o'clock so I'm heading down for that to log all the Post Mortem forensic exhibits. I take it, you'll be attending?'

'Wouldn't miss it,' smiled Jack. 'Will you bring the extra strong mints or shall I?'

Jack regarded post mortems as a necessary evil. As much as he hated attending them, he realised that they could provide the details to not only establish a cause of death, but often provide clues as to what, and occasionally who, to look for in an investigation.

The sights he had witnessed in the clinical confines of the dissecting room had never bothered him but as always it came down to the smell.

Whilst some cops doused handkerchiefs in aftershave or menthol vapour rub, Jack had always favoured the extra strong mint approach to combating the problem, and always kept a packet in his inside jacket pocket.

'Well, she has been in the river so she'll not be smelling at her sweetest,' said Jackson, twisting his face.

'At least this should be the shortest P.M. I've been to. There's not that much left of her to be dissected,' countered Slade.

Jack looked up as Dave Armstrong strolled into the Incident Room clutching several sheets of A4 paper, and made his way towards Jack.

'I'm just about to interview Sample on video boss if you want to watch it on the remote monitor.'

'Has he said anything so far?'

'Nothing different from what he told the first uniform cops who attended. They're downstairs writing up their statements as we speak.'

'There's no chance this Sample guy knows more than he's saying? I take it from his mug shot that he has some form?'

'I've done the usual computer checks on him and he has a little for minor stuff. A bit of shoplifting… that sort of thing. I don't think he's up to making the leap from petty thief to a head severing psychopath just yet.'

Armstrong held out a sheet of paper.

'Here's a copy of his I.S. printout.'

The Information System was the locally based computer records of criminals and their associates within the force area, but also included data on missing persons and people who, although not criminals, had come into contact with the police for various reasons.

By inputting a name and date of birth, details would flag up any contact that person had with the police.

Jack nodded. 'So, you don't reckon he's going to be our man then?'

'Afraid not. Shame really. If he fancied coughing to it, we could have this all wrapped up in a few hours and still get down the club for a pint by the end of shift.'

'Well,' said Jack, 'I suppose we better go down and see if he can help us find the real murderer then.'

With Slade watching the interview room on a monitor, Sample sat opposite Dave Armstrong. Although still being recorded this was to be a 'soft' interview to get Sample's account and initially treat him as a witness.

Sample did not prove to be much of a help in moving the investigation forward. Although he had never been one to voluntarily speak to the police, this time he was more than happy to do so, almost falling over himself to tell his story to Armstrong. It was just that he didn't have anything very useful to say or that wasn't already known to the investigation team.

Sample had been back to the river with uniformed officers and pointed out exactly where the box had been lying. The only thing that might prove useful was that he regularly walked the same route and had never spotted the metal box before, so it was possible that it had only been there a day or two.

He was clearly still quite shaken by his experience and clutched a cup of sweet tea between unsteady hands. He complained that whenever he closed his eyes he could visualise a disembodied head staring up at him from his kitchen table.

After the interview Slade contacted Steve Maitland, an old friend he knew from the Marine Section, to quiz him about what effect the constantly changing tides might have had on depositing the box.

Inspector Maitland had worked the river for several years. From experience when a body had gone into the river and been sucked down by the undercurrents, Maitland could often predict where it would eventually wash up.

The Marine officer briefed Jack that the underwater current in the river at that point was very strong so, despite the weight, it was not beyond possibility that the box could have been moved by the incoming or outgoing tides. Unfortunately, he could not say with any certainty how long the box may have lain there.

'I can get some divers to cover the section of the river bed a little further out towards the mid-river. However, because of the murky water conditions and poor visibility it would have to be a fingertip search.'

'I'd appreciate it if you would do that Steve. Get me on my mobile if they locate anything.'

After hanging up Slade immediately rang through to Ged Kirkby at C.S.I. to see if the forensic team had found anything of note.

Kirkby answered on the second ring and quickly brought Jack up to speed.

'There were several fresh well-defined footprints left in the mud by the side of the river. One of my lads has taken photos and a three-dimensional cast of what looks like a size nine trainers. He's busy as we speak checking through pattern records to try to identify a maker.'

'Were the prints where the killer could have stood to throw the box into the river?'

'That would be my guess Jack, but we have to be aware that because the area is a frequent route for dog walkers, there's nothing to show for certain that the footprints are those of your killer. I would take a guess that your best bet is a press appeal for any possible witnesses who were down there, and then a very long process of matching footwear to see if the casts recovered can be eliminated.'

'Anything else?'

'Just the usual mountain of detritus, discarded bottles, cans and the like. It's all been recovered, recorded and bagged. Your exhibits officer Jim Jackson is about to experience a great increase in his workload.'

Slade mused that in real life murders were solved by the painstaking gathering of evidence most of which proved of no use. It was all about the meticulous collection of minutiae, where just one tiny piece out of the hundreds recovered might be the clue that linked everything together, and point to a suspect.

Remembering the post mortem, he glanced at his watch.

'Thanks for that Ged. Will you ring me immediately if there's any developments? If my phone's off, speak to Dave Armstrong and leave a message. I have to go now. I have a date with a young lady... or rather what's left of her.'

The post mortem was held at the small annex mortuary at the Lemington cemetery to the west of the city where bodies recovered from the river were usually taken.

The red brick building located at the far end of a sloping graveyard was well away from the gated entrance. From the outside it had the appearance of some kind of storage facility, which was indeed one of its functions. Windowless and with no signage it gave nothing away concerning its real purpose; the location for dissection of bodies too decomposed or contaminated to be kept at a hospital mortuary.

Inside, the room was dominated by a large polished stainless steel dissection table angled down at one end to allow waste fluids to be flushed away. It smelled strongly of antiseptic but underneath there was a vague musty smell that was difficult to identify.

As Jack entered, the Home Office pathologist Paul Clifford was already waiting with Jim Jackson.

Slade and Clifford were well known to each other and Jack greeted him as he would an old friend. Sudden and unexplained deaths were a part and parcel of both of their lives they had had met many times over the years.

Tall and slim with a thick head of salt and pepper hair, Clifford's ready smile and deep laughter lines gave no indications of the gruesome tasks that he undertook on an almost daily basis.

With a well-earned reputation for being methodical and meticulous in performing forensic examinations, Clifford was often the favoured pathologist in serious cases. When it came to a murder, the all-important 'chain of evidence' could make or break a case, and Slade had confidence that it would always be maintained when it came to any autopsy exhibits recovered by Clifford.

Over his years, as a forensic pathologist, Clifford had carried out thousands of post mortems. This was certainly one of the most unusual of them.

Already dressed in surgical theatre robes he started by announcing the date and time into a small black microphone hanging down from the mortuary ceiling.

As he went about the dissection all his observations would be recorded digitally, and this would form verbal notes from which he could later prepare a written report for the coroner.

Unclipping a flexible hose from a stand, he began washing away the mud and grime deposited on the head by the river water. As the dirt ran away into a drain at one end of the stainless-steel platform, Clifford was able to get a better view of what lay in front of him.

'The skull is that of a late adolescent or adult female…between sixteen to twenty-five years old at time of death. The flesh is in the early stages of decomposition.'

He leant in closer, studying the severed head from several angles.

21

'The skull appears to have been removed from the torso using a serrated blade. I would suggest a household saw or similar.'

Reaching out with a gloved hand he began checking for signs of injury.

'An examination of the anterior and facial area of the deceased's skull shows no signs of any contusions, abrasions or laceration that would indicate any kind of blunt force trauma. On turning the skull around there is likewise no evidence of trauma to the posterior cranium.'

To the pathologist the face seemed oddly shrivelled and the eyes appeared sunken, bringing to mind the Egyptian mummy he had once seen on display in The Great North Museum in the city centre. The skin appeared in parts almost brown instead of the usual waxy yellow.

'I note that the epidermis has an unusual discolouration and scarring.'

The pathologist took swabs from inside the mouth for any trace evidence and using a small plastic brush obtained a sample for DNA analysis. Each item was handed to the stony-faced Jim Jackson for forensic packaging and recording.

Clifford pointed out a strange grey-brown patch on the skin on one side of the head. 'Take a look here Jack.'

Slade leant across for a closer view and despite sucking on strong mints still got a strong whiff of the rancid river water. 'What do you think it is, Paul?'

The pathologist twisted his face in a grimace. 'An educated guess…I think it's a freezer burn.'

Jack was startled. 'She's been kept in a freezer?'

'I'm pretty sure but there are further tests that can be done to make certain. Deep freezing and subsequent thawing causes extended extracellular spaces and shrunken cells, so it should be possible to verify it histologically.'

He glanced across at Jack and gave a smile. 'That means under a microscope to you Jack.'

'Can you give any estimate as to how long she was stored?'

'Well, the cell shrinkage would be more pronounced in tissue stored for longer durations…' He paused '…but just by looking at the state of the skin I suggest that we're not talking just a few weeks. I'm thinking about months … maybe even years.'

'Years. That's not looking good for the investigation.'

'If it's only good news you're after Jack you've come to the wrong place?'

'Well just a little bit of good news would be nice.'

22

Clifford gave a smile.

'Well if it helps… I'm guessing you can rule out suicide.'

Chapter 5

Later that afternoon, back in his office, Jack sat quietly contemplating the preliminary results of the post mortem and considering how the samples gathered were going to impact his crime investigation.

If the pathologist Doctor Clifford was right and the body part had been stored in a freezer for some time, then not only was a time of death going to be impossible to establish, but checking through missing persons might turn out to be a nightmare.

How far would they have to go back?

With no possibility of fingerprints, it was clear that the best way to identify his victim was going to be through DNA.

What if the body part had been frozen since before the regular collection and retention of DNA samples? That procedure was relatively new in terms of police forensic records. She might not even have her DNA recorded in the system.

In that event there would be the labour intensive task of tracking down relatives for every missing person and then trying to match them using familial DNA. Even starting with the Northumbria Force and extending outwards it would be a huge task.

The only other records that might prove useful were dental records, but with nowhere to even start, that could also prove a long and possibly fruitless effort.

And what if they did find a possible victim that fitted the profile?

The prospect of showing some grieving relatives the severed head of their loved one was not something he wanted to consider.

Would they even recognize the frozen body part as their once living daughter or sister?

There were too many questions… and nowhere near enough answers.

Slade decided to ask Parker if the budget would extend to having an artist prepare a representation of the victim that could be used for press circulation. It might trigger some response from the public and help in establishing the identity of their victim. Once a possible I.D. had been made, they could then obtain DNA from relatives which could lead to a positive identification.

As this was all going through his mind Dave Armstrong knocked on the door and came in. Slade apprised him of the disturbing new development.

'In a freezer? For how long?'

'Doc Clifford's saying months… possibly years. He has taken some samples that he wants examined by a forensic cryobiologist for a second opinion, but he seems fairly confident.'

'What's a cryobiologist when he's at home?'

'Some lab rat geek type that studies the effects of low temperature on biological samples.'

'Well, I guess it means we're going to have to re-assess the search parameters for our 'misper'. You say possibly stored for years? Do you want to give D.C. Henderson the good news or should I?'

'I'll leave that pleasure to you. It should give him something new to complain about.'

Detective Constable Mike Henderson was not best pleased when Dave Armstrong passed on the latest news.

'You have got to be bloody joking.'

Henderson, a twenty-year veteran of C.I.D was the type of detective that other cops described as "old school". On the slippery downward slope to retirement, some of his not so generous colleagues described him as a dinosaur who would fit well into an episode of 'Life on Mars'.

Overweight and round faced, his bulbous reddish nose was indicative of several years of over indulgence in alcohol, begun at a time when cops meeting contacts in bars over pints of beer provided the bulk of Confidential Informants. Back in those days pub visits became a habit. It was one that Henderson was very reluctant to give up.

Despite his faults he was still regarded by many of the other cops as a very competent detective, who could smell a lie in an interview like a shark could smell blood in water. Over the years he had possessed an enviable record for nailing the bad guys.

Today however, he had his grumpy face on and was considerably less enthusiastic about the job in hand.

'So how many years back are we talking?'

Dave Armstrong shrugged. 'How long is a piece of string?'

Each year there are over a quarter of a million reports of missing persons and over half those reported are aged fifteen to twenty-one. A tiny number are murder victims, an increasing amount commit suicide, but the vast majority return or are located after a short time.

'Are we talking five years…ten? Where do I stop?'

'You're asking me to tell you something that I don't know myself. Obviously we're only interested in any open missing person cases, so that should narrow it down considerably. Most 'mispers' come back after a couple of days.'

Henderson frowned at his computer screen. 'Well, I've just gone back twelve months up to now. Not counting those in the past couple of months, there's about a dozen long time outstanding 'mispers' in our force area alone. Thankfully only four females match the approximate age and description.'

'Dig out what you can on those four and do a summary for the boss. See if you can find hair colouring and maybe even photographs to compare with the victim. That might eliminate a couple. Can you also get details circulated of our victim to other forces to see what that throws up? We're particularly interested in any from any nearby forces so Durham would be a good place to start. Maybe even contact Cumbria and Police Scotland.'

'It'll take some time.'

'Well, it should keep you out of trouble for a while,' said Dave.

'Once I start going back over the numbers will start to mount up.'

'Best make a start then.'

Henderson turned back to his computer scowling.

'Slade doesn't bloody want much does he?'

Chapter 6

Jack Slade stood with his back to the Murder Wall and looked around at the room of detectives, ensuring that he had the attention of them all. A hush descended on the room as everyone focused on what he had to say.

As well as Armstrong, Henderson and Jackson, about half a dozen others of the Homicide and Major Enquiry Team were sitting in on the briefing.

Donna Shaw, at twenty-three was the youngest member of the H.MET. squad. Although she had only been in C.I.D for a year before joining the team, she had proved herself an excellent interviewer. Donna had quickly become invaluable, especially in dealing with female victims of crime where the perpetrator had been male.

Despite first appearances, the slim attractive young cop was no pushover and many violent offenders had found themselves flat on the floor and handcuffed before they knew what had happened. Donna Shaw was not someone to be underestimated.

In sharp contrast was Gavin Oates, a stocky young detective of twenty-seven who had only recently joined the team. He had been a detective in one of the outlying rural areas of Northumberland, but ambitious to progress had applied to transfer to the city where he quickly established himself as a hardworking and efficient detective. When a vacancy came up in H.MET he had applied for and been given the job.

Armstrong sat off to one side with the small team dotted around the Incident Room sitting at, or standing by, their desks. Everyone was hanging onto the Detective Inspector's words.

'There's not much to go on so far, but I want to make sure that we're all up to speed. The head recovered is that of a female aged between sixteen and twenty-five. It hasn't been very easy to establish a more accurate age because of the method used to store it. The freezing process has had an impact on the skin integrity and without sounding in any way flippant, parts of the face have what the pathologist says can best be described as "freezer burns".'

Everyone remained silent. Slade indicated to DC Henderson.

'Mike here is going through any missing persons who fit the profile, but we don't know whether our victim went missing weeks, months or even years ago. I should say that Dr Clifford is inclined to the latter. We also don't know whether she went missing from

Northumbria Police Force area or another… so as you can see, we all have a massive task on our hands.'

Jack turned to the white board and pointed at one of several recently added colour photographs of the metal box.

'The head was found inside this box. It looks like it has at one time been a tool box of some sort. There is no manufacturer's mark so it may have been put together in some home workshop. We need to raise an action to trace its origins.'

Jack indicated the next two photographs showing the severed head. One showed it lying on the table in Sample's kitchen and the second, taken against a white background in the mortuary, showed it from directly in front.

'Identification based on these photographs would prove problematic to say the least, so Superintendent Parker has agreed to authorise a sketch artist to give us a reconstruction of what the victim may have looked like prior to her death. We intend to release that image to the press and see if it sparks any reactions.'

A few groans could be heard around the room.

'Look I know we have to expect the usual cranks and "nutters" but someone somewhere out there must be missing this girl.' He paused. 'The press have already gotten wind of the story so expect it to be featured in the late edition of the local paper and on tonight's regional news.'

Slade looked around the room. 'Any questions so far?'

Gavin Oates spoke up.

'Are we certain she was murdered?'

'She didn't bloody well chop her own head off,' muttered Henderson sarcastically.

'What I mean is, there's been a lot on the news recently about people having their bodies frozen until they find a cure in the future for whatever is killing them. Could this be from one of those places?'

'They don't just freeze their heads man,' responded Henderson.

A couple of the detectives began to laugh.

'They do! I've heard that they try to preserve the brain,' protested the young detective whose face had begun to redden.

Jack held his hands up and everyone went quiet.

'I won't rule anything out…' he glanced at Oates, '…no matter how bizarre.'

Donna raised a hand and Slade looked across in her direction.

'I've heard that something similar happened in America a few years back. Body parts were being found on a university campus. It turned out to be a sick prank carried out by a group of medical students using body parts that had been left for medical science. We have one of the top medical universities in the country. Could we be looking for a student?'

'I don't think so but it's a possibility. However, at this stage we're working on the trophy theory. We all know that murderers like to take trophies as souvenirs of their crimes. Often something from the victim, a lock of hair, a piece of clothing or jewellery. It helps them relive the crime. Allows them to prolong their fantasies.'

Jack pointed again at the photograph of the victim.

'Maybe this time the killer went one better. This time he kept the victim's head. It wouldn't be the first time. Dennis Nilsen, the Muswell Hill Murderer, kept his victims under the floorboards and would get them out to talk to them, and even to sit with him as he watched television. He only got rid of them when they began to decompose.'

'There are some sick bastards out there,' Henderson growled.

Jack continued. 'I want checks done on any firms in the area that have large freezer storage facilities. We're looking at small to medium firms where not everyone has access to all the freezers… or maybe one is permanently locked.'

'It could just be a domestic chest freezer,' said Gavin Oates.

'Yes, it could be, but we have to start somewhere,' responded Jack.

A hand went up and Jack nodded towards Jim Jackson.

'Boss, is there anything further from the fingertip search of the riverbank?' Jackson was clearly thinking of his rapidly growing list of exhibits.

'The ASG are packing in for the day but the area is to remain sterile and secure until they're back in the morning. As you know, they've recovered plenty of discarded items but nothing of significance yet. Don't worry Jim, I'm sure they'll have plenty more exhibits for you to log in.'

A couple of the officers laughed, pleased that they hadn't been given that particular job.

'A word of warning for the wise. I'm sure I don't need to say this but nothing about the head having been frozen leaves this room. At the moment only the pathologist, senior C.I.D and people on this squad know about it,' Slade smiled. 'Apart from the killer of course. If we have someone in the frame keeping back that detail may prove crucial in weeding out any fruitcakes from the enquiry.'

In high profile cases, people often admit to a crime that they did not commit. Frequently it is an attention seeking misfit, but sometimes it is someone suffering from a mental illness who has convinced themselves that they are responsible. Differentiating the true killer from the fantasists can be a difficult task, so it has become common practice in major investigations to withhold a piece of evidence only known to the investigators and the murderer. By doing so it is possible to discredit any false confessions and prevent an enquiry needlessly spinning off at a tangent.

'OK!' Jack glanced around the room, 'If no-one else has any further questions we'll wrap it up for tonight. I want everyone back in here for eight tomorrow morning. Get some decent sleep. I think we may be in for some long days ahead.'

That night, after a last check of his paperwork, the thought of a microwave meal for one didn't appeal, so Slade picked up a takeaway pizza from one of the many Italian restaurants in the city centre, and headed straight home.

The night was clear and not too cold and the walk along the Quayside allowed him to wind down and shake off some of the stresses of the day. Passing the Pitcher and Piano pub by the side of the Tyne, he peeked down at the boxed pizza and resisted the temptation to call into the bar for a pint. Instead, he ambled onto the Millennium Bridge crossing the black river below, and made his way towards his apartment.

Opened in the year two thousand the Millennium Bridge is a futuristic tilting structure that allows pedestrians and cyclists to cross the River Tyne. The design enables the walkway to tip at an angle to allow ships to pass and gives an impression of an eye opening and closing. It is known to the locals as "The Blinking Eye Bridge".

Once over the river it was a short walk to the modern apartment block and Jack's home on the seventh floor.

On entering the hallway Jack kicked off his shoes, pulled off his tie and made for the kitchen where he grabbed a wine glass and a bottle of Malbec from the rack.

Heading into the lounge with his pizza, he settled down on the sofa and poured himself a large glass of the deep red wine.

The diet of most cops was not the healthiest. Long days, late nights and the irregularities of shift work, meant that food had to be grabbed when time permitted. Often it would consist of stodgy sandwiches or greasy takeaways. With a social life that usually revolved around alcohol it was surprising that more cops didn't just keel over dead with heart attacks.

Jack recalled that his father used to claim that most cops in his time only lasted about three years into retirement before they were appearing in the obituary of the "Northumbria Bobby", a magazine for local Police Officers.

Certainly, since retirement over ten years ago his father claimed to have attended more funerals than he had weddings.

The thought of his father reminded Jack of how long it was since he had visited, or even been in contact with him. Although he lived fifty miles away there was no excuse for the lack of telephone conversation. Since his mother's death his father had retreated into his own world, which seemed to revolve around his garden and the local pub in the village where he had settled.

Jack looked at his mobile phone lying on the glass coffee table and wondered if he should call or whether to put it off until tomorrow.

Guilt got the better of him.

Slade senior took some time to answer. It was a land line number as the mobile reception in the village was notoriously bad. When he did pick up, he sounded at first suspicious. He explained that it was the result of too many unsolicited calls from accident solicitors or double-glazing salesmen.

'I thought you'd opted out from all that.'

'I did but they still get through. If I can be arsed I try to get my own back. Last week I kept this double-glazing guy on for twenty-five minutes discussing styles and types of conservatories. Eventually I got bored and asked him if it mattered that I lived in a fifth floor flat. He sounded really pissed off and hung up.'

'I'm never in the apartment long enough to get hassled by them.'

'Speaking of that, how is work in the big city.'

'Much the same as in your day… with the additional mix of a long list of illegal street drugs to make life more interesting.'

There was a pause on the other end before his father spoke.

'Have you heard from Elaine or young Dale?'

Jack hesitated. Since the divorce Elaine had moved away from the area. The only good thing that had come out of their brief marriage had been his son Dale, and although Jack had joint custody, the pressures of running H.MET seemed to constantly scupper his plans to see more of him. There had been several last-minute cancellations, and it had become a constant source of friction between Jack and his father… not to mention annoyance from Jack's ex-wife.

'You do know that it's the bairn's birthday next week? Weren't you supposed to be having him down to stay for a few days?'

Jack was taken off guard. With the events of the last couple of days it had slipped his mind that he was supposed to telephone Elaine to finalise the arrangements.

'Actually dad… something's come up. I might have to cancel.'

'With you something always comes up. Every time the job comes first. Well, maybe if you had put your family first a few years ago you wouldn't have been such a disaster as a dad.'

Jack felt chastened and muttered something about arranging to meet up with Dale when the current investigation was over, but then quickly changed the subject.

For a short while they managed to exchange small talk about work and how Slade senior was glad to be out of it. Since his mother's death, conversations with his dad could sometimes be fraught and stilted, but so long as they avoided any contentious subjects they could rub along agreeably.

After about five minutes Jack felt he had fulfilled his dutiful son role and made the excuse to hang up. A decision that met with little resistance from his father.

On putting the phone down Jack considered ringing Elaine, but decided that he would postpone that particular confrontation until another day.

He clicked on the television, more for background noise than any real interest in the content, hoping to be distracted from thinking about work and his disastrous domestic situation. The news just seemed to be the usual political name calling so, after a few minutes of channel hopping and convinced that there was nothing worth watching, Slade switched it off.

Thoughts of having again to disappoint his son were doing nothing for his appetite. Abandoning the pizza he reached for the wine and poured another large glass.

Jack forced himself to think instead of the day's events and what to make of the enquiry so far. He considered Donna's suggestion about a medical student prank. He couldn't one hundred per cent dismiss the theory, but it was nowhere near the top of his list.

Reflecting that the Post Mortem had not revealed any blunt force trauma to the head or the presence of anything having entered the skull, he was nonetheless sure in his own mind that this was a case of murder.

The preservation of the head in a freezer had prevented any estimate of a year of death let alone a time. Despite Doctor Clifford's meticulous evidence gathering he was sure that the subsequent disposal in the river had removed any possibility of the killer's DNA.

Slade was confident that Ged Kirkby's crime scene officers would find any forensic evidence that was available, but was sure that this would be restricted to footprints. With that area of the riverbank frequented by dog walkers, adventurous kids and the local glue sniffers it was going to mean a lot of footprints to check out.

Jack had faith in his team with whom he had worked with on several previous major incidents. Despite their foibles and quirks they had always managed to come up with results.

He was well aware that this would be a difficult case to solve, but it was early days yet, and once the victim was positively identified the enquiry would immediately change up a gear.

But how long was that going to take?

Chapter 7

The next morning Slade was out of bed early. The sun poking through the apartment blinds left strips of sunlight on the lounge floor heralding the start of a bright and sunny day. Pulling back the blinds revealed a cloudless sky that made the river look almost blue instead of the normal black. It was a perfect morning to walk to work.

The stroll along the quayside and the light easterly breeze helped blow away the cobwebs and by the time he arrived at Forth Bank Police Station he was ready for whatever the day would throw at him.

What it threw up were several messages that had come in overnight in relation to their investigation.

Following the previous day's media circulation there had been more than a dozen calls about 'mispers' from other forces throughout the country matching the description that had been circulated.

Jack read through the details of each of them, before allocating them to DC Henderson to add to the growing pile of 'possibilities' for their unidentified victim.

In addition, there had been a call from a dog walker who lived in the river bank area where the box had been found. A man in his sixties had telephoned the non-urgent Police 101 line giving a story about being out and about on the night before the head was recovered.

It was dusk and he was just about to make his way home with his dog, when he heard a loud splash coming from the river. The area was very wooded so he hadn't actually seen who or what had caused the noise. At the time he put it down to just kids messing about by the water's edge. However, the following day after reading in the local paper of the discovery of the head, he was now wanting to speak with an officer.

It looked to be a promising lead but Slade wasn't getting too excited. Sometimes people make stories up just to be at the centre of something interesting. It seems to make them feel important. Slade put the message aside as an "action" for one of the detectives to follow up with a home visit and a written statement from the caller.

"Actions" were particular tasks or lines of inquiry. Sometimes they were requested by the Senior Investigating Officer, or they may result from some information received, or even be thrown up from the result of a previous query.

Just before eight o'clock the HMET detectives started to arrive. The kettle was boiled, teas and coffees passed around and with the usual cop banter, the room began to get a familiar buzz about it. It appeared that everyone was keen and ready to crack on with the job at hand. Even the usual grumpy Mike Henderson was allowing himself the occasional smile.

Slade informed them of the overnight callers and allocated any "actions" that required following up. Henderson was informed of the new leads and asked to research the dozen or so additional missing persons.

'I'll add them to the pile boss. Some on the list have arrests on file, so once we get a DNA profile from our victim, I'm hoping a few of those will be eliminated.'

'Thanks Mike. Make sure you highlight any that you think might be connected and get them onto my desk.'

Jack turned to DC Shaw. 'Donna, can you collate any sex offenders within a five-mile radius of the scene. Get one of the others to go along with you to give them a visit. Some of them get very chatty when a woman is asking the questions.'

'Will do boss.'

'Dave…' Slade nodded in Armstrong's direction, '…chase up a preliminary copy of the pathologist's report and see if you can get him to commit to a time of death…' Slade allowed himself a smile '… I'm guessing to the nearest year would help.'

Once all the other enquiries had been allocated Jack left them to it and headed out along the corridor to the office of the Detective Superintendent.

Thomas Charles Parker was perched behind his desk speaking on the phone and hung up when Slade knocked at his door. 'Come in Jack. I was just about to give you a call. I've been talking to Command Block and the Assistant Chief has been in contact with the Press Office. There's going to be a media conference at eleven o'clock. We're going to give them this.'

He handed over to Jack an A4 sized artist's impression of what the victim might have looked like "ante mortem". The reconstruction showed a pretty girl with shoulder length fair hair and fine features. The sketch certainly looked different from the almost mummified remains that Jack recalled.

The artist is either very talented or has a bloody good imagination.

'The damned press have already got information that the only thing we have of the victim is her head. They've been doing their own house to house, and getting quotes from residents in the area.'

'Do you want me to be at the press conference?' Jack enquired, hoping against hope that the answer would be no.

35

'Aye! You're up to speed on the enquiry so it would be best. I'll take the lead but hand it over to you for the facts. We'll tell the buggers as little as possible. Just enough to give them their story and get our sketch out there in the public domain.'

Parker took a sip of coffee from a large mug. 'Have there been any developments since yesterday afternoon?'

Slade told him of the dog walker and of the additional missing persons.

'It's possible that it could have been the suspect dumping the box. I think that at the press conference we should make an appeal for any other people who were in the area the previous night, or walk there regularly to come forward. Someone might have seen a person leaving the scene after they'd dumped the box in the river.'

'Right Jack. I'll let you get back to your troops but I'll see you at headquarters fifteen minutes before the conference.'

Slade headed back to the incident room where Dave Armstrong was just hanging up the telephone.

'Boss, that was Inspector Maitland at Marine. There was nothing of any value found on the river bed yesterday, so that looks like another dead end.'

'Thanks Dave. Can you also chase up the results for the A.S.G. search of the river bank for me and arrange to widen the house to house to take in a radius of a quarter mile from the scene. I've got to go to a press conference with T.C.P. at eleven. Hold the fort and give me a call if anything urgent comes in.'

'No problem. Anything else boss?'

'Just to give you a heads up. Once we release the artist's sketch to the press you can expect quite a few calls into the incident room. Most will be false leads but with a bit of luck, amongst the deluge of calls from cranks ringing in, someone out there has a name for our victim.'

The reality was… without an identity for their victim it was going to be almost impossible to trace her murderer.

Chapter 8

The press conference was held at a large hall at the new Northumbria Police Headquarters at Middle Engine Lane in Wallsend which had replaced the old rambling mix of blocks that had made up the former Ponteland HQ.

Whereas the old array of buildings had been given the nickname of "Fantasy Island" the new Headquarters had been given the unofficial moniker of "Middle Earth". Both were an indication that, to the cops on the street, anyone who worked in the cosseted world of headquarters, was distanced from reality.

To the far end of the hall a stage was set up covering most of the width and below a backdrop of blue boards emblazoned with the force logo, stood a long table and three chairs.

In front were several rows of seating stretching back to either side of the room and down the centre aisle were a number of television and press cameras mounted on tripods. All eyes and cameras were focused on the stage in anticipation of the forthcoming briefing.

It was the usual lively affair with the reporters and television crew packing the large hall, jostling for position; each wanting to get their questions answered in the hope of a unique angle on a juicy story. The hubbub died down as Parker, Slade and a representative from the Police Press office climbed the steps of the stage and took their seats.

Parker had prepared the briefest of circumstances concerning the discovery of the remains.

The press had already tracked down the finder Joe Sample, who had been 'doorstepped' that morning by Liz Harmon the crime reporter for the local paper.

She had picked Sample's brains to find any angle that she could use to put a spin on her article in that evening's edition.

From what Slade had seen on meeting him there were very slim pickings to be had. However, where Harmon was concerned, there was no doubt that anything that he did say would be tagged as 'an exclusive' and suitably embellished for effect.

When it came to getting a headline Harmon's motto was clearly 'Why let the truth spoil a good story?'

Harmon had arrived early. Slade thought that she waddled in about as gracefully as a pig on ice. She glanced across at him and smirked. She was clearly still pleased with her success in tracking down the police's main… and so far, only witness.

She positioned herself in the front row so that she was impossible to ignore… no matter how much you wanted to. Slade thought that she appeared even more corpulent than the last time he had dealings with her. Looking at her, flanked by two weedy men on either side, he struggled to suppress a smile at the comical image, during what was intended to be a serious press briefing.

Liz Harmon was known to be a tenacious journalist with a nose for a good story and had more than her fair share of contacts, both outside and inside the police force. Although not very well liked by many police officers, she had a reputation for wheedling out stories from the slightest snippets of gossip or offhand comments. She was always determined to get her front-page scoop… whether by fair means or foul.

During a previous murder enquiry Harmon had obtained some inside information from an Inspector with whom she was having an affair. When he was discovered to have been leaking material he crashed and burned. Following an internal investigation the Inspector was given the opportunity to resign quietly, to save the Force any embarrassment. Many said that he was lucky not to end up in jail. Instead, there had followed a hastily arranged early retirement, and following a messy divorce, Jack had heard he was living alone in a rented flat in the east end of the city.

Harmon however seemed to float away from the scandal unscathed.

Like a bad fart on a windy day.

Following this, many cops were very wary of even speaking to her but she somehow still managed to have some informants willing to feed her little snippets of information.

The press briefing began with Parker describing the recovery of the metal box from the River Tyne. He told the assembled reporters that it contained the severed head of a young female but that information had already leaked into the public domain. He told the gathered reporters that, following the discovery, a murder enquiry had been launched.

Harmon, not wanting to shy away from the more gruesome aspects of the case, stuck a fleshy hand in the air and Parker nodded towards her.

'Yes, Miss Harmon.'

'So, are you telling us that the only part of the victim that has been found so far is a head enclosed in a metal box?'

'That's correct. Now, if I could refer to the box for a moment, it is an unusual container and we're appealing for help in tracing its origins. At the end of the conference, we will be providing photographs of the item for circulation. I would like anyone who has seen it, or a similar box to get in contact with us at the telephone number in your briefing notes.'

Parker turned to catch the eye of a different reporter but he wasn't going to get away so easily.

The same hand went up again and Harmon called out.

'Are you any further forward in tracing the victim?'

Parker glanced across at Slade who took his cue.

'Not at this time but we have prepared an artist's impression of the victim which is also for circulation, and we would ask for anyone who knows or believes they recognise her to come forward. Copies of the sketch are available at the back of the hall for you to take away following the conference. Digital images are available from the force website. It is vital that we trace the identity of this female.'

There followed several questions from the other reporters, all of whom wanted to find their own angle on the investigation.

'Was the decapitation an indication of some kind of ritual murder?'

'How long had the head been in the river?'

'Could a serial killer be on the loose?'

'Has a cause of death been established?'

To the last question Harmon had been heard to mutter just loud enough for the questioner to hear, 'Chopping her bloody head off didn't help …you prick.' There were sniggers from the people on either side of her.

When the press conference was over those present from the media scurried away to file their copy and report back to their relevant newsrooms. As the camera operators dismantled their gear Jack spoke briefly to Parker.

'I see Harmon is still keeping herself at the forefront despite losing her main informant in the Police.'

'The loss of her inside contact won't hold her back. What she doesn't know she'll just make up. That said, I'm reasonably happy that we should get widespread press coverage.'

'A severed head in a box. The readers will lap up the grisly details.'

'Just so long as it brings us in plenty of leads.'

Cops may not like the press but it was at times like this that they could have their uses.

Liz Harmon, if truth be told, was not a great fan of the police. She had scored many a headline from highlighting some botched enquiry or missed clue in a major investigation and was more than happy to plaster police failings across the front page to increase newspaper circulation and promote her own ambitions.

The public seemed to revel in tales of police cock ups; loving to read about the gaffes and blunders of the boys in blue. It was as if they enjoyed the contrast between the coppers they watched on television and what happened in real life. They had become conditioned to believe that a murder could be solved in a two-hour episode at most.

That said, as Chief Crime Reporter, Harmon needed to have a working relationship with cops in order to carry out her job effectively.

In better times, she used to gather her informants in the police through the various drinking venues that she knew cops frequented and found that the more they drank the more they would let slip. Her mounting bar bill at times could be daunting but so long as the newspaper covered her expenses, the results when measured in exclusive headlines were well worth it.

When the private Police Club opened, she had occasionally been asked to visit but following her problems involving a certain married Inspector at headquarters, all invites had dried up and she was finding herself "persona non grata".

After her ex-lover had been unceremoniously booted into retirement he had tried contacting her, no doubt expecting to continue their relationship.

Unfortunately for him she had no use for an ex-cop.

She told him their relationship was over and blocked his calls.

The younger, more trendy cops, could still be seen around town but now preferred the busy Quayside venues with the noisy 'thump thump' music and wall to wall unattached partygoers. They were rarely seen in the police club mingling with 'the oldies' except for the occasional promotion or leaving do.

As the cops got younger and she got older, the feminine charms of the middle-aged crime reporter had lost much of her allure.

Increasingly it was only at scenes of crime and press conferences like today that she had any opportunity to chat to police officers and attempt to cultivate new sources.

Looking around, she had spotted several familiar faces of cops that she knew from the old days but all of them appeared to be avoiding eye contact. It was clear that she was now considered bad news in many police circles.

She wished she could get back to being at the centre of things but God knows how. It was becoming increasingly unlikely.

She did not know at the time that her wish was very soon to be granted.

Chapter 9

Back at the incident room Dave Armstrong was sifting through the 'action' results. As he saw Jack entering the office he called across. 'How did it go, Jack?'

'Not too bad. Liz Harmon was there as usual. She was, as always, about as welcome as Herod at the nursery Christmas party but I can put up with having to look at her for a few minutes if it gets the results we're after.'

Armstrong handed him a printed list of exhibits.

'These are the results from the A.S.G. search. They've wound up now. Nothing startling was found but they've gathered more assorted rubbish, bottles, cans and the like to add to the growing collection.'

Jack shook his head, 'Doesn't anyone down there know what bins are for?'

He scanned down the long list. 'Anything new from forensics?'

'Ged Kirkby has been back on. His guys have obtained some more good casts of footprints from a muddy track which may have been used as an escape route for whoever dumped the box. Ged is quite hopeful that they might prove evidential.'

The door swung open and they were interrupted by Henderson striding over. He was holding aloft a sheaf of papers. 'The lab did a hurry-up job on the victim's D.N.A. so I've managed to eliminate several of the outstanding mispers from the list. I'm concentrating on local Northumbria cases at first. There's always time to spread the net later.'

He seemed to be hesitating.

'What's up?' Jack asked.

'It's just how far do I go back boss. I've gathered stuff from three years back so far and the further back I go the longer the list gets.'

'That's not something I can answer at the moment Mike. You just have to keep going.' Jack tried to sound sympathetic.

Henderson nodded but clearly not happy with the response, frowned and wandered away back to his desk and a large teetering stack of paperwork.

Dave Armstrong watched him go.

'He's right Jack. It's like looking for an honest man at a lawyer's convention. We're on a hiding to nothing.'

'We've just got to keep at it. That's how these things get resolved in the end. Let's see what the press appeal manages to throw up.'

At one o'clock Slade came into the Incident room carrying a small portable flat screen television. Setting it down on a desk he switched it on as the detectives gathered around.

The murder and press conference had made second item in the national news and was the lead item on the local coverage. Photographs flashed up on the screen of the box and the artist drawing of the girl. It was stressed that identifying her was a priority and that so far the police were no further forward in doing so.

'I see that they've stopped short of saying the police are baffled,' muttered Henderson sarcastically.

'Best stand by for the usual "nutters" and "oddballs" to start ringing in,' grumbled Jim Jackson.

'And with it being on the national news we're going to get calls from all over the bloody country,' Henderson growled.

'And maybe further afield,' agreed Armstrong.

Jack switched off the television and looked around the room. He could tell from the glum faces staring back at him that the enormity of the task ahead was beginning to sink in with his team.

Most murders are solved in the first forty-eight hours. That is because the majority are domestics or drunken brawls and the offender is obvious. More often than not, they were still at the scene when cops attended and in many cases, might even be the person that had made the call to summon the police.

"Stranger murders" were a much tougher prospect, needing extensive investigation and sometimes were only solved by getting the right break at the right time. They were the most manpower intensive and time-wise could drag on for months or even years.

'We could do with a bit of good luck on this one.' Gavin Oates said, glancing across at the photographs displayed on the murder wall.

'Yes. But I've always found the harder I work the luckier I get,' said Jack. 'And if just one of those calls identifies the victim, then it will all have been worth it. So, let's just get on with it and pray for that little piece of good fortune.'

Two hours later their prayers were answered.

Dave Armstrong came hurrying from the Incident room into Jack's office and from his smile Jack guessed it was some good news for a change.

'We've had a woman on from the West End's area. She claims to have recognised the artist sketch on the afternoon news as her sister. She's given her name as Jacqueline Marshall.'

'How sure is she?'

'Sobbing down the phone certain. I think we have our victim.'

Jack stood up. 'That's great news… for us if not for her. When was Jacqueline Marshall reported missing and have we got all the details on our database?'

The sergeant's smile faded.

'There's a bit of a complication with that,' he said looking down at a piece of paper in his hand.

'Come on … spit it out!'

'Well…if she is our victim …she's been missing for almost forty years.'

Chapter 10

He saw the report on the afternoon news and cursed his choice of a dumping ground. He had never intended the head to be discovered at all, never mind this quickly. It was all because he had panicked when the dog started to bark. He wasn't sure whether or not he had been seen by that damned dog walker.

On the plus side, after this length of time he doubted whether they would ever discover the victim's identity. It was obvious from the television coverage that the police had no clue as to a name for her.

The truth was... neither had he.

The television screen was filled with a sketch showing a very pretty young girl. That was probably what she looked like about four decades ago. He wondered if the people watching would recognise her and come forward, or whether she was long forgotten by any family and friends that had known her.

Whilst at first, he had been annoyed that the head had been found so quickly, that initial irritation was slowly being superseded by an odd thrill. He was suddenly finding himself the centre of attention in such a widely talked about news story. The discovery had featured prominently on both local and national news with senior policemen almost begging for help. It felt strange to know that he alone held all the answers to their problems.

Not that he was ever going to help them.

He had never liked policemen; all the ones with whom he had come into contact with he regarded as arrogant and aggressive bullies. They used to always claim that it was down to his attitude. Now it was amusing to see them floundering in their fruitless search for clues.

After nearly being spotted the other night, he knew that it was probably too dangerous to try to dispose of the other body parts whilst there was so much press attention. However, seeing the effect he was having, he began to wonder how funny it would be to confuse the struggling 'bizzies' even further. It would give him enormous pleasure to watch them squirming on television each night as they gradually caved in under the relentless press furore.

Getting up, he walked along the hallway to the end door. Turning the old-fashioned key in the mortice lock, he clicked the switch just inside the entrance. The old fluorescent tube flashed several times, before coming to life and illuminating the basement.

It was months ago when he had first ventured down into the subterranean room. Now as he walked down the creaking wooden steps and entered the dusty basement it had become very familiar to him. Windowless and neglected, with a concrete floor, the room stretched the width of the house, and was crammed full of assorted junk.

At the far end under dirty brown canvas sheeting were two chest freezers. One looked positively ancient but the second appeared a few years newer. He didn't suppose many people bothered these days with chest freezers. Most belonged, as did these, in the eighties or nineties. Now everyone wanted to have those modern American style upright things with double doors.

Pausing for a while he gazed at the two appliances standing side by side and imagined their frozen contents. Dumping just one head had brought unbelievable attention. Yet he was still nowhere near solving his problem.

There was still a hell of a lot more to get rid of.

He began to fantasise about posting pieces of the bodies to the police a bit like Jack the Ripper was supposed to have done with his victim's kidney.

Unable to suppress a grin he conjured up images of the copper's shocked faces if they were to open a parcel and found a leg, an arm or even another head.

It would be very entertaining.

Of course, as much as he would love to do so, he knew he couldn't possibly do it. It would be far too risky.

Or would it?

Chapter 11

Driving away from Forth Banks, Dave Armstrong headed across town towards the West Road; the main thoroughfare heading west out of the city.

Jack was deep in thought as they passed several motorcycle shops where on a Saturday morning crowds of bikers would gather to show off their high-performance machines, or stare in envy at those of others. It amused Jack to think that half the young men strutting their stuff in full leather gear, mixing with the bikers and gossiping about the latest race bike, probably didn't even own their own machine.

Several had likely come into town by bus.

The further West they travelled, it struck Jack that the West End of the city was and always had been, a strange eclectic mix of housing.

With the accommodation went a similar mix of occupants.

The further one got from the city centre, rows of terraced housing had been converted into flats or businesses and still further on, in the streets running off from the main road, were the "Tyneside flats". They were purpose built twin apartments with two separate entrances but sharing a communal backyard.

Further on again there were side roads of neat semi-detached houses with well-kept lawns and flower beds. Then amazingly in amongst all this mixed housing there might be a small section of two-thousand-year-old Roman Wall. A remnant from the reign of Emperor Hadrian and upon which parts of the West Road had been built.

Both Jack and his father had worked at the West End nick at one time or another. Jack recalled having attended a burglary in a neat crescent of houses set back off the main road and being astounded to see the out of place remains of an ancient Roman Vallum crossing, standing in a neighbour's garden.

The thirties brick built semi-detached house that he and Dave Armstrong now pulled up in front of, was in one of the long streets of semis that ran off to the North of the main road. From the outside the building looked well cared for.

The freshly painted front door was answered by a woman in her mid-fifties with greying hair and a slim figure. She gave her name as Marie and ushered them inside and through to a lounge at the front of the house.

The room was clean and tidy but appeared dated with patterned wallpaper and dark wooden furniture in a style that would be more suited to the nineteen eighties. A bay window looked out onto a patch of well-kept lawn surrounded by colourful plants.

The atmosphere in the room was tense. Jack was sure that somewhere in the back of her mind Marie had always hoped that her sister might still be alive.

He was about to shatter that illusion forever.

Dotted around the room were several family photographs. Marie picked one up from on top of the faux Adam fireplace and handed it to Slade.

'This is Jackie. She was my sister.'

Jack registered that she had used the past tense and realised that Marie had come to an acceptance that she would never see her sibling alive again.

He studied the photograph which showed a fair-haired girl of about eighteen with bright blue eyes and a smile that displayed a row of gleaming white teeth. She was sitting on a wall next to a younger girl who looked similar in features. Some distance below was a large expanse of golden beach and Jack recognised the remains of Tynemouth Priory in the background.

'That was taken near Long Sands about a month before Jackie disappeared. That's what the family called her. We used to joke that Jacqueline was only her name for Sundays.'

She seemed a little lost in thought and glanced out the window at two young children passing in the street outside, before turning her gaze back to the two detectives.

'It was a Sunday. The most gorgeous sunny afternoon. We had taken the metro down to the coast to celebrate the results of Jackie's A levels. She is... she was... a year older than me. My big sister.'

Marie O'Connor had a softly spoken voice which exuded melancholy as she told the detectives about the closeness between her and her older sister. Despite the passage of time Slade had easily recognised her as the younger girl in the photograph.

Jack was also in no doubt regarding the similarities between the older girl in the photograph and the artist's impression of their victim.

He felt a deep sadness for this woman's loss and felt pangs of guilt that her anguish was giving him some relief. He was certain that he had at last identified his victim.

'I was called Marshall in those days. O'Connor is my married name.' she explained in a voice that at times was close to breaking.

'Can you tell me how Jackie went missing?' Slade said softly.

'She had gone down to Newcastle to meet up with some of her school friends.

They were going to visit a couple of the bars. In those days most of them called last orders at ten thirty so we expected her home by half eleven at the latest. When she wasn't back by twelve thirty my mam began to panic. People didn't have mobile phones in those days so we couldn't just ring her.'

Marie's voice was beginning to crack but she took a deep breath and continued.

'Mam left it until two o'clock and then dad rang the Police.'

'Was Jackie worried about anything? Maybe exam results? A boyfriend? Was there any reason for her to go missing voluntarily?'

'No. Jackie was a daddy's girl. We both were. After she went missing dad knew something really bad had happened. He just sensed it. After that he seemed to go downhill quickly. He died less than two years later. The doctors said it was cancer that took him in the end but I know it was brought on by losing our Jackie.'

Slade saw the tears forming at the corner of the woman's eyes and patiently waited for her to continue.

'I lost mam a few years later. She never gave up hope but I think she always knew in her heart that she would never see our Jackie again. Jackie never even got to have a funeral. We never got to say goodbye properly.'

She stopped speaking to discreetly wipe the corner of her eye.

'I'm sorry to ask this but we need to be absolutely certain that it is your sister.'

She looked worried and leaning forward whispered, 'Will I have to identify her?'

Jack's thoughts flashed to the mummified head lying in a plastic box in the mortuary.

'No, that won't be necessary. What I'd like my colleague here to do is take a simple mouth swab which we can compare with the DNA evidence we have. That way we can be sure that it is your Jackie.'

He paused. 'We'd also like you to provide details of her dentist.'

Sitting back in her chair Marie simply nodded.

'You must do what you have to do.'

Slade studied the photograph and wondered how someone could just snuff out a young girl's life, robbing not just her but also her family of their future. It may have been almost forty years ago but he was determined to track down her killer and ensure that he gave the family some closure.

He handed the photograph to Armstrong who looked down at it and said quietly, 'May we take this. We'll make copies and I promise you that we'll bring back the original.'

Marie O'Connor silently nodded.

Slade glanced around the room at the many photographs of Jacqueline Marshall. Evidence that despite the passage of time she had not been forgotten. In each and every one she seemed bright and happy; her whole life ahead of her.

'Did the police at the time have any theories as to why she was missing?'

'At first, they suggested that she might have just run away, so they checked out all her friends, especially the ones she had been out with on the night. Then suddenly after a couple of days the Police really seemed to step things up. There was a lot of media coverage on television and the newspaper ran a two-page story about the missing girls... but nothing ever came of it.'

Both Jack and Dave stared across at the woman and sat forward. Jack was the first to speak.

'You said "missing girls". What did you mean?'

'The police didn't tell us at first but Jackie wasn't the only girl to have just disappeared like that. That's why the press made such a lot of it. I think there were three. All of them within a year.'

In the ensuing silence Jack could feel his heart thumping.

The enquiry had just taken on a whole new direction.

Chapter 12

Sitting behind his desk Parker was his usual sullen self. 'Why the hell am I just finding out about this now?'

'It was almost forty years ago, boss. They were recorded in the files as simply Missing Persons. We're talking back in the day when having no body meant not having a murder.'

'So, what are you doing to pull together the details of all three of the girls?'

'Henderson was already working through all the outstanding missing persons but there are dozens and he's only gone back about six years so far. We are now talking about three young girls from the nineteen eighties. A trawl through newspapers from the time will get us some background. We can also dig out the historic missing person reports from the archives.'

Jack took a deep breath. 'We also need to make sure we're only talking about three, so I've asked Henderson to change his search parameters. He's now working forward starting in 1984, a year before Jackie went missing, and concentrating on the Northumbria Force area. We can extend the search as and when we feel the need. It's a pretty large task and we're talking about forty years ago. It was a different world back then. Although there were extensive enquiries at the time on the three girls that we know about, they were never classed as murders. With no evidence or any scene of crime they were simply three girls who for whatever reason had left home.'

'You've had a positive identification on our victim?'

'I've asked for another "hurry up" on the DNA and Dave Armstrong is making enquiries at the dentist Jackie attended to trace her dental records. That said I've seen the family photos. She's a ringer and I know in my gut that it's her.'

'And we have names for all three of them?'

'Yes. The sister kept all the original newspaper articles that linked the girls. They give us names and ages for the two other possible victims. The photos are black and white and pretty faded but all three have a remarkably similar description. Slim, blond hair, blue eyes and all about eighteen at the time of their disappearances. I've got Gavin Oates checking with the newspaper to see if they have the original photos still on file in their archives.'

'Who is collating the historic missing person reports?'

'Donna Shaw is up at headquarters as we speak, searching through the archives. She will pull together the old reports and any

51

ancillary documents she can find relating to the initial enquiries. When DC Oates is finished at the newspaper offices, he's been 'actioned' to head over to the Central Library and the Civic Centre to check through all the newspaper reports from the period. All the old newspaper records at the Civic are on a microfiche system so it's going to take some time.'

'Let's hope to God that there are only three we're dealing with,' muttered Parker.

'That's enough don't you think?'

Parker fixed him with a cold stare. 'You know what I mean. Are you anticipating more turning up?'

'It's a possibility, but far too early to say at this stage.'

'Serial killers don't stop after three. There might be others out there. If he did stop forty years ago, why has he suddenly started disposing of the bodies now? There's a lot of questions that need answering Jack.'

Parker got up and striding across to the window stared out across the wide expanse of the city. Below him cops were strolling out the Police station to make the short walk into the centre, probably hoping that the worst they might have to deal with was a violent shoplifter. Meanwhile three floors up Parker was silently contemplating the possibility of three unsolved murders and a potential serial killer.

Parker broke the silence.

'It's before my time but in 1990 Northumbria got that evil bastard Robert Black in for four murders that he'd carried out back in the eighties. It still felt fresh when I joined the job. All the cops that I spoke to said that they had a gut feeling that he'd done many more. Black died in prison in 2016 without revealing how many poor kids he murdered or where they're buried. Right now, I hope he's burning in Hell!'

'Black's profile was completely different boss. He went for prepubescent children. At eighteen these girls are much older than any of Black's victims.'

'Eighteen is still young.' Parker seemed lost in thought. 'You know Jack, I've got a daughter not much older than these kids.'

Slade had never heard Parker mention his family before and a heavy oppressive silence descended upon the office.

Eventually Parker turned back and stared hard at Slade.

'I know that you've pulled some strokes in the past and we've not always seen eye to eye but this is different. I want this bastard. We need him off the streets and, just at this moment, I don't really care how we do it.'

52

Slade nodded his understanding and silently stood up and headed back to the Incident room, leaving Parker alone to his thoughts.

That night sitting in the lounge of his apartment, Jack stared down at the dark waters of the Tyne and slowly sipped from his second large glass of Glenmorangie.

Although the river reflected the lights of the quayside bars it still exuded an air of menace as it raced past, black and dangerous, on its way from the city down towards Tynemouth and the North Sea. The same Tynemouth where a happy and carefree Jacqueline Marshall had posed for the photograph a short time before her disappearance.

Jack thought about the investigation and wondered how far and wide the enquiries might stretch. So far they had three possible victims but Parker was quite right when he said that serial killers don't usually stop at three... unless forced to.

Maybe he hadn't stopped. Maybe there were more victims out there waiting to be found.

Maybe not in the Northumbria area.

Perhaps not even in the UK.

Had the serial killer simply moved away to a different area or even a different country and carried on?

If so, why come back?

Although it was what cops called a 'cold case,' it was still as current for the family of Jackie Marshall as on the day she had gone missing, four decades before.

Superintendent Parker had referred to Robert Black, the paedophile serial killer responsible for a child murder in the Northumbria Force area in the eighties. The investigation had been an epic undertaking for Northumbria Police and had involved close liaisons with a number of forces, before the murderer was eventually detained as he attempted to carry out yet another child abduction.

In 1994, Black was convicted of three child murders throughout the UK spanning more than a decade. However, it wasn't until another seventeen years after his convictions that he was found guilty of another child murder in Northern Ireland. That murder had occurred thirty years earlier.

Parker had mentioned that he himself had a daughter the same age as the current victim had been. Jack's thoughts drifted to his own child; the ten year old son he had hardly seen since his wife had left, taking him to Scotland. He imagined what it would be like if someone had abducted his child and he had to come to terms with the realisation that he was destined never to see him alive again.

It felt too dreadful to contemplate.

He lifted his glass and downed what remained, before returning to the bottle and pouring another.

Talking to the sister of Jackie Marshall had been a disconcerting experience. Although he had delivered many death messages before, he had never met anyone who had waited nearly forty years to be told the dreadful news that they hoped never to hear. It must be a mixture of intense grief, contrasting with a deep relief at finally knowing the truth.

Now, there was the possibility that two further families might be faced with the same scenario. Was it better not to know? Was it easier to live in hope and yearning, or would they prefer the knowledge that their loved ones were never ever returning home? Loved ones that had most likely died alone and in terror at the hands of some psychopath.

Jack tried not to get too emotionally involved in cases he dealt with. He always went out of his way to portray an image of the professional hard-nosed detective, who viewed every case dispassionately.

The reality was that cops like that didn't always get results. Sometimes it was only by allowing yourself to get involved, by taking on board some of the grief and to feel the anger of the family left behind, that you were spurred on to get results.

Such intense involvement can take a toll. Many cops had trouble sleeping, suffered stress and more than one, overwhelmed by depression, had taken their own life. Others sought to dull the pain and seek solace in drink.

With that thought still in his head he glanced down at the amber liquid in his glass and considered pouring it down the sink. He resisted the thought. Instead, he swirled it around and drained the glass.

Now, that would have been a terrible waste of a good malt and a real crime.

Chapter 13

The following morning the Murder Incident room was buzzing.

The photograph that Dave Armstrong had taken from Jacqueline Marshall's sister was now enlarged and up on the wall replacing the one from the morgue. Below was her full name, date of birth, description and the West End address at the time of her disappearance.

Jacqueline was no longer nameless remains.

She had become a person.

Having a name, a face, a personality, made her someone that the team could relate to. It made all the difference.

Next to the photograph were two other images that Donna Shaw had unearthed from the archives. The two other missing girls. Below each were their personal details.

Elizabeth Mortimer had disappeared from the Walker area in the east of Newcastle in January 1985. She was followed four months later by Elaine Robinson who had disappeared from Gosforth to the north of the city. Following that the last of the known victims, Jackie Marshall, went missing in September from the West End.

The disappearances had each been almost exactly four months apart.

Following Jackie Marshall, there appeared to have been no further reports. It was as if something had occurred that suddenly stopped all the disappearances.

But what?

Looking at the array of photographs, all the girls were strikingly similar in appearance and all had gone missing in similar circumstances; walking home from the city centre after a night out with friends.

Slade turned from the murder wall to face the assembled detectives and the general hum of conversation in the incident room died down.

'Right! Mobile phones to silent! You should be all up to speed on the latest developments. We're still waiting for DNA confirmation but believe me on this one… I'm ninety-nine per cent certain we have a name for our victim.'

He pointed to the photograph of Jacqueline Marshall.

'Jacqueline Marshall, known to her friends as Jackie, disappeared in 1985 after meeting friends in Newcastle City centre. Nothing was seen or heard of her until her head turned up, just a few days ago, in a metal box dragged from the River Tyne. One of the key things that we need to know is…where is the rest of her?'

Slade turned and pointed to the other photographs.

'The other two girls Elizabeth Mortimer and Elaine Robinson went missing over that same year in similar circumstances. Both were making their way home after a night out in Newcastle city centre. Nothing has been seen or heard of either of them since.'

He then moved to a flip chart and turning to a fresh sheet of paper wrote on it the three names of the missing teenagers and the dates that they had gone missing.

The room was silent, every pair of eyes focused on the chart waiting for Slade to continue.

'Why has the murderer suddenly started up again after almost forty years? Why choose now to dispose of Jackie's remains and why just the head. Where is the rest of her? Has anyone got any theories to explain why the killer has suddenly resurfaced?'

Dave Armstrong was the first to speak, 'More than thirty odd years boss. Maybe he's been banged up for life on another murder and just got out.'

Slade scribbled on the flip chart, "Prison?".

Jim Jackson called out, 'Are we sure he did stop? I mean, we haven't found the remains of the first two girls yet. Maybe he just slowed down but continued in a different part of the country.'

Slade nodded and "UK wide circulation" was added to the list.

Gavin Oates chirped up from the back. 'Maybe he's been working abroad. He could have shifted his kill zone somewhere else. Europe or even further afield.'

Jack thought of Robert Black and the murder in Ireland. He scribbled on the chart, "Abroad? Europe? Check with Interpol?"

'Right!' said Slade, 'so why dispose of the bodies now? Why not at the time or even ten or twenty years ago?'

This prompted a number of suggestions from the team.

'Maybe the location in which she was stored is no longer available. Perhaps it's changed hands or has to be demolished,' volunteered Donna Shaw.

'The freezer equipment he's using has broken down,' put forward Gavin Oates.

'What if he thinks someone is on to him and has been panicked into disposing of the evidence,' said Mike Henderson.

With each suggestion Slade made a note on the chart from which he would later plan their strategy and determine allocation of 'actions' for the following days.

Fairly soon the brainstorming session left the chart a crisscross of words and arrows.

Jack turned from the chart to the assembled detectives.

'Anyone anything else to add?'

Dave Armstrong raised a hand.

'There's one other possibility, boss...'

As one, all eyes turned to the detective sergeant.

'... maybe he's just making some room in the freezer.'

The room went silent as everyone considered the implications of his words. The silence was broken by the ringing of a telephone in the background.

Gavin Oates picked it up and shot a glance at Jack.

'Boss, I think we have an answer to one of your questions. Control room are saying that a torso has been found by kids playing in the woods at Jesmond Dene.

Chapter 14

Designed in the 1860s by Lord Armstrong, Jesmond Dene is a densely wooded park area, in a narrow steep sided valley to the north of Newcastle City Centre.

On sunny days it is usually crowded with an eclectic mix of people, enjoying leisurely strolls and taking in the scenic wooded vista. A rural idyll within a short walking distance of the bustling metropolis. Joggers can be spotted pounding the miles of winding tracks, casting surreptitious glances at their smart watches as they go about their fitness regimes. Children excitedly explore the trees and foliage, making dens or playing beside the small Ouseburn stream that meanders down, through small pools and waterfalls, in a relentless journey towards the River Tyne.

Today was one of those days and happened to coincide with a half term holiday for the local schools. The mild weather had brought out dozens of people eager to enjoy the late spring warmth of a mid-week morning. Sunlight filtered through the leaves onto blankets and picnic hampers, as families seeking shade, watched their children playing and exploring the park.

Those families had been moved a considerable distance away from the blue and white Police tape that now festooned the location.

It had been a couple of twelve year old boys walking their dog who had come across the body... or rather pieces of it. Three packages containing a torso and two severed arms were wrapped in thick polythene sheeting and bound tightly with parcel tape. At first the youngsters were unsure of what they had uncovered. Maybe they were parts of one of those tailor's dummies; like the ones that they had often seen in the city centre shops. Perhaps they had been abandoned in the undergrowth as a prank.

It was only when they began to unwrap one of the arms that they realised their discovery was something quite different.

By the time Jack Slade and Dave Armstrong arrived, the crime scene had already been taped off, with the obligatory young probationer constable standing sentry and scribbling into an attendance log. Inside the cordon white suited forensic officers carrying plastic evidence bags were sifting through a number of items recovered from the trees and bushes.

Many of the families, who an hour earlier had been setting up a picnic, had now left, ushering away their children... several leaving before their details had been obtained. Slade frowned. That was something which would clearly hinder the search for any potential witnesses. To add to his annoyance, they had been replaced by the usual 'rubberneckers' armed with mobile phones and eager not to miss out on a photo that they could share on Facebook or Instagram. All hoping for their fifteen minutes of fame.

A local television crew were just setting up their cameras and Slade wondered how the press vultures managed to get their information so quickly.

Social media had a lot to answer for.

Glancing across, Slade spotted one of the reporters whom he recognised from the early evening news.

As Jack and Dave walked towards the police tape, a photographer with a lens as long as his arm was snapping away at the scene. On seeing the detectives arriving, he turned around and focused in on them. Jack heard the rapid clicks of multiple digital images being snapped.

Suddenly, a microphone was thrust in his face, and one of the reporters was shouting questions at him.

Jack responded, 'No comment,' forcing his way past the journalist, as a uniformed officer came over and tried to keep the photographers and reporters at bay.

On spotting Slade and Armstrong, one of the CSI officers ducked beneath the crime scene tape and made his way towards them. Despite being head to toe in a white forensic suit, Slade recognised the familiar gait of Ged Kirkby.

'Morning Jack. Some presents for you,' he said, handing the two detectives white coveralls, gloves and some forensic shoe coverings.

It took them a few minutes to pull on the coverings, and all the while Jack could hear reporters shouting questions at him. He tried to ignore them and when suitably attired, Kirkby indicated for them to follow him.

Ducking under the fluttering police tape, the detectives walked silently along on carefully laid out tread boards. A short distance into the thick vegetation, they came to a stop beside three wrapped packages.

Lying a little way apart, in the shade of a large pink flowering Daphne shrub, two of the body parts were close together. A third was a distance away. Jack guessed that it was the one that had been partially unwrapped by the children who had found it. Even before he got close, he could see that it was an arm.

'It was found by a couple of bairns walking their dog,' said Kirkby.

'That's why I don't have a dog… the buggers are always finding bodies,' replied Slade.

'The young kid had a job unwrapping it because it was bound by quite heavy-duty packaging tape,' Kirkby explained, pointing down at the tightly wrapped parcel.

'I hope you're going to tell me it's a rare type of tape only sold by one shop in the country?'

'Sure Jack. And the killer left a sticker on the torso giving a return address. I wish it was as easy as it is on the bloody telly. No, the tape isn't rare Jack… just unusual. It's not what you use to parcel up and post stuff off on ebay.'

'What about the actual body parts?'

'Other than that, they are a torso and two arms, it's going to be down to the pathologist. It's female. I'm guessing late teens early twenties but that is just a guess. I'm also assuming they're all going to be a match for your head from the other day.'

'If you're looking for a bet you've got no takers.'

'They've probably been dumped overnight. With them lying at the bottom of a steep bank there's every possibility that they were dumped in the dene from above. From the flattened grass I'd suggest that the torso rolled down to where it ended up and the two arms were thrown down after it.'

Jack glanced up the steep bank rising up from the dene, before turning his attention again to the discarded body parts.

Kirkby continued. 'I've had a quick look and although the exterior of the torso is showing very early signs of defrosting, it appears as if the inside is still frozen solid.'

He looked Jack in the eye. 'It's not rigor mortis. The body has definitely been frozen and is starting to thaw. We're taking a couple of photographs in situ before we take a closer look.'

'Have the uniform checked the area at the top of the bank?'

'They've already taped it off Jack. There's a uniform cop up there keeping people away, and C.S.I. will move to that location after we've finished here.'

'Anything else found in the vicinity?'

'Nothing obvious, but I'm assuming you'll be calling the Area Support Group boys and girls in for a fingertip search of the immediate area.'

'A.S.G. is already being sorted by control room. Are the two young kids alright?'

'Bit shocked. They've been taken home and are with their parents now. There's a cop been allocated to recover and package up the kids' shoes and outer clothing until we pick them up. I don't expect to get anything from their clothes but I'm just covering bases. The cop on the cordon has their details. There's another uniform cop who went home with the lads. She's trying to coax anything she can get from them before one of your detectives takes a statement.'

He glanced down at the discarded remains.

'There are a couple of partial fingerprints clearly visible on the packaging but they're small, and probably from one of the kids. We're going to need some elimination prints from them, but it'll be easy to verify.'

'I'll get one of the team on it,' replied Jack.

'When we get the wrappings back to the lab, we can have a cyanoacrylate test done to see if we can get any more prints.'

Cyanoacrylate, better known as superglue, gives off fumes when heated in an airtight container. The fumes then settle on the oil residue left by a finger and reveal any latent prints.

Ged Kirkby again glanced back to where the remains had been abandoned. 'Well Jack, I suppose we're only missing the legs and we can complete this sick jigsaw.'

'It would at least allow the family to bury her whole.'

The other Crime Scene Investigator had finished taking photographs and was now crouched down, peeling back some of the wrapping and looking closely at the packages.

He began to shake his head and called over to Kirkby and Slade. 'I wouldn't get your hopes up just yet.'

Jack sensed a problem. 'What's up?'

'See for yourself boss.'

Slade moved in for a closer look at the body parts and saw what he meant. 'Oh shit!'

'Aye Boss. Unless your missing lass had two left arms… we've got more than one victim here.'

Chapter 15

That afternoon Jack stood again in front of the white murder wall. There were now several additional photographs on the wall showing the assortment of body parts recovered from Jesmond Dene. Alongside was a Google map image highlighting the general location of the deposition site and surrounding area.

'Donna. I need you to arrange interviews with the relatives of the two outstanding 'mispers' from the same time as Jacqueline Marshall. The result hasn't yet come back for the familial DNA test to positively link Marie O'Connor with the first body part who we believe to be her sister Jackie Marshall… but I think that we're in little doubt they'll find a match.'

He looked at two of the photographs behind him.

'We need to trace and interview the relatives of the other girls so we can do further familial DNA tests to confirm whether any of the latest body parts from Jesmond Dene match. The worst possible scenario is that they could be from other victims that we don't yet know about… but for the moment let's go with what we've got.'

Jack pointed at the image of the arm where the wrapping had been partially removed.

'As you can see from this photograph the way the body parts have been packaged is interesting. The tape used is not rare but according to Ged Kirkby it is a little unusual. I've raised an action to trace the manufacturer and see if we can narrow down which outlets they supply to.'

A hand was raised and Jack nodded towards Gavin Oates. 'The head was in a metal box and there was no packaging tape used. Why the change boss?'

'A good point but something that I haven't yet got an answer to. It's a very significant change of M.O. in respect of the body disposal. Obviously with the head being dumped in the river the killer never intended us to find it, but this latest disposition site is different. The arms and torso were left in a busy park where he must have known they'd soon be discovered. That's a hell of a change of Modus Operandi. He obviously intended them to be found.'

'You think he's taunting us?' said Henderson.

'Let's keep an open mind on that one.'

Dave Armstrong glanced down at his phone.

'Boss, I've had a text from Ged Kirkby. The partial prints on the packaging do match the elimination prints taken from one of the kids, so that's a dead end. They're doing further tests as they remove the wrappings and will get back to us as soon as they have anything else.'

'Thanks Dave.'

Slade turned and pointed to the enlarged google map showing Jesmond Dene. 'A.S.G. are still doing a fingertip search of the immediate area but the Dene is such a vast space that we've been forced to limit the search parameters at this time. There were several footprints found from adult size trainers not too far from the disposition site. Casts have been taken but Ged Kirkby is pretty certain that the body parts were probably rolled down the steep bank so the footprints may be yet another false trail. That being said I still want an action raised concerning an ID for the make and size, and for any casts obtained to be cross checked against those found at the riverbank where the head was recovered. There might be a match. There's always a possibility that the killer may have been careless.'

'That might be a lot of casts to find storage for,' said Jim Jackson imagining a mounting mass of exhibits.

'But just one of them might be our murderer.'

'I know the park's extensive and it would take some time but it might be worth bringing in cadaver dogs to do a sweep of the whole area,' suggested Oates. 'Especially if we think he may have disposed of other body parts in nearby locations.'

'Good idea Gavin. Can you get on to the dog section after the briefing?'

'He or she,' said Armstrong quietly.' We don't know if the murderer is a man or a woman.'

Mike Henderson raised his hand, 'Any chance of CCTV from the area?'

'Not anywhere near the scene but I've asked the uniform Inspector to allocate a couple of his guys to do some door to door on any premises in the vicinity of entrances to the Dene. A torso is heavy, so I'm guessing our killer transported the body parts in a vehicle. There's a lot of high value properties overlooking the area. It's quite likely that several of those have their own security cameras.'

Jack looked across the room at the gathered detectives. 'We don't know yet whether the body parts recovered this morning are recent but indications are that they may be from one or more of our missing girls from the 1980s.' He turned to look at the white murder wall and frowned. 'There's something that's niggling at me. The key to this is working out why suddenly, after forty years, our killer is disposing of the bodies. We need to know the answer to a very important question. Why now?'

Jack stared at the photographs and when he spoke it was softly as if he was talking to himself. 'Maybe he has become spooked and is disposing of evidence...' Jack turned back to the officers, '... or perhaps Dave is right.'

He scanned the faces of the detectives. '...Maybe he's clearing his freezer to make room for more!'

Chapter 16

He sat clutching a can of beer and watching the television news. The discovery of the body parts had been the lead story on the local channels at lunchtime but had not yet made the nationals.

There was no doubt that it would.

He recognised the location on the news as being the steep banked area below where he had disposed of the body parts. Snatching up the remote he turned up the volume and listened to a female newsreader reporting on the discovery of the dismembered body.

The camera operator was zooming in on a uniformed police officer standing next to blue and white Police tape marking a cordoned off area of undergrowth.

He smiled as he saw the detectives ducking under. There was one of them who clearly didn't look very happy.

What's that cliché that the writers use in their cheap "potboiler" books?

Oh yes. 'The grim-faced detective.'

If I was writing the book he would be 'The seriously pissed off detective who clearly hasn't got a bloody clue.'

He felt some satisfaction knowing that he was the reason for the copper looking so hacked off. All the annoyance that he had initially felt when the head had been found was disappearing. With hindsight it was serendipity. The discovery of the head had thrown his actions into the limelight and suddenly made him the centre of attention. It felt as if he had total control over the developing situation.

It was like being the director of his very own television drama.

He had the ability to set the scene and then come home, sit down in front of the television, open a can of beer, and wait for the spectacle to unfold.

It was all very gratifying.

It reminded him of his favourite true crime magazines. He could be just as famous as one of the serial killers that featured every month in the lurid factual stories that he so loved. With the obvious major difference that was going to set him apart from the others.

I'm not going to get caught!

Getting up from the chair he ambled into the kitchen and put on a fresh pot of coffee. As the filter machine hissed and bubbled his mind wandered to the untidy basement and the remaining contents of the freezer.

It had been a struggle up the stairs but the oldest freezer had now gone to the refuse tip… along with any forensic traces it had contained.

At first he had wanted to get rid of all of the evidence as soon as possible. Ensure that there was nothing to link him to the murders.

With the thrill that he had experienced following the first headline news report, all that had now changed. He was now enjoying this cat and mouse game with the Police.

Sitting down on one of the tall stools next to the wooden breakfast bar, he considered different ways of which to dispose of the other body parts. It would have to be for maximum impact. Something that would generate plenty of television coverage. Some place or in some way that would have everyone talking.

A smile spread across his face and he began to chuckle away to himself.

I wonder what they thought when I left them two mismatched left arms? That should keep them on their toes, wondering how many bodies there are.

I bet they're shitting themselves. I wish I could see their faces.

Chapter 17

Parker was sitting behind his desk wearing his familiar scowl as he considered the latest developments that Slade had presented to him.

The ham and cheese sandwich he had just been about to tuck into had lost much of its appeal. The cause of his sudden lack of appetite wasn't Jack's description of the body parts. It was the realisation that he would have to pass the news on up the pyramid to the Assistant Chief Crime, who was already pressing for some positive results.

Serial killers may provide fodder for sensation seeking journalists, but they never went down well with the bosses. They stretched what was already limited resources to breaking point and cost barrel loads of taxpayer's money... not to mention the intense press scrutiny they attracted. He looked at the Detective Inspector standing in front of him and signalled to a chair.

'Body parts from at least two victims, you say Jack?'

'Two... maybe three. There's no saying that the two limbs recovered today match with the head from the other day. DNA will either confirm or negate.'

'And you think he might be about to start off on another killing spree?'

'That's just one of the theories. To be honest we don't really know why he's suddenly clearing out the previous victims. Is he getting rid of evidence... or is he making way for more bodies?'

Jack cleared his throat before continuing.

'Either way we're going to need more resources. The enquiry warrants it. It's getting bigger. We need more cops to share the load.'

Parker got up and wandered to his window. Looking down he could see a group of half a dozen kids walking in the direction of the nearby Centre of Life building. Lively and leaping around they didn't seem to have a care in the world.

They were probably only a couple of years younger than the missing girls.

'We need this bastard caught soon so I suppose it makes sense.' He turned back to Slade. 'A couple of C.I.D. sectors might throw their dummies out of their prams. With all the bloody cutbacks God knows we're all short but they'll just have to get on with it. We're all under pressure here.'

Which means you're under pressure from the ACC thought Jack.

'If I can get you a couple of Detectives, do you think that you could persuade one of the shifts to give you a uniform cop to help out in the office. Preferably one with some good knowledge of the workings of C.I.D?'

'I'm sure they will be willing to help. I'll sort out task allocation as soon as I know who we're getting in to bolster the team.'

He got up and was just turning to leave when Parker spoke.

'Jack, I can get you a couple of detectives but you know I can't guarantee the quality. The Sectors are hardly likely to send you their star detectives. You'll have to make do with what you get.'

Jack nodded. He had already thought of that. If he was in the same position he would be reluctant to lose one of his best officers for an investigation that might leave him short of a cop for weeks or even months.

'I'll cross that bridge when I come to it,' he said, making his way out of Parker's office and heading for the H.MET Incident room.

Five minutes later Slade was running his proposed strategy past Dave Armstrong.

'We have three missing person reports. I'm going to allocate a detective to each 'misper' and treat them as three separate enquiries. That will allow one cop to concentrate solely on their particular aspect of the enquiry without any distractions. We'll deal with them from scratch as if we've just got them in, but with a fresh look at each, using the latest profiling and technical developments.'

Jack looked up at his friend, 'I know it means a load of work. It's going back to base and requires re-interviewing any witnesses, tracking down and speaking to friends, family and any associates. If possible, I want a timeline for each girl's movements for the twenty-four-hour period before they disappeared.'

'After so many years there might not be many witnesses left to interview,' said Armstrong. 'Those still alive may have moved elsewhere in the country or even abroad.'

'That's a strong possibility but something may have been missed the first time around and if we get lucky, we might find that one person still out there who might hold a vital clue.'

'And the rest of the team?'

'Jackson remains as exhibits officer. Everyone else deals with the abandoned limbs and all actions that arise out of that aspect of the enquiry. I'll assign individual tasks, once I get to know how many additional detectives, I'm getting allocated, and exactly who we've got.'

Jack glanced across at the mounting paperwork in his tray.

'At the end of each day we all debrief and everything we have gets fed into H.O.L.M.E.S. 2. That way it's all recorded on the computer and we can still maintain an overview of the whole enquiry.'

H.O.L.M.E.S. is the acronym for "Home Office Large Major Enquiry System". It is the computerised method first introduced in 1985 as a direct result of the Yorkshire Ripper enquiry following the murders committed by Peter Sutcliffe in the 1970s. Several forces were involved and a case review highlighted the lack of coordination making it impossible for the Senior Investigating Officer to have an overall view of the enquiry.

Sutcliffe had been interviewed several times by different forces, but no link was established because each area had its own computer system, incompatible with the other forces.

H.O.L.M.E.S, later updated to HOLMES 2, provides an integrated computer system to collect and collate the results of all 'actions' ensuring that major investigations are carried out in a thorough and organised manner.

After the briefing Jack returned to his office and took a call giving the details of two additional detectives who had been assigned to the investigation.

Etal Lane had sent a former Newcastle North detective Simon Walters. Tall and good looking he had a reputation as being a bit of a lady's man. Rumour was that on one occasion he had almost been caught in bed with the wife of one of the local burglars from the Kenton area. The burglar had been detained in police custody but was released early. Walters had only narrowly escaped by scrambling down a drainpipe and clambering over some garden fences.

He had joked to other detectives that the next time he would ensure that her husband was safely remanded in custody before he went a-calling.

It was just a rumour, but if true Slade guessed that it wouldn't be long before Professional Standards came knocking on Simon Walters' door.

A drainpipe wouldn't allow him to escape so easily when that happened.

Walters had at best an average arrest record and could perhaps do better if he concentrated on banging up villains and not banging their girlfriends.

The other cop was Christopher Tait, a young man in his mid-twenties. From what Slade could see had a good arrest record and appeared on paper to be a hard worker. Slade being a cop was immediately suspicious. Why would another sector send such a good 'thief taker'.

What's the catch?

In addition to the two detectives, one of the Shift Inspectors Peter Worthen had volunteered P.C. James Dalton. A keen young cop who had expressed interest in an attachment to one of the local crime teams he had come well recommended. Dalton came across as bright and intelligent and a short secondment to H.MET wouldn't do his career any harm.

Jack's thoughts were interrupted by a sharp rap on the door as Dave Armstrong entered with Mike Henderson following closely behind.

'Boss, we've got a lead off one of the CCTV enquiries,' said Henderson.

'We could do with a break. Give me some good news. What have you got?'

'One of the large houses near the Freeman Road entrance to the Dene captured a van on camera in the early hours heading towards where the body parts were dumped the night before they were found.'

'Have we got a registration number?'

'It's not like the cop programs on telly, Boss. The recording quality is shit. The camera has been there for years, mainly as a deterrent. We're lucky it was even running. So, no registration number.'

'Well, what have you got me?'

When Dave Armstrong responded he did not sound confident.

'Not a lot. All we have is a fuzzy image of a Ford Transit. Dark blue colour. No signage.'

'There must be thousands of dark blue transits in the North East area.'

'I took the image to the local Ford dealer and he is pretty certain that it's a recent model Ford Transit Custom with a nearside sliding parcel bay. We can get into the PNC and try to narrow it down with a Vehicle Online Description Search.'

'Well that sounds a little more hopeful. Ask one of the Analysts to set off the VODS. Start initially with Newcastle and Northumberland postcodes. If we need to we can expand the search to Durham and Cumbria.'

'Aye. But there's still nothing to actually link it to the disposal of the body parts.'

'Well, that's all we've got at the minute, so let's chase it up.'

'Will do Boss,' said Dave, turning to leave.

'Hang on. Before you go. Check this out.'

Jack held out a piece of paper. 'These are the new secondments to the team.'

Henderson glanced over Armstrong's shoulder at the names Jack had written down. 'That Dalton lad that uniform is sending has a good reputation as a thief taker. But if the other two are what you're being given, then you've been dealt a right crap hand there. There's neither of them I would give the time of day to.'

He gave a grimace and jabbed a finger at the paper.

'Walters might have been a good detective if he could keep his dick in his pants. He's got an ex-wife and two young kids to support and still chases anything in a skirt. He's also a bit of an "overtime Bandit" grabbing anything he can get. He even works in uniform at the Newcastle games when he can get it. Mind you, it's no wonder. Between the missus, the pub and the bookies in four weeks he probably spends more than an average cop earns in three months.'

'What about the other one… Tait?'

Henderson gave an involuntary frown. 'Aye Tait! Well, everyone's heard about him.'

'Enlighten me,' said Jack, looking distinctly unhappy.

'You must know Tait … he bats for the other side. I heard that he even lives with another bloke in a flat down St Peter's Basin area. I heard his boyfriend's supposed to be a teacher.'

'Aye. I've heard that about him,' echoed Armstrong glancing down at the list. 'I was told that it was just gossip.'

'No smoke without fire,' Henderson muttered.

'If he's a good cop I don't care what he does in his private life,' said Jack, folding up the paper and tucking it back into his pocket. 'So long as he does the job right.'

Henderson gave a resigned shrug.

Jack nodded to Armstrong. 'When young PC Dalton from downstairs arrives, get him to follow up on the VODS. As soon as we get the results start allocating a couple of detectives to start visiting the owners. Also ask the uniform Inspector if he would task one of his cops to widen the door to door enquiries; checking for any other CCTV in the area. Freeman Hospital for a start… and there's a row of nearby shops. Let's see if we can get a better image of the van. Hopefully a registration number … maybe even the driver.'

As Armstrong walked towards his desk in the Incident Room Henderson hurried up behind him and tapped him on the shoulder.

'Hey Sarge! Do you know how we can tell if Tait is gay or not?'

Armstrong turned and paused.

Henderson was grinning. 'Give him a kiss. If he closes his eyes, he's Gay… if he closes yours… he's not.'

'Well listen to you,' replied Armstrong. 'Here you are part of the cutting edge of a twenty-first century crime investigation and you're still making inappropriate comments that belong back in the nineteen seventies.'

'Howay man, lighten up. I'm just having a laugh.'

'Yeah! Well just be careful because if Slade hears any homophobic shit when the new guy gets here, you'll be back on the beat wearing a pointy hat and a black chequered jacket before you can say 'employment tribunal.'

Later that afternoon the three new additions to the team arrived and Jack got the squad together to introduce them, bring everyone up to speed and to outline his plans for the next stage of the investigation.

James Dalton on loan from uniform shift would answer phones, take messages and be a general dogsbody in the Incident Room.

Of the three 'mispers', Jacqueline Marshall was allocated to Donna Shaw as she had been instrumental in tracking down the initial report.

Simon Walters was asked to do a full review of the report on Elaine Robinson as he had worked the Gosforth area, whilst Christopher Tait was allocated to do the same for the Elizabeth Mortimer missing person enquiry.

The others would continue to respond to any new leads that emerged but everyone would collate their results at the evening briefing before having them fed into H.O.L.M.E.S.

The rest of the day passed uneventfully and that evening the debrief was relatively short. As the detectives clocked off Slade decided to try a little team building with the new members by asking everyone to go to the police club for a drink.

Needing some stress relief, they all readily agreed.

The Newcastle Police Club was a private social club where off duty cops could meet and relax without constantly looking over their shoulders to see if the guy at the next table was some tattooed villain that they had locked up in the past.

It had been formed twenty years previously when all existing clubs located on police premises had been closed down; supposedly to make use of all available workspaces.

More cynical cops thought the real reason was to cut down on the amount of beer that cops drank, so a few disgruntled but determined cops decided to set up their own independent club. The Newcastle Police Club was the result, with the current premises discretely tucked away above an Italian restaurant in the Newcastle city centre.

A large bar ran half the length of the room and to the right of the counter were assorted tables and chairs, where several serving and retired officers could usually be found telling 'war stories' and supping pints.

Off to the left was a large open plan room, which was also set out with tables and chairs but was quieter and further away from the bar.

As they entered Jack spotted Paul Brunton pouring a pint for one of the regulars. Instrumental in the formation of the club, Paul was now retired from 'the job' and could often be found helping behind the bar, or doing other tasks to keep running costs to a minimum.

'Pint of the usual Jack?' Brunton called out on seeing Slade at the head of the group.

'Cheers Paul, and whatever this lot are having,' Slade replied, indicating the group of thirsty detectives piling in behind him.

'If I'd known the Murder Investigation Team was coming, I would have ordered an extra tanker load of beer.'

'That was our name when you were piloting panda cars Paul. Now we're called the Homicide and Major Enquiry Team.'

Brunton twisted his face in mock disgust.

'There must be a whole bloody department sitting at "Middle Earth" just coming up with fresh names for old teams. If half of them got their arses back on the streets we wouldn't be so short of polis.'

Brunton began pouring pints as the detectives crowded into the bar but he clearly wasn't finished with his diatribe.

'What was that they were planning on calling that team at the West End? Oh aye! The Fast Action Response Team.' He said placing a pint in front of Jack. 'The F.A.R.T. What a team to be attached to.'

'Well, we're now H.MET. You need to keep up with the times, Paul.'

'No Jack. You need to… thank God I'm retired.'

Jack held up his hands in mock surrender. 'OK. Don't rub it in. You win.'

'Whatever you're calling yourselves you're still a bunch of piss heads and risk drinking the place dry.'

'Just clam up and do what you do best… pulling pints and thinking of the club profits,' grinned Jack.

Once everyone had been served drinks, they moved from the bar to the far end of the club where it was quieter, and there were fewer people to overhear their conversation.

This section of the club had originally been two rooms with each half having a marble fire surround topped with black mirrors. Three of the walls were painted cream whilst the walls with the fireplaces were a bright pillar box red. To one side was a large wall mounted television with the sound muted. The screen silently flickering with images of a rugby match.

The detectives pushed some tables together and settled in a corner of the room. Jack enjoyed the camaraderie in the police club and hoped that the relaxed atmosphere would allow him to gauge the mood of the officers on his team.

The setting might gain him an insight into how the squad truly felt the investigation was going. A little alcohol had the benefit of loosening the vocal cords and reducing inhibitions, allowing them to comment, in a comfortable social environment, on things that they might feel too restricted to say in the formal setting of an incident room.

This time it would have the added advantage of allowing him to suss out the new members of the squad; see how their minds worked, and find out how they might fit in with the team.

Simon Walters was in his late twenties, six foot tall and solidly built; displaying the build of the regular gym user. His thick dark hair was in a modern style shaved at the sides and the tanned clean-shaven face and dark eyes gave him a Mediterranean look.

Jack could see why women might find him attractive and noticed Donna Shaw occasionally casting glances in the young cop's direction.

The second addition to the team was different again. Christopher Tait was about five ten, slim build and in his mid-twenties with fair hair and a centre parting that brought to mind some of the students from the nearby university. To have been appointed to C.I.D. with only three years' service he must have something about him that shone out. Disconcertingly Jack had noticed that he too cast the occasional surreptitious looks in the direction of Simon Walters.

James Dalton the young cop sent from Uniform appeared a little in awe finding himself amongst the team and had little to say. Jack noticed him looking around and listening carefully to everything being discussed. Obviously he was keen to learn all he could about the workings of the squad.

The conversation naturally revolved around the current case and the progress, or rather the lack of progress, in the investigation. It would help to give the newcomers an up-to-date overview of the enquiry.

'I'm leaning toward our murderer just getting out of nick after a thirty year stretch,' suggested Dave Armstrong sipping his beer.

'That list shouldn't be too extensive,' said Mike Henderson. 'There's not many that get that length of sentence… not these days.'

'If I'm right,' continued Dave, 'It might not be long before he starts up again.'

'Once he clears space in his freezer?' said Henderson smiling and taking a large swig from his glass.

'I can see a flaw in your argument Dave,' responded Slade and everyone switched their eyes to him. 'Thirty odd years is a long time to leave the freezer running. What if it packed in? That's a lot of smelly meat you're going to have inside starting to rot.'

Armstrong considered this carefully.

'OK! So maybe he has an accomplice and there were two of them killing the girls.'

'And the accomplice just thought he'd wait forty years until his mate got back out before starting up again?' exclaimed Henderson shaking his head. 'I don't buy into that.'

The group fell quiet until the silence was broken by Gavin Oates. 'Well…'

Everyone looked across at him.

'… who's for another pint. I'm still clamming.'

That finally managed to bring a smile to Mike Henderson whose glass was already drained.

As Oates went to the bar to order the drinks from Paul Brunton, Chris Tait, who until then had been content to sit quietly on the edge of the group, raised his hand to speak.

It amused Slade to be reminded yet again of a reticent student or schoolboy wanting to ask a question in class and he couldn't help but smile.

'Yes Chris?'

'What if he isn't planning to start up again. Could he have stopped after the three? Maybe now that he's getting old, he needs to get rid of the evidence for some reason?'

'It's something to be considered,' admitted Jack, 'But the consensus is that it's unlikely.'

'Why unlikely?' enquired Tait.

'Because serial killers don't usually stop until they're either caught, locked up or dead,' interjected Henderson, his scowl returning.

Tait despite his youth was not one to be intimidated and stood his ground.

'Dennis Rader the BTK killer in the States had stopped fifteen years before he was eventually traced and arrested.'

'What's a BTK killer for God's sake? It sounds like some kind of fucking sandwich,' barked Henderson, who clearly thought that Tait should sit quietly and know his place.

'It stands for "Bind, Torture, Kill." which is what he did to each of his victims. It could easily be what our killer was doing.'

'Maybe he modelled himself on that Rader bloke,' suggested Dave Armstrong as Gavin Oates re-appeared at the table balancing a tray loaded with drinks.

'Well, you might all get a chance to float your theories tomorrow,' said Jack. 'I've asked a Professor Alistair McNaughton from Newcastle University to come along to the briefing. He's their top lecturer in Criminal Psychology and I hope that he can give us an insight into what sort of person we should be looking for.'

Just at that point Paul Brunton called across the room.

'Jack, you've made the national news.'

Turning to look up at the television mounted on the wall Jack saw that the rugby match had been replaced with a BBC newsreader. There was some film of the press conference at headquarters, followed by more recent cutaways to shots of Slade in Jesmond Dene where the torso and limbs had been located.'

Oates put the tray down and walked across to the television to turn up the volume and a hush descended as everyone focused on the news report; each cop lost in their own private thoughts.

They had all known that this case was going to be a hard one to crack.

It was going to be all the harder with the intensive press intrusion.

Chapter 18

He put down the latest true crime magazine that he had been reading and looked at the television images of Jesmond Dene intercut with shots of Police HQ.

It was just a repeat and rehash of some of the earlier local footage complete with the usual clichés; 'gruesome find', 'shocked residents' etcetera. The difference was that it was now all over the national channels.

So far it had been on Sky News, BBC News 24 and there had even been an extended feature on the local television channel. He couldn't help but break into a grin. He felt very important, knowing that he was actually at the centre of all that coverage. Everyone was talking about who was behind the murders, and the fun part was that he knew that they would never catch him.

It was just so perfect.

He had always been fascinated by true crime books and magazines and particularly loved those featuring real life murderers. His favourite was Ted Bundy the American serial killer who confessed to thirty murders but had probably done more.

Can you have a favourite serial killer?

The bookcase was full of magazines on several of his favourites, and then there were those documentaries on television that he watched over and over again. He gorged on it all, but especially the forensic side of things. He considered himself quite an expert on police procedure and detection techniques, and had learned all the tricks that the police employed to catch murderers.

Which is why they'll never catch me.

A face filled the screen and he saw a detective having a microphone thrust in front of his face. He smiled thinking how pissed off the detective looked as the press shouted questions. Even the reporters could tell he hadn't got a clue.

A caption at the bottom of the screen gave his name as 'Inspector Jack Slade'. He would remember that name for the future. Maybe he could send him a letter written in red ink. No! Better still. Written in blood like the original Jack the Ripper did. That would get everyone interested. Ensure even more coverage. Not his own blood of course. That would be a forensic faux pas. Chicken blood... something like that. This was really becoming fun.

A sudden thought struck him and he couldn't help laughing out loud. And then there's my other little surprise. They might not have even found that yet.

Chapter 19

The following morning Jack was surprised to see that, for once, he wasn't the first cop into the office. Even as he reached the top of the stairs to the first floor he could smell the rich aroma of freshly brewed coffee drifting along the corridor from the open office door.

Entering the room, he spotted one of the new detectives Chris Tait huddled over his desk, deep in thought and sifting through some paperwork, a cup of coffee on his desk next to him. Jack shot a quick glance across at the coffee pot, registering that it was already half drained, and he wondered just how long the young detective had been at his desk.

He was just about to call out a greeting when he noticed Tait screw up a sheet of paper and throw it angrily into the bin.

'Good morning,' Jack said with a smile. 'That's the way I sometimes deal with the boss' memos.'

Tait looked up startled. He glanced back towards the bin and Slade got the faintest impression that he appeared a little guilty. If so, he quickly recovered his composure.

'Good morning, Inspector,' Tait replied, adjusting a pile of reports in front of him. 'I'm just clearing the decks of the routine rubbish and making sure I'm up to speed. Can I get you a coffee?'

'Very kind of you,' Jack said, wandering across to the 'In Tray' and starting to go through any new messages that had come in during the night for the team. There was nothing of particular note. Night shift had increased patrols around the Jesmond Dene area and had recorded several "Stop and Search" checks of people acting suspiciously in the vicinity of the dumping ground. Other than two students found in possession of a small amount of 'weed' there had been no positive results. Certainly there had been nothing whatsoever that would impact on Jack's enquiry.

'Here you are Boss.' Jack turned to find Chris at his side holding out a coffee mug which he accepted gratefully.

'So Chris, how do you feel you're fitting in so far?'

'Early days yet sir, but I'm hoping to be able to contribute. I hope that I'm going to learn a lot from the investigation.'

'I'm sure you will,' Jack said, taking his first sip of the freshly brewed coffee. 'And I'm sure that you'll fit in well with the team.'

Drink in one hand and the paperwork from the 'In Tray' in the other, Slade headed off in the direction of his office.

I wonder if he left teacher an apple on my desk.

There was no apple on the desk. Instead, there was a ringing telephone. It made a very poor substitute.

Putting down his coffee, Jack picked up the receiver.

'D.I. Slade, Major Enquiry Team.'

'Good morning, Inspector. It's Ged Kirkby here from forensics. We have some good news and some bad news.'

'I need some good news. We can save the bad stuff 'til I'm at least half way through my coffee.'

'We've found two full sets of prints on the inside of wrappings covering the body parts. They were clearly visible on the inside of the sticky tape.'

'Two full sets?'

'Aye. Thumb to little finger for both.'

'That sounds very unusual. I could understand one or even a partial print. A full set smacks of a real amateur. Which package were they on?'

'All of them. On the torso package and on the wrappings of both arms.'

'We are never normally that lucky. I'm ready to grab at any straws at this stage but either our killer has suddenly become the most careless and inept murderer of the last hundred years or there's something else to tell me.'

'There's something else to tell you.'

'Which is the bad news no doubt. Let me guess, they're not in the database and we can't identify them?'

'No Boss. I can identify them. I've matched them already.'

'That's brilliant news Ged.'

'Aye. You would think so, wouldn't you?'

There was silence on the other end and Jack knew he wasn't going to like what Ged had to tell him.

'Come on Ged. Spit it out.'

'The fingerprints on one of the wrappings come from the hand of the arm in the other package... and vice versa. Just to confuse us further, the torso has both sets on it.'

There was a silence for several seconds. Slade broke it.

'The bastard's just taking the piss out of us!'

Ten minutes later Dave Armstrong was sitting in Jack's office looking very unhappy.

'It makes no sense.'

Jack sat forward in his chair and gave a wry smile. 'It does to me. Our killer wasn't being careless. Obviously, he deliberately left the

80

prints for us to find. He used the severed hands from each victim to do it.'

'But even if they were defrosted enough to do that, they were so old they were almost mummified. They wouldn't leave any traces of oil residue, would they?'

'Which is why he did it on the sticky tape. It would be sure to pick up the ridges.'

Armstrong took some time to consider this. 'So far from being sloppy he knew exactly what he was doing. But why? What's the point of all that?'

'He's saying to us "I'm clever and you're all thick. I know what you're going to be looking for… so I'll give it to you. Except it won't help you because it's planted and I only did it to screw with your heads." The sick bastard is having some amusement at our expense.'

Dave looked aggrieved, 'So he's just screwing with us?'

'That's not how I'll phrase it in my report.'

Armstrong looked straight at his friend and locked eyes. 'He obviously has some knowledge of forensics and what we're going to be looking for. Do you think he's a cop? Maybe an ex-cop who got the sack.'

'Back in my old man's day that was the rumour concerning "Wearside Jack" who sent the false Yorkshire Ripper tape. Many of the detectives were convinced he would turn out to be a bitter cop with a grudge. In the end he turned out to be a labourer from Sunderland. I prefer to keep an open mind.'

'The murderer's knowledge of forensics points to the possibility.'

'Yes, but these days with all the stuff on the television, everyone and their granny are forensically aware. You're right though, it is something that we need to be considering.'

'The possibility that it might be a cop isn't exactly going to please the big cheeses up at Command Block.'

'Yeah, but there is an upside.'

'Which is?'

'He thinks he's intelligent. He is convinced that he's cleverer than all of us. That's going to make him cocky and arrogant. Sooner or later, he'll become over confident and screw something up.'

Jack smiled, 'And that's when we'll get the bastard.'

Chapter 20

That afternoon Jack was finishing the umpteenth coffee of the day and wondering if he should go for a lifestyle change and shift to decaf when his phone burst into life.

It was the downstairs front reception to tell him that his guest from the university had arrived. Telling the support officer that he was on his way, Slade headed downstairs to the reception desk to greet the caller.

Alistair McNaughton was in his late fifties and looked every inch the academic. Short, a little overweight, with a rounded face and thinning black hair, he wore a pair of steel rimmed glasses perched on the end of his nose. McNaughton was smartly dressed in a dark blue box jacket and neatly pressed grey trousers. A blue and black striped tie and polished black shoes completed the ensemble. He reminded Jack of one of his old headmasters.

When he spoke, McNaughton's voice was quiet and measured, as if every thought and word was being carefully vetted before being allowed out into the wider world. Whilst talking his eyes were continually darting around, taking in his surroundings, and committing every detail to memory.

Jack introduced himself and shook his visitor's hand. It had the softness of someone who had not experienced a great deal of manual labour but Jack was nonetheless surprised at the firmness of the grip.

'Good to finally meet you Professor. As I told you over the phone, I'm hoping that you will be able to assist us with our enquiry.'

McNaughton nodded and smiled. 'I understand that you're hoping for an insight into the mind of your offender. As you know I have a deep interest in the field of criminal profiling. My specialism is in the field of Psychopathy… the detailed study of psychopaths or what we now prefer to refer to as sociopaths.'

'I believe that you have written the foremost study on it.'

'Ah, Inspector! Flattery will get you everywhere.'

'Follow me Professor.' Slade escorted him up to the Incident room where the team were already sitting around waiting for the briefing to begin.

Slade and McNaughton entered and a hush descended as everyone turned to look at them. It was clear that they were all making their own appraisals of the professor. Several were convinced that he wasn't going to be any help at all.

'OK guys, listen in! This is Professor Alistair McNaughton. He is Head of the Criminal Psychology Department at Newcastle University. I've asked him here to give us some background on the sort of individual that we are looking for. Hopefully he will give us some clues and pointers as to how we can go about catching our killer.'

McNaughton gave a wide smile which creased up the corners of his eyes.

'Good morning officers. I've been asked just to give a general background into the minds of the people who carry out these types of murders.' He glanced around at the sea of faces. 'And perhaps dispel some of the common myths that might send you or your investigation off on the wrong track.'

They were all ears as he continued.

'Believe it or not we even have an accepted definition of what qualifies a person as a serial killer. He or she has been defined as a murderer who kills three or more people over a period of more than a month… with a significant break or cooling off period in between.'

McNaughton, as a university lecturer, was well used to talking to large assemblies and the room was silent as he expertly drew in his audience.

'Strange as it may seem the crazed gunman, who in one single horrific incident, murders a dozen or more people at one time in what I believe the Police now refer to as a 'Marauding Terrorist' scenario, falls short of the classification. He, and it usually is a male, is not a serial killer. He does not fit the definition.'

McNaughton paused. He knew that he had his audience in the palm of his hand.

'No. We must look to your Nilsen, your Sutcliffe, and your Dahmer. They are the true serial killers.'

As he spoke McNaughton became more animated, warming to a subject on which he was clearly an authority.

'Research has also shown that the biological relatives of sociopaths were four to five times more likely than the average person to be themselves sociopathic. Now, firstly I should point out that whilst the majority of serial killers are men, the possibility that you are looking for a woman must never be discounted. The ratio amongst known serial killers is approximately fifteen per cent women as opposed to eighty-five per cent male.'

McNaughton gave a quick glance at the three girl's photographs displayed on the murder wall.

'In this particular case, the fact that your offender has targeted females is strongly indicative of a male killer.'

83

McNaughton looked around the silent room and seeing that he had everyone's attention continued.

'Serial killers are usually driven by sexual urges and it's estimated that sex is a leading motive for approximately fifty percent of all male serial killers.'

McNaughton turned and pointed to the white board behind him.

'Taking the sexual motive into account, a male homosexual murderer almost exclusively targets gay men and boys, such as in the case of Jeffrey Dahmer and John Wayne Gacy in America. Of course, the United States does not have a monopoly of gay serial killers as demonstrated by Dennis Nilsen and recently Stephen Port here in the UK.'

Mike Henderson asked, 'Would you say a large proportion of serial killers are gay?' He shot a quick sidelong glance across at Christopher Tait.

'Definitely not,' responded McNaughton. 'Criminologists estimate that at least eighty-six per cent of male serial killers are heterosexual.'

McNaughton did not turn around but indicated over his shoulder at the Murder Wall.

'Based on the profiles of these three victims that you know of, I would say your killer is almost certainly heterosexual.'

'That gives Tait an out.' Henderson muttered under his breath so that only Oates sitting next to him could hear.

'So, what about gay women?' asked Oates.

'There are even fewer lesbian serial killers and they usually fall into two categories; the nurse who kills her patients and the prostitute that murders her customers.'

'Hey Simon! I heard you're going out with a nurse,' grinned Henderson.

'And I've heard you've taken to collecting those cards in telephone boxes,' responded Walters. 'That puts us both in the at-risk group.'

The room dissolved into laughter and Slade had to calm them down.

'Save the jokes for the Police club. This information might be what cracks the case. I'm sorry Professor. Please carry on.'

'Thank you, Inspector. Let me start by dispelling some common myths.'

The room had grown quiet again.

'Serial killers are not always white as was initially suggested by research in the States. That was flawed research which at the time appeared to make sense, but it was only because at the time statistically about eighty percent of the American population at the time was Caucasian. However, it has also been shown that it is rare for serial killers to target people from another race. Consequently, in this case, it is highly likely that your offender is white.'

'Why did he keep the body parts?' asked Tait who had been making notes on a pad as the professor talked.

'Ted Bundy, the American serial killer who murdered more than thirty victims in a four-year period in the seventies, decapitated twelve of his victims and kept their heads in the fridge as souvenirs. He also took photographs of his victims and when questioned as to why he had done so told investigators, "When you work hard to do something, you don't want to forget it".'

'So, they were most probably kept as trophies?' asked Armstrong.

McNaughton nodded. 'That would be the obvious conclusion.'

'So why after four decades is he now disposing of his trophies?' enquired Slade.

'That I can't tell you. It does point to a dramatic change in his circumstances. It's quite possible that some sudden change has led him to believe that he may be in danger of being discovered. The fear of discovery is overcoming his desire to keep souvenirs. He is getting rid of the evidence.'

'One of my officers has a theory that he's clearing his freezer for more victims.'

'I can't discount that, but for you and your detectives it would be a nightmare scenario.'

'If during enquiries we come in contact with our offender then how will we recognise him?' asked Simon Walters.

This was what the detectives really wanted to know.

They were about to be disappointed.

'You won't,' replied McNaughton. 'Serial killers are not the reclusive social misfits of the movies. They do not keep their mothers mummified in rocking chairs in the basement Hitchcock style...' He allowed himself a smile, '... well not all of them.'

'So, he'll just look like an ordinary bloke?' asked Oates.

'Yes, look like and act like... as you say... "an ordinary bloke." Over the years he will have become adept at hiding in plain sight...' He paused for effect, '... and gentlemen make no mistake, it is the ability to blend in that makes him all the more dangerous.'

'If he's so normal looking then how the hell will we catch him?' grumbled Henderson.

'Unfortunately for you, many serial killers are only caught by chance. Nilsen was caught when a company cleared his drains, the Ripper was detained for a traffic violation over his number plate, and James Dale Ritchie following a dispute over a taxi fare.'

'Are you saying we have to wait and hope that he somehow drops himself in it? He's managed to avoid doing that for forty years so far,' declared Henderson, causing a general hubbub of conversation to begin again.

McNaughton held his hand up and the room went quiet.

'You may not know where he might strike again. You may not know whether or not he will make a mistake in the future…' The Professor looked around the room at the detectives, '…but I can tell you where he is.'

The room was silent. Everyone was waiting to hear what he was about to say.

'He is more than likely already in your files.'

The detectives exchanged glances and Dave Armstrong spoke up. 'Why do you say that?'

'Serial killers do not start their crime career with murder. They build up to it. They practice… they hone their skills.'

McNaughton paused and the silence was almost palpable.

'Additionally, from a young age many serial killers are intensely driven by various forms of paraphilia…'

'Give us that in plain English,' called Mike Henderson from the back.

'Paraphilia is used to describe abnormal sexual behaviour. Fetishes that they find sexually arousing such as transvestitism, exhibitionism and most often voyeurism. They may commit sexual offences whilst juveniles. They may have come to notice for animal cruelty. Almost all serial killers admit that they started acting out their violent fantasies killing or torturing small animals before moving up the scale. I repeat…a serial killer does not start by killing people.'

He glanced again at the murder wall before continuing.

'Search your files. Because somewhere within them is a record of an indecent exposure or a peeping Tom. Perhaps an incident of animal cruelty that has in the past brought your offender to police notice.'

The room had become still and calm with every detective focused on McNaughton.

'So, gentlemen…and lady… somewhere in your files is your killer.'

Chapter 21

Liz Harmon was feeling very pleased with herself, as she tucked into some squares of chocolate from her desk drawer stash. The diet might not be going so well but as Chief Crime Reporter on the newspaper, her standing in the office was going up by the day.

Last night her article had dominated the front page, with an account of the dismembered body parts being found around the city. It was the sort of macabre sensationalist article that her readers lapped up.

It hadn't gone unnoticed by her that Detective Inspector Jack Slade was taking the lead on the enquiry, so she made sure that she inserted references to how the police were clearly struggling.

It was an added bonus for her to be able to get a dig in at Slade. In the past there had been run-ins between her and that particular detective. She blamed him for the loss of one of her best informants within the Police Force. She didn't like the man... and she had good reason to believe that the feeling was mutual. On the rare occasions that she had managed to get through to his extension he rarely responded to any enquiry.

It would give her great satisfaction to see Slade fall flat on his backside by failing to make progress in such a high-profile case. There was no doubt that when he did flop, she would be there for maximum press coverage.

She allowed herself a little smile. She might even go with that old clichéd banner, 'The Police Are Baffled'. That should rub salt in the wound.

Picking up a copy of the previous day's paper she proudly looked at her name emblazoned as the "By Line" below the banner "Grisly Find In City Park".

Following the identification of the head from the river she had wanted to run the feature article as, "The Jackie in the Box Murders" but the editor thought it too lurid and in bad taste... even for her.

There was still time yet to convince him.

She was just pouring herself a third cup of filter coffee to wash down another square of chocolate when the letter arrived.

It was addressed to her at the newspaper offices and was in an A4 sized business envelope. She stared at the way it was addressed on the front. An odd block letter style, as if it had been done by a child using a stencil.

Curious, she wandered back to her desk and tore it open. She was startled to see that the letter inside had been written in red ink, in the same block letters as on the envelope.

As she slipped the letter out, a large cutting dropped onto her desk and she immediately recognised it. The cutting was from her newspaper article; the first one following the discovery of Jackie Marshall's head in the river.

Taking a quick slurp of coffee but careful not to spill any on the envelope, she sat back in her chair and began to read the accompanying letter.

Dear Miss Harmon
I see that you have taken an interest in my work.

That Inspector Slade is to (sic) stupid to catch me and should get another job.
So far you just have the head but I am just getting started. I'm having fun.
I look forward to reading more of your storys (sic) about me and if your (sic)   good
I might send you a piece of the next lass in the post.

The letter was unsigned and as she had been reading it she found it difficult to contain her excitement.

The latest front-page scoop had just landed on her desk.

A few minutes later, she was sitting in the office of Harry Sharpe, the paper's editor. He seemed pleased but still a little cautious. 'What if it's a hoax?'

'That's not our problem. Let Slade and his band of keystone cops sort that one out. What's important is that we have the story,' declared Harmon eager to get her next By-line.'

Sharpe frowned, 'Talking of the police… what plans do you have about informing them?'

'I'll write up the editorial. We'll get photographs of the letter and envelope. Only after that do we inform Slade and ask him for a comment. We can hand over the letter and show what good citizens we are… even get a photograph of the handover to prove it. All I see here is a win-win situation.'

Harry Sharpe came out from behind his desk and began pacing the room, Alright, but I don't want any hassle from the bloody police complaining that we should have contacted them immediately. You've already pissed off that Slade copper in the past. It's not that long ago that he threatened to arrest you for withholding evidence.'

Harmon thought back to her last run in with Inspector Jack Slade several months before, and vowed that she would soon see her day with him, just like she eventually did with anyone who crossed her.

For Liz Harmon vindictiveness was a hobby. One that she had become proficient at over the years. One she enjoyed.

'They'll never be able to know when I opened it. For all they know I've come straight down to the cop shop like a concerned citizen.'

'They'll want to do tests on it.'

'So, we're giving it to them. They can test the damned thing 'til the cows come home.'

Sharpe thought about it for a few more moments before announcing his decision. 'Right … do it. Sort out the handover with one of the Detectives and get a photographer there as you do it. Make it soon and we could still make the late edition.'

For Liz it couldn't be just "one of the Detectives". That would never do.

It would have to be Slade.

Chapter 22

Slade was about to call Parker and update him on the latest progress when one of the admin staff came into the incident room to inform him that Liz Harmon was downstairs at the counter wanting to speak with him.

'Tell her I'm very busy and take a message.'

'She's very insistent. She says that she has important information about the murder and must speak to you.'

'Well just tell her I'm out and she can talk to one of the other detectives.'

'Sir, she's saying that she has received a letter and will only hand it to you.'

Jack hesitated. It just might be important.

'Damn that woman! Alright, tell her I'm coming down.'

A few minutes later he was standing on the police side of the reception with Liz Harmon on the other side of the counter. She was clutching a letter to her chest like a Victorian lady clutching her pearls.

'This arrived for me today at the paper,' she said, holding out the letter.

Slade accepted the proffered envelope holding it gingerly by the edges. As he did so Harmon stepped slightly to the side and a man who had been sitting quietly in the corner of the reception, stood up and began snapping off a few photographs.

Slade glowered at him but Harmon said chirpily, 'Oh don't worry about Stan. He's with me.'

'Take a seat for a few minutes,' Slade said, glaring in turn from Harmon to her photographer.

Leaving the reporter and the over eager photojournalist, Slade returned to the secure area where he sat down at a desk to study the letter and the envelope that it had arrived in. The post mark indicated that it had been posted second class two days previously in Newcastle upon Tyne.

The handwriting was in block capitals and there had clearly been a crude attempt to disguise it. The red ink used looked to have been a cheap ballpoint pen. If it was meant to look like blood it failed miserably.

Inside there was also a front-page newspaper cutting of an article written by Harmon in the local newspaper. It was about the discovery of the head from the Tyne; the first body part recovered.

Slade took some clean plastic forensic bags and carefully popped all three items in as potential evidence, sealing them individually and endorsing each as an exhibit.

On returning to the counter Harmon was in deep conversation with the photographer but looked up as Jack reappeared.

Slade spoke directly to Harmon.

'I see it has been opened. How many people have handled it?'

'The envelope… God alone knows. The staff in reception, the trainee that brings the post, my editor Harry Sharpe, the photographer that took copies… and me.'

'And the actual letter?'

'Just my editor Harry and myself.'

'Before you go, I'm going to need your prints for elimination purposes and I'll get a detective down to your offices to do the same for your editor and anyone else we need to. Please prepare a list of any person at your building who may have handled the envelope.'

'And what about all those at the Post Office sorting office? There could be dozens that touched it before it ever got to the newspaper offices.'

'Let me worry about that… if it is genuine.'

'You're saying you believe it's genuine?'

'I'm not saying that. We treat any possible evidence as such … until proven otherwise.' He looked down at the letter. 'Have you any idea who sent it?'

'No. But you do think it might be from the killer? Can I quote you on that?'

'No. You may not. Why was it sent to you?'

'Maybe he trusts the press more than he does the police.' She paused and caught his eye. 'We get a lot of that these days', she said with a sarcastic smile.'

Slade glared back.

'Well thank you for bringing it in. If you get any more communication, please let us know.'

'So have you a quote for my readers?'

'Are you seriously thinking of running this as a story without any idea if it's a hoax or not?'

'The public has a right to know. Do you have anything to say to the press about the letter?'

'Yes! If you ever get anything like this again, can you put it down and call us first … before half the population of Tyneside have had their paws on the evidence.'

As he turned to leave he gave her a crooked smile.

91

'Oh! You can quote me on that.'

Slade and Armstrong sat in Jack's office and stared down at the letter enclosed in a clear plastic evidence bag.

'Well Jack, what do you think?'

'You want my frank and honest opinion?'

'Yes.'

'It's most likely a load of bollocks.'

'And that's your professional judgement?'

'Based on several years of experience of dealing with crackerjacks and time wasters… yes.'

Jack pointed to the letter. 'I mean, just look at the spelling. He's spelled "too" with one letter O. He doesn't know how to spell stories and has written "you're" as Y.O.U.R.'

'Why is that a problem? I've got "A" Level English and I'm still crap at spelling. I've even been known to spell crap with a K.'

'Our guy is clever. Forensically aware. This letter has been written by some "numpty" who is after his fifteen minutes of fame. It's pure attention seeking which is the reason that he sent it to the press and not to us.'

'Come on Jack, these days even the dumbest of car thieves is forensically aware. You've said it many times yourself.'

'There's something else. There's nothing in that letter that hasn't been in the papers or on television. More importantly there's a glaring omission.'

'Which is?'

'Don't you think that if the killer had written it, he would have mentioned the torso and two left arms that were found yesterday. He would taunt us with it. He only refers to the head. The letter was posted a couple of days ago. At the time that it was written he didn't know that there would be more body parts turning up the next day.' Slade shook his head. 'No Dave, I have a feeling that this is a distraction.'

Armstrong did not seem as convinced.

'He does say in the letter that he's just getting started.'

'Not specific enough. My gut feeling is it's a hoax. Unfortunately, we haven't got the luxury of simply dismissing it… just in case it is genuine.'

Slade looked annoyed and continued. 'As much as I think it's a wild goose chase, we can't take the chance of not playing it by the book. Get it down to forensics and see what they can find for us.'

'But you're convinced that it's a waste of time'.

'If it's not, I'll show my arse in Fenwicks shop window as part of their Christmas display.'

'That should make a change from the usual Snow White. Not sure the kids will be as impressed.' Armstrong muttered, picking up the evidence bag.

'I'll ask them at the lab to do the usual rush job,' he said over his shoulder as he left the office.

Chapter 23

The following morning Jack woke early. A bright late Spring morning had been promised by the forecast, but when he looked out of his seventh floor apartment across to Newcastle Quayside it looked unlikely. It was still not yet light and he could see the black river below and the Millennium Bridge looking sad and deserted in a steady drizzle of rain.

After coffee and a breakfast of scrambled eggs prepared in the microwave, he headed down to the car park and over to his blue B.M.W. for the short drive to the station.

Despite Slade's misgivings that it would ultimately turn out to be a hoax, Liz Harmon had run the story about the letter in the previous day's late edition.

Much to his annoyance, she had illustrated the article with the photograph of her handing the letter to Slade in the foyer of the police station. In it Harmon stood looking suitably serious, whilst Jack looked like a startled rabbit caught in headlights.

On the drive up to the office he considered the letter, but no matter which way he looked at it he couldn't get away from the feeling that it was going to be a momentous waste of time, diverting investigators from more important leads. He would have preferred Harmon not to have published but that was too much to hope for from that self-promoting harpy. Now that had a ring to it and he might adopt it as his new name for her. "Harpy Harmon".

At the nick Jack arrived early but Chris Tait had once again beaten him in and was already sitting at his desk going through some paperwork.

'Did you wet the bed or something? Why so early?'

Tait looked startled. 'Morning Inspector. Just clearing away some stuff I had left over from the West end. I like to keep the decks clear for whatever gets thrown at us today.'

'Commendable… but don't put in a Fin 11.'

Tait smiled at the slang reference to the submission form for overtime; which for many detectives was the most important form in the police force.

Slade began pouring himself a coffee from the already brewed pot and headed through to his office.

The truth was that he was about to do exactly the same as Tait with the increasing amount of paperwork that was accumulating on his desk. The pile was looking in danger of tipping over. Firstly, he had to wade through the results of the previous day's actions so that he was up to speed and able to plan the day ahead.

Looking through the tray he gave a little smile. D.C. Donna Shaw was proving herself a star and had located all of the original missing persons reports for the outstanding girls. They consisted of three printed Missing Person Investigation Forms with several sheets of handwritten A4 paper stapled to each. Such was the paper record keeping used before the introduction of computers.

There were quite a lot of original handwritten sheets to go through, so Slade decided to delegate it to one of the detectives rather than allow himself to get buried in it.

He had just jotted down some instructions to Dave Armstrong, when there was a knock on the door and he walked in.

'Morning Jack. I see that Tait is out to make a good impression.'

'He's succeeding so far. He was in before me… again.'

'You'll have to start setting your alarm for half an hour before you go to bed if you want to beat him in.'

'Come in and shut the door,' said Jack quietly.

Armstrong did as he was told, but Jack closing his office door was not a good sign and he sensed that it signalled trouble.

'Whatever it was. It wasn't me. You didn't see me and you've got no evidence.'

'Sit down and shut up,' smiled Jack indicating to the chair.

Armstrong noted that the Inspector's smile quickly faded.

'Is there a problem Jack?'

'I hope not.' He paused for a couple of seconds. 'It's about Tait. What do you make of him?'

'He seems very keen.'

'Maybe a bit too keen.'

'Just because he beats you in each morning?'

Jack looked down at his desk and rearranged some paperwork.

'Yesterday he was in at his desk and looked a bit shocked to see me so early. Even a bit… guilty.'

'You think he's up to something?'

'I don't know. Just keep an eye on him for me won't you.'

'Will do Jack,' nodded Armstrong but Jack could see that he had a slightly worried look on his face. There was something that he was holding back.

'Is there something you want to say Dave?'

'It's just these rumours doing the rounds about him. You know… living with another bloke and all that.'

'What's your point?'

'I'm just saying. How's some gay bloke going to fit in with the team.'

'If he's a good detective then he's going to fit in very well.'

'Come on Jack. Sometimes things like that can cause disagreements in a squad.' Armstrong hesitated. 'It's just I've heard mutterings.'

'From who… Henderson?'

'I'd rather not say.'

'Dave, you're the Sergeant. If you hear anything unprofessional then stamp on it quickly. I don't want any distractions… especially if it leads to any allegations. The last thing we need is some bloody internal investigation into discrimination. We have a murder to investigate. So far as I'm concerned at the moment, he's one of the team. Anyone wants to make an issue of his sexuality then they'd better start looking for another job in another team… and that includes Henderson.'

'OK Jack.'

'That being said, I still want you to keep an eye on Tait. My gut is telling me that there's something on the go and I don't know what it is.'

'No problem.'

'And what do you make of the other one, Walters?'

'Well, I've asked around. Other than that he likes the odd bet and fancies himself as a bit as a ladies' man I've heard nothing negative.'

'Well, so long as he keeps it in his pants when it comes to anyone on this investigation then I'm not bothered.'

'Don't worry Jack. I'll keep a close eye on both of them.'

'Thanks Dave. We've got two unknowns on the squad so let's run a tight ship until we get to know what we've been landed with.'

'My job's sounding less like management and more like running a pirate ship.'

As Armstrong turned to leave, Slade stopped him.

'Just a minute Dave. Here's the three original "mispers". Have a look through them for me. See if you can spot anything that might have been missed the first time around.'

'Will do Jack. I'll see you at the briefing.'

The team arrived just before eight and when everyone was sorted with the obligatory hot drinks, Slade stood in front of the whiteboard to update them on the current state of the enquiry.

'Donna's done some great work tracking down the three original historic "Misper" reports. I've passed them to Sergeant Armstrong to go through them to see if he can spot any obvious gaps.'

Slade looked across to Armstrong.

'Dave, when you've done can you get someone to photocopy them for me. I need one copy handed out to each of the detectives allocated to the follow ups. Then pass the originals to Jim to be logged as exhibits.'

'Will do Boss.'

'Simon, good work on tracing Elaine Robinson's family. Sgt Armstrong will give you a copy of the original report. I see that Ged Kirkby's crew have already been around the house to complete a forensic search. Apparently the girl's bedroom was preserved like a shrine. Can you check the exhibit list for what SOCO recovered from inside? Then chase up C.S.I. to see if we've got a match yet on any of the recovered body parts. Up 'til now we've just assumed that Elaine Robinson will be one of our bodies. We need to know for sure. Let's get that 'action' bottomed.'

'Boss.'

'When you go along to visit the family I'd like to come with you. Just to get a feel for what Elaine's home life was like. Was she abducted or did she go missing willingly?'

Simon Walters nodded.

'Chris! Anything yet on the third girl, Elizabeth Mortimer?'

'Not so far boss. The family moved away from the area and I'm told they may be up in Berwick or the Borders but no joy as yet.'

'Thanks. Keep me informed.'

D.C. Gavin Oates went through the results of his enquiries at the library, explaining that he had trawled through the microfiche of old press reports for any potential witnesses who might assist. He already had a couple of names but needed to trace addresses.

One of the detectives was tasked with making a list of all the officers in charge of, or having significant roles in the initial reports.

'Let's see if they have anything to add to what was recorded on the forms. I'm particularly interested in the Inspectors who were in charge when the reports first came in.'

It would be a difficult task as all three were long retired, and Slade knew for a fact that the 'Officer in Charge' of the Elaine Robinson case would prove most problematic to speak to.

Jack had attended his funeral six months before.

Slade picked up a sheaf of printouts. 'I've got a list from PNC of all the Ford Transits that match the description of the one seen near the

Jesmond Dene disposition site. Donna, can you take the list and make a start?'

Donna nodded and took the wad of papers. It was going to be a task and a half. Slade dished out the other actions for the day and the team set about their enquiries whilst he returned to his office to make some calls.

After fifteen minutes Simon Walters appeared at Jack's office door.

'Sir, I'm heading off to visit the mother of Elaine Robinson. I've already telephoned ahead so we're expected. You said you wanted to come along.'

'Yeah. Let's go.' Jack said, grabbing his jacket and heading for the door.

The drive out to Gosforth took about twenty minutes and once they hit the High Street, the pedestrians and shoppers crossing at lights slowed them down to almost a crawl.

It was with some relief that they turned left off the main road into one of the side roads. A couple of minutes later they pulled up outside a large terraced house.

Woodbine Road was a long road in an upper middle-class area of Gosforth where houses went for up to half a million pounds. DC Walters having telephoned ahead, their knock on the door was answered almost immediately by a woman in her mid-seventies, who looked as if she was in late eighties. Mrs Robinson had once been tall but now walked with a pronounced stoop and the thin and lined face was pallid and surmounted by a mop of white hair.

Mrs. Robinson lived alone; her husband having died over two decades before. She exuded the melancholic aura of a woman who had lost any interest in life and for whom death might come as a blessed relief.

Jack wondered how much the loss of her daughter had led to her decline.

The detectives were shown to a spacious lounge filled with dark wooden furniture that reminded Jack of the home of Jacqueline Marshall's sister. It seemed like both relatives were stuck in a time warp as the result of their loss.

The room itself was clean and tidy but lacked any kind of warmth. On one wall was a picture of The Madonna and Child and on another a photograph of the current Pope, below which was a small crucifix.

Mrs. Robinson had been informed that new lines of enquiries had been opened into the disappearance of her daughter and Jack wanted to prepare her for what he believed would be the news that she had been dreading for so many years.

'I watch the television Inspector. I assume that the sudden new interest and the visit of your forensic policemen is to do with the body found in Jesmond Dene.'

Jack nodded.

'I thought as much. Why would you think that has anything to do with my Elaine? It's been so long now.'

'I'm not able to say just at the moment but there is a link with another enquiry. I just wanted to prepare you for...'

The old woman cut him short. 'I've been preparing for almost forty years, Inspector. To tell you the truth it might be a relief to know the truth.'

'I was told that Elaine's room has been kept as it was on the day she went missing.'

'I clean it and dust but other than my husband... my late husband and I, no-one else was allowed in. That is until your forensic people arrived yesterday.'

'I was wondering if we might have a look in... if you didn't mind?'

Mrs. Robinson nodded and showed them to an upstairs bedroom that had pink and white wallpaper that was beginning to peel away in parts.

Elaine Robinson's bedroom had remained virtually untouched despite the passage of time, her mother hoping against hope that her daughter would one day return.

There was a large colour poster on the wall of George Michael and on another wall was a small wooden shelf stacked with CDs of various eighties pop groups.

Glancing around, Jack wondered how anyone could live so much in the past and never even try to move on. Then again, he had never suffered the loss of a child.

He thought of how he would cope if his son Dale went missing.

He supposed for any family there must always be that vaguest of hopes that one day a loved one would just come strolling back through the door. To change things and move on was to accept that such a return was never really going to happen. He didn't want to think too deeply about the effect it might have on someone's mental health, and that of the rest of the family who also had to acquiesce to it.

The pristine room would however, hopefully turn out to be a welcome bonus for the investigation. The bedroom had been examined by C.S.I. and although it had been regularly cleaned of fingerprints, they had managed to locate several personal items from drawers including a hairbrush and toothbrush which, even after this length of time, held the prospect of having recoverable DNA on it.

If that failed a mouth swab sample had also been taken from Mrs. Robinson to test for familial DNA.

Slade wasn't sure what information he had hoped to glean from his visit that the previous detectives hadn't. He just felt the need to learn a little of what Elaine Robinson might have been like. It helped him to personalise his victim; made him even more determined to track down her killer.

Later, as they left Mrs. Robinson to reconcile herself to the thought that her daughter's body may have now been found, Slade promised to keep her up to date and that he would do all in his power to find the person responsible.

Driving off he wondered whether he would be able to keep his promise or were they just so many more empty words.

When Slade returned to the nick Dave Armstrong was waiting for him and asked to speak to him in his office. As they entered the young detective closed the door behind him.

'I've been going through the "misper" files as you asked. Something has come up on the one for the first missing girl, Elizabeth Mortimer that you need to know. The Inspector who was in overall charge of the case is retired as you might expect, but it was one of his cops… a uniform cop who got landed with doing the bulk of the enquiries.'

'And…'

When it was eventually linked to the other two "mispers" the uniform cop came in for some criticism that he perhaps hadn't put as much effort as he should have into the enquiry.'

'A lazy cop in the eighties. Not exactly earth-shattering news.'

'You need to see the name of the cop.'

Armstrong handed over a photocopy of pages from the initial report and the name seemed to leap off the paper.

Jack felt as though he had been punched in the stomach.

The cop's name was P.C. Charlie Slade.

'My dad!'

'He was allocated the day-to-day enquiries, but when the press linked it to the other two and ran a big feature there was a lot of scrutiny from Command Block about how much work he had done on the case. His Inspector threw him under the bus and he was given a Superintendent's warning. The case was handed on to a C.I.D. officer but by then was six months old.'

'From what his colleagues have always said, my dad was conscientious. This doesn't fit in with what I know of his methods.'

'Maybe he screwed up that time Jack. I just thought you should know. Opening cans of worms and all that.'

Jack sat down and began to look in detail through the report. The silence of the next few minutes seemed to Dave to be hours as he waited for his friend to speak.

Finally, Slade placed the report down on his desk and looked up.

'Look into it Dave. Report directly back to me. But listen, no matter what you find there's going to be no cover ups. Keep it straight. Understood?'

'Will do.'

Jack looked down at the file of stapled papers.

'The Inspector supervising was Mark Porter.'

'You know him?' asked Armstrong.

'Just by reputation. My dad occasionally mentioned him. He said that Porter's nickname was 'The Lotus Eater'. Partly because of his love of Chinese food which he "blagged" for free at The Lotus Chinese Takeaway, but also because he seemed to be dozing his way through his service.'

'How did he get to be Inspector?'

'God knows. Back in the day it could just be knowing the right people, drinking in the right bars… joining the right lodge.'

'Could he have just coasted through the investigation?'

'From what dad used to say he was a lazy sod and probably drifted through his whole career. He was never going to set the world on fire. As a P.C. he'd spent more effort trying to avoid recording crime, than if he'd just investigated it in the first place.'

'Maybe your dad had a grudge after the way Porter threw him to the dogs?'

'It's possible.'

'So, how are we going to play this?'

Jack seemed thoughtful.

'I'll get in contact with the pensions department for a current address for Inspector Mark Porter. Tomorrow we'll both pay him a visit and get his take first hand on the way the investigation was handled.'

'That works for me.'

'Thanks for this Dave. Leave it with me to go through again. We'll speak later.'

Armstrong left and Jack turned his attention back to the sheaf of papers.

Before I get to see the retired Inspector Porter there's someone else that I'm going to need to speak to.

Chapter 24

That evening immediately after the late briefing Jack eased his BMW out into the early evening traffic. Instead of turning right out of the nick and dropping down towards the Quayside to cross the Tyne for the ten-minute drive home, he turned left and made his way out of the city.

The sun was still bright as Slade drove past the towering edifices of the Cruddas Park flats, eventually joining the main A1 and the route north into the county of Northumberland.

Once he was away from the nose-to-nose city traffic Slade started to enjoy the drive through the northern countryside. He had done the journey so many times before that he could practically do it in a trance.

It was less than an hour's journey to his father's retirement cottage in the small village of Belford. He put his foot down. Tonight was not the night for a leisurely drive. He had questions that he wanted answered.

On previous occasions, if he had plenty of time on his hands, he would sometimes cut away from the A1 to take the scenic coastal route through the many villages dotted along the North East coast. Driving through Beadnell past the pretty bay and into Seahouses where pleasure boats ferried tourists to the nearby Farne Islands, he would cruise along to Bamburgh dominated by the magnificent castle. Then, dropping down to Budle Bay he would finally cut back across narrow country lanes and into the village of Belford.

He remembered as a young boy running through the dunes between Seahouses and Bamburgh, leaping off them to land in the soft golden sand below. Although the coastal drive took longer, the memories of his childhood could always cheer his mood.

Slade's family had always loved the stunning Northumberland coast. It was no surprise when, on retirement, Jack's parents had sold the family home in Newcastle to settle in a small village in the Northumbrian countryside, far away from the crowded city and rising crime rates.

It had always been a longstanding dream of his parents to live a more rural lifestyle and they had hardly finished the left-over buffet from his father's retirement party before they made their move.

Both had looked forward to spending their sunset years in a countryside idyll. They had imagined visits from their little grandson Dale; day excursions where they could take him to explore the area. As

Jack was growing up Charlie Slade had spent less and less time with his son. The job had seen to that.

Once retired, he had hoped to have more time to spend with his grandson than he had ever had with his own boy.

Unfortunately, in the words of the Lennon song, "life is what happens whilst you're busy making other plans".

Less than a year after the move Jack's mum was diagnosed with lung cancer. Within six months she was dead. She had never smoked a day in her life.

The last time Jack had spoken with her she had said in a rasping voice, 'I've only really had your dad for eighteen months. The job had him for the other thirty years.'

After the funeral Jack had tried to persuade his dad to sell up and move back to the city where he had friends; people he had known from work.

Slade senior would have none of it, seeming to have lost interest in everything he preferred to see out his days in the cottage, dwelling on what might have been and passing on his love of Northumberland to his grandson.

Jack's split from his wife Elaine and her subsequent move away with Dale to Scotland put paid to even that.

Jack suspected that his father had never forgiven him for the break up and that it was one of the reasons that they had drifted so far apart. He was sure that his father blamed Jack and his career for the current domestic situation, whilst conveniently forgetting his own absences during Jack's childhood.

"The job" had a lot to answer for.

Slade kept a wary eye on the road as, although the A1 is the main road from London to Edinburgh, it is a single carriageway for a good part of the journey through Northumberland.

He also kept a close check on the speedometer as the route was becoming notorious for speed cameras and despite the public perception, cops did not have any kind of 'get out of jail free card' when it came to speeding tickets.

Thankfully, other than getting stuck for five minutes behind an HGV on a single carriageway section just north of Morpeth the drive up was relatively smooth and fast.

Jack had not telephoned ahead and as he pulled up outside the stone-built cottage, he wondered what sort of mood his father would be in. Catch him on a good day and there was still the spark of the old Charlie Slade, the cheerful raconteur full of old war stories about policing in the eighties. Visit on a day when his black dog was on the prowl and the depression could ooze from his pores and slowly suck the joy from you.

Knocking on the door he waited a few minutes before his father answered. He was dressed in soiled jeans and an old blue police shirt from a bygone age.

Charlie Slade was beginning to look his age. Since his wife's death he did not seem to have the same appetite for life... or food. He existed on microwave meals and takeaways usually washed down with beer... or sometimes whisky. He appeared to be more stooped and to have lost even more weight than on his son's last visit and Jack noticed that the old shirt now hung loose around his neck.

He seemed a little surprised to see Jack but covered it well.

'Come in son. I've spent the afternoon in the garden. Put the kettle on and I'll get cleaned up.'

Whilst his father wandered off Jack poured out a cup of tea for his father and a coffee for himself. Wandering to the kitchen window he looked out onto the neatly kept garden. The fruit trees at the end had started to come into leaf and several spring flowers were poking their heads out from the freshly turned soil.

He was lost in his thoughts, when after a few minutes a noise behind him heralded his father returning, now dressed in casual trousers and a clean short sleeved shirt.

Picking up his cup of tea from the kitchen bench Charlie Slade walked through to the lounge and settled himself into an old armchair.

Jack followed and sat down opposite.

Lifting the drink to his mouth his father stared over the rim of the cup at Jack. 'To what do I owe this pleasure?'

'You make it sound like I hardly ever come up here.'

'You've only been a handful of times since you and Elaine split'.

'I'm very busy these days. You know how it is.'

Charlie Slade raised his eyebrows. 'Too busy to see your own son? When did you last see Dale? Twice... three times since Elaine took him to Scotland?'

His dad had wasted no time in straying into a contentious area.

The divorce from Elaine and the estrangement from his son were still open wounds to Jack. The memories were raw and painful and not something that he wanted to revisit. He had not travelled a hundred mile round trip for an argument.

Jack changed the subject. 'Actually dad, there is something that I need to speak to you about.'

'Fire away.'

'Back in the eighties you were stationed for a while in Walker in the East End when you took a report of a missing girl.'

'I dealt with hundreds, son. I can't remember where I put down my glasses this morning and you're asking me about a missing person from almost forty years ago.'

'Most young lasses that go missing return after a day or two. This one didn't.'

Charlie Slade nodded, and clutching his drink in both hands he stared down into it, avoiding Jack's gaze.

'You'll be talking about young Elizabeth Mortimer then?'

'I am.'

'I always knew that one day that subject would raise its ugly head again.'

Jack reached into his jacket and removed a photocopy of the missing person report. He handed it to his father who dragged his eyes away from his cup. Putting down his cup and taking his glasses from the table beside him, he put them on and glanced down at the paperwork.

'Where the hell did you get this?'

'It wasn't easy. It was buried deep in the archives at headquarters.'

His father began to look through the copy of the report.

'I was at Welbeck Road in those days. A little substation that I think had been a police house at one time. It's gone now... like so many of the small local nicks.'

'Your name appears several times in the report.'

'Aye I remember taking the report and I also remember doing quite a lot of follow up enquiries.'

'What were your impressions?'

Charlie Slade sighed and removing his glasses began twisting them around his fingers as if stirring his memories. He stared off into the distance

'You know what it's like. You go to hundreds of those reports. Almost all of them return in a day or two. But just occasionally you get that twist in your guts that tells you this one's different. This one's the real deal.'

Charlie Slade turned back to his son.

'The parents sensed it too. It was as if they knew their daughter wouldn't be coming home. Knew they wouldn't see her again... leastways not alive.'

'Did you think they were somehow involved?'

'No. Their grief was genuine. It's just that they knew...'

'What can you tell me about Elizabeth?'

Slade senior folded his glasses and placed them carefully down on the arm of the chair. He fixed his son with a long stare.

'Why are you interested now… four decades later?'

'Have you seen the news about the body parts that have been turning up in the city?'

'I never watch the news. It's all bad these days. Wars and viruses. The only magazine I read is the local one "The Bobby" that they send out to retired cops… and that's just to keep up with who's dropped dead since the last edition.'

'There were two other girls of similar age and appearance that went missing at the same time as Elizabeth Mortimer. I think it's those girls who are now being left in packages about the city.'

'I read about the other two going missing after young Elizabeth disappeared. When the second girl was reported as a misper I raised it with supervision but my Inspector at the time Mark Porter would have none of it.'

'Why was he so set against it?'

'Because he was a lazy bastard. If he did bugger all on Monday, he'd spend Tuesday finishing it.'

'What did you do?'

'What didn't I do? There weren't the CCTV cameras all over the place that you have today and Porter wouldn't allocate any additional resources. I spent a lot of time checking out friends, neighbours and even suggested arranging one of those reconstructions but Porter wouldn't have any of it. It was only when the third lass went missing and the press started linking the three, that he sat up and took notice. Shortly after that the enquiry was taken off me and given to one of the C.I.D to follow up.'

Slade senior's face darkened and he frowned at the report.

'When the flak started flying Porter started taking in water. He needed to bat it sideways. Started hinting that any failings were down to me, whilst doing everything he could to distance himself from what was starting to look like one almighty balls up.'

'Porter did a back covering exercise?'

'No doubt. He was looking to avoid any criticism of the investigation landing at his door. I was a very handy scapegoat and as we all know, in the police force shit always rolls downhill.'

Jack wondered how much he should tell his father about the current investigation. He decided to let him know the plan for the following day and watch for any reaction.

'I'm calling to see him tomorrow about the missing person's report.'

'Well good luck with that. Do me a favour… don't bother passing on my best wishes.'

'I take it there's no love lost there then?'

'Some funeral's you attend out of friendship. His is one I'll attend just to make damned sure the bastard's really dead.'

'Were there ever any real suspects in the disappearances?'

'Not that I recall but as I say it was taken off me. I think a couple of names cropped up during the C.I.D. review but nothing ever became of them.'

Jack tried quizzing his father some more but it was clear that everything there was to know was already in the report.

After a while Slade senior levered himself slowly out of his chair and suggested that they should take a short stroll to the nearby Black Swan for something to eat.

'I haven't cooked meals much since your mum…' his voice tailed off. 'When I do it's usually in the microwave. Besides, all this talk of police work has made me thirsty for a pint.'

Jack remembered the dynamo that had been his dad when he was younger, and realised how much his mum had been part of that energy. He had an early start the following morning and had eaten nothing but a takeaway sandwich since breakfast, so the lure of a decent hot meal was too much to resist.

'That sounds a good idea to me.'

'That's agreed then. You can pay. You're on an Inspector's wage and I'm just a poor pensioner,' he said, a glimmer of the old Charlie Slade humour shining through. 'Now, where did I put my glasses?'

Later that evening, as Jack drove back towards the city, he went over everything that his father had told him. It was clear that someone had failed during the early investigation into Elizabeth Mortimer's disappearance.

It was also clear that Charlie Slade thought the blame should rest with his supervision at the time… Inspector Mark Porter.

It would be interesting to see tomorrow what slant Porter would put on it.

Chapter 25

The following morning after the briefing Jack indicated for Dave Armstrong to follow him to the Inspector's office. Once they were both seated, he told him the details of the previous night's conversation with his father.

'I suppose that means that it's time to pay retired Inspector Porter a visit,' said Armstrong. 'Where does he live?'

'Morpeth area. I've just got the address from the finance department at Gateshead that deals with his pension. Hopefully it should only take us a half hour if we set off after rush hour. We can go in my car.'

Just after ten thirty, having first telephoned ahead to inform the former Inspector of their impending visit, Slade eased the blue BMW through the city and, taking the route as he had on the previous night, headed north. The drive took slightly longer than expected but after thirty five minutes they drove into the centre of the small market town of Morpeth, past the seventeenth century clock tower and a little further on until they came to a pleasant leafy modern estate just on the outskirts of the town.

Although there was a slight chill in the air the sun was shining out on a bright morning as they headed towards the address.

Mark Porter was living a comfortable retirement, in a smart double fronted detached house with a large drive, double garage and well-kept lawns.

Porter was expecting them, and greeted them at the door, before politely ushering them into a clean and tidy open plan living room, with views out over the rear garden and a patio.

Jack saw a woman who he took to be Mrs. Porter, kneeling beside a flower bed, carefully digging out weeds with a small metal trowel. She was slightly built and stooped over her task, so that it was difficult to assess her age.

Seeing where Jack was looking Porter said jovially, 'The garden is the wife's domain. I'm not much of a gardener myself. All that digging and planting. Too much bloody work. If it was up to me, I'd just have it all paved.'

Jack looked across at their host. Porter was on the wrong side of seventy. In stark contrast to his wife, he was very overweight with a round fat face and flabby jowls. When he walked every step seemed a Herculean effort. Jack expected at any moment for his corpulent belly to explode out of the dangerously stretched shirt, sending buttons pinging around the room.

Porter was the sort of overweight man that fat people like to stand next to.

The retired police officer collapsed into a large arm chair that groaned under his weight and waved to a leather settee indicating to the two detectives to do the same.

Porter looked at Jack thoughtfully. 'Inspector Jack Slade you said? Any relation to Charlie Slade who worked at Welbeck Road in the mid-eighties?'

'My dad,' said Jack quietly.

'Aye! I remember him. A canny polis was Charlie Slade.'

That's not what he said about you, reflected Jack but kept the thought to himself.

'What's he doing with himself these days?'

'Retired. You know… living the dream,' responded Jack with not a little trace of sarcasm.

Porter studied Jack's face looking for any subtext. 'And now his young lad has made the rank of Detective Inspector.'

'I'm not so young anymore.'

'None of us are,' smiled Porter. 'So, what can I do for you… Inspector Slade?'

Jack told him about the missing girl Elizabeth Mortimer and that the case was being reopened because some new evidence had come to light.

'What sort of new evidence?' Porter asked, trying not to sound too wary.

'We think that she may be connected with a body that has been found.'

Porter gave a good impression of someone trying to remember something long forgotten. When he spoke, it was soft and measured as though choosing each word with great care.

'Can't say I remember her… but we dealt with lots of missing persons back then. I don't suppose it's changed much these days.'

In my day we deal with them properly, Jack thought to himself.

'She disappeared in eighty-five whilst you were a uniform Inspector covering the Byker and Walker area.'

'Eighty-five… Elizabeth Mortimer,' murmured Porter squinting his eyes in a theatrical display of concentration.

'Maybe these will help,' said Armstrong handing over photocopies of the missing person report, 'You make reference in it to her having most probably run off to London.'

110

Porter took the sheaf of papers and studied them for some time.

'Now this vaguely rings a bell. I think someone might have said something of the sort about her running away. I'm fairly sure London did get a mention.'

'There's no indication in the report of who this supposed person was.'

'I think that it was all a bit hazy at the time,' he said, handing back the file. 'But to be honest it was so long ago. I don't think I can be of much help.'

The detectives tried several different tacks but it was apparent that Porter was not going to add anything to their case. It was clear that any mistakes made during his investigation would remain in the eighties, along with the yellowing missing person report.

He had no intention of allowing two young detectives, raking over the dead coals of a failed investigation, to upset his happy retirement.

Frustrated, but not too surprised, Jack made a show of thanking him for his time. With the prospect of their imminent departure, Porter seemed to become more amiable.

As Jack and Dave were shown to the door he smiled and said, 'So how is your dad's health these days?'

'He's doing OK but not getting any younger.'

'Well…' smiled Porter, 'Don't forget to pass on my regards.'

'I will do,' lied Jack.

Once they were in the car and pulling out of the estate Armstrong shot a glance across at Slade. 'What did you make of him?'

'He was about as useful as a glass door on an outside netty.'

Dave grinned at the use of netty; the Geordie term for a toilet.

'You're not just a little biased because he tried to stitch your dad up for his own failings in the investigation?'

'He's a lazy prick who couldn't detect a fart in a perfume factory. Come on Dave… what's there to like?'

'Do you think he was bullshitting about not remembering Elizabeth Mortimer?'

'I've not the slightest doubt he was talking crap. He remembers her alright. He probably also remembers that he walked through the investigation and never got off his fat backside long enough to ensure all the right enquiries were done. If he had put the effort in at the start then, when the second girl went missing, someone would have spotted the link sooner.'

'There's not much we can do about a botched missing person enquiry from forty years ago.'

'No, but I still think that lazy bastard has a lot to answer for.'

Much of the rest of the journey was taken up with discussing what direction the enquiry might take. Nothing useful had been gained from Porter. The passage of time meant that many witnesses were no longer around and those that were would have hazy recollections at best.

Once back at the station Dave Armstrong went off to check up on any progress from the lab results. Slade made his way to Parker's office to update him on the visit to the former Inspector Porter.

Parker frowned. 'I don't think it will do us much good to point fingers at botched enquiries from so many years ago Jack. It will smack of trying to shift attention from the current lack of progress. It might also give the press another stick with which to beat the force.'

'I'm not suggesting that Boss. It's just the poor investigation back then means everything has to be gone over as if starting from scratch. I'm getting information from the detectives reviewing the reports that witnesses may have been mentioned at the time who were never even spoken to. Forensic opportunities were missed… leads ignored.'

'Even after the enquiry was passed over to C.I.D?'

'Uniform cops didn't have the monopoly on cutting corners in the eighties'

'Murder enquiries were always thorough. Not many went unsolved back in the day.'

'Except that this was never ever classed as a murder enquiry. It was always just three unconnected missing girls. If it had been small children maybe it would have been dealt with differently. But we're talking about older teenagers. There was no way it was going to be classed as murder unless a body turned up.'

Parker slapped his hand down hard causing the photo frame on his desk to jump.

'Well, they're bloody well turning up now… aren't they.'

Jack sat silently in front of Parker's desk. It was obvious that he was feeling the pressure. Slade felt just as frustrated as his Superintendent but seemed to be keeping it more contained. Then again, it wasn't Jack who was getting daily calls from Command Block demanding explanations about the lack of progress.

'OK Jack. Keep at it, but ring me as soon as there is anything positive to report back to headquarters.'

Jack left Parker to his thoughts and returned to his office. He prepared a short precis on that morning's visit to Porter and recorded his belief that the retired Inspector probably knew more than he was letting on.

He was just scanning through the other 'action' returns, sorting out those requiring further enquiries, when he heard the sound of footsteps coming rapidly down the corridor.

Slade looked up to see Dave Armstrong suddenly framed in the doorway, clutching a letter in an evidence bag along with a sheet of typed A4 paper.

'It's the result from the lab on the letter sent to Liz Harmon. There were no prints on the letter or any usable prints on the envelope. The lab also did a DNA test on the seal... but there were no traces of saliva.'

'I'm hoping that there's a 'but' coming.'

Armstrong gave a smile. 'But... he slipped up Jack. They got a partial print from the newspaper cutting that arrived with it. There's a positive match with a known offender and he has previous for indecency.'

'Thank God. This could be the break we've been waiting for. What's the name?'

'John Paul Bell. He's in his late fifties, and living in the Walker area... just two streets away from Elizabeth Mortimer's old address. He would have been in his late teens at the time she disappeared.'

Armstrong grinned, unable to hide his excitement. 'Jack, I think we might have just nailed the bastard!'

Jack read through the report as Dave stood impatiently shifting from one foot to another.

'I know Bell of old. If you look at his arrest screen you'll see it was me that locked him up for the indecency conviction. I got him a three-year stretch. If you'd asked me I would have said that a murder was way out of his league... but in other respects he certainly seems to fit the bill.'

Jack got up and hurried through to the Murder Incident room with Armstrong following close on his tail.

The rest of the team were at their desks having returned from their allocated enquiries. They were all busy updating the results of their actions in advance of the late briefing but sensing something important stopped what they were doing. The room went quiet and all eyes turned to Slade who was holding aloft the sheet of paper from the lab.

'At last we have something positive to go on. It looks like our letter writer has screwed up.'

Jack informed the gathered detectives about the discovery of the fingerprint.

The room suddenly erupted and everyone was wreathed in smiles, with the exception of Slade who appeared cautious. He held a hand up and everything quietened but the cops were still all smiling.

'It's good… but let's not get ahead of ourselves. We might have evidence linking the person who wrote the letter… but that's not necessarily our killer. It could conceivably be that we have another "Wearside Jack" hoaxer. One more nonentity desperate for his fifteen minutes of fame.'

The atmosphere in the room calmed down and Armstrong began to protest. 'Boss, he's old enough to be around at the time of the murders. He's local to one of the 'mispers' living only streets away… and like that Professor McNaughton guy said, he has two convictions for indecent assault on kids. I'd put money on him being our man all right.'

'We have to keep an open mind. There's no doubt that he needs to come in. However, if we go for him now, by the time he's processed he'll have to have his eight hours lie down during the night. That would mean we lose eight hours out of his twenty-four… and it gives him the whole night to think up a good story for the morning.'

'With it being such a serious offence we could go for a Super's authority to take us up to thirty six hours,' protested Armstrong.

Jack nodded. 'I'm going to update the Super so that we can put things in place for the morning. Meantime, I want you all to gather as much background as we can on John Paul Bell. We'll give him an early morning knock and when we lift him, we'll spin his place. Let's see if we can find any forensic evidence to link him to our mispers.'

Slade's voice took on a hard edge. 'Listen carefully! Nothing about this must leave this room. I don't want a word of this to get out until Bell is cooling off inside a cell. At this stage the less people that know that he's in the frame the better.'

'Let's do as much as we can today concerning checks and tonight get a good sleep. I want everyone back in here bright eyed and bushy tailed for six thirty in the morning. Tomorrow is looking like it's going to be a busy day.'

The detectives began to smile again. They were no longer treading water. They had a name. They had a suspect in their sights.

They were already scenting blood.

Chapter 26

At six o'clock the following morning as Jack made his way to the car, the streets appeared deserted and the only sign of life was the calls of the Tyne Bridge kittiwakes as they began their dawn chorus.

There was a slight breeze and several of the seabirds were pirouetting in the shadow of the Tyne Bridge, occasionally swooping down into the dark waters in search of small fish.

The birds clearly now regarded the buildings of the Quayside as manmade sheltered cliffs and had nested there since the nineteen fifties.

He had read on one of the tourist signs by the bridge that the birds were the furthest inland nesting colony in the world, and as such had attracted international interest from many ornithological groups.

To the Quayside residents forced to suffer the noise and guano they were just eating/ shitting machines.

Setting off it only took a few minutes to cross the Tyne Bridge and cut up behind the Central station to the "nick".

Jack had slept fitfully the previous night; his mind turning over the upcoming morning raid. He felt sure that some of the others on the team would have also had difficulty sleeping but despite the early hour and lack of rest he knew that everyone would be wide awake, psyched up and ready to go.

Before leaving the previous evening he had spent some time with Dave Armstrong putting together a risk assessment for the early morning raid.

A background check on John Paul Bell with the Computer Information System had not thrown up any firearms warning markers but there had been a previous incident of a severe stabbing and a couple of convictions for possession of a knife.

Concerns had been raised that because of the seriousness of the latest offences Bell might not want to come quietly and may put up a fight. He could easily arm himself with a knife or weapon from the flat and nobody wanted the arrest to end in a siege situation.

Working on the premise that it was better to be safe than sorry, Jack decided to err on the side of caution and, as a precaution, firearms officers had been requested to attend the early morning briefing. Hopefully they would not be required.

Slade pulled up outside the Forth Banks station and was climbing out of his car when he heard his name called. Turning he saw a stocky figure just emerging from a BMW 530 traffic patrol vehicle.

Jack couldn't suppress a grin at seeing his old friend Mike Robson. 'Well Mike! You're a sight for sore eyes. The Control Room didn't tell me that they were sending you.'

'I guess that you just struck lucky.' He indicated to a second uniformed officer. 'This is the other half of the team. Steve, meet my old pal Inspector Jack Slade. Jack, meet Steve Black. Steve here is under the mistaken belief that he's a better shot than me but apart from that he's a canny polis.'

'Good to meet you Steve.'

Mike gave Slade a wide grin. 'Now firearms cops don't mind getting up at stupid o'clock in the morning to give you a hand Jack but I've checked C.I.S. and the punter I'm told you're going to lock up isn't exactly Mr Big. Are you expecting some trouble that we are unaware of?'

'Not really… but I find that it's the unexpected trouble that can really screw up your day.'

'Let's make sure we spoil his day first then. I might get to try out my new toy,' he said, tapping the bright yellow Taser strapped to his belt. It was the newer X2 model; the two-shot replacement for the X26 version that had been used for many years.

'Let's hope that it doesn't come to that Mike, but as my dad used to say. 'That's what Police work is all about. Hope for the best… plan for the worst. Either way it's great to have you along for the ride.'

Robson and Slade had known each other since crewing Pandas together in the early days at the West End. Over six foot tall and powerfully built Mike had short cropped hair, a goatee beard and a ready and infectious smile.

Where Jack had only ever been interested in detective work, Mike's love of fast cars had marked him out early as a potential traffic officer.

After three years in traffic and much to Slade's surprise, Mike had suddenly applied for a placement on the Armed Response Vehicles.

'What the hell brought this on?' Jack had exclaimed at the time.

'Come on Jack! It's ARVs. Think of the 'Street cred'. I get to drive big cars… and carry a gun. Now…how cool is that?'

With his imposing figure, quick wit and gallows sense of humour, there was never a doubt that Mike Robson was always going to stand out in a crowd. On Armed Response he quickly earned the reputation for keeping a cool head in a crisis, but it was an incident six months into his posting that had sealed his reputation.

In the early hours of the morning on a dark winter night shift, Mike had been on routine patrol in the Benwell area, when he spotted a car parked up on a narrow darkened back lane.

Spinning his car around he pulled the traffic vehicle up short of the junction, got out and cautiously approached the vehicle on foot.

In the shadows he could see two male occupants sitting inside and a gut feeling told him that there was something very wrong.

As Mike stepped out into the lane he had felt vulnerable silhouetted against the street lights on the main road behind him and as he approached the driver looked up and spotted him.

Suddenly the car engine sprang to life and Mike heard the crunch as the panicked driver botched shoving the stick into first gear.

In the narrow space of the alley there was little room to jump aside should the vehicle launch towards him. Mike knew that he was in real danger.

Reaching for the Glock nine-millimetre strapped to his waist he raised it, pointing it directly at the windscreen on the driver's side.

The driver froze, eyes wide with fear as Mike walked slowly towards him, the semi-automatic rock steady and pointed directly at his face.

Walking to the side of the vehicle Mike tapped twice with his knuckles on the driver's window. The barrel of the firearm never wavering as he motioned for the driver to wind down the glass.

As if in a trance the stunned man did so. All the while his eyes never left the barrel of the weapon.

'That's a good boy,' Mike said, a slight smile on his lips as he nodded in the direction of the passenger. 'You have just saved your mate's life.'

'My mate's life?' the driver managed to stutter.

'Aye… your mate. I know that you were thinking of running me down. If you had tried, I would have felt quite justified in putting a nine-millimetre round right between your eyes.'

The driver began to shake.

Mike leant closer and smiled.

'And you don't think I was going to leave a witness… do you?'

A search of the vehicle had revealed two kilos of uncut heroin concealed under the rear seat, and next to it an adapted Baikal IZH-79 handgun, machine bored out to take nine-millimetre rounds.

The two occupants turned out to be known drug dealers from Manchester who had travelled to the North East for a meet with their local counterparts and managed to park in the wrong place at the wrong time… for them.

After the incident, Mike had received a commendation but more importantly his reputation spread far and wide, ensuring his legendary status amongst the other firearms officers.

Jack headed into the station closely followed by Mike and Steve and all three made their way to the H.MET Incident Room.

They had only had time to pour three cups of coffee when the other detectives began streaming into the office.

Jack gave a quick briefing, mainly for the benefit of the Firearms officers, after which all the officers including Jack pulled on their P.P.E.

The Personal Protective Equipment of the detectives were the usual stab proof vests worn by street cops, whilst Mike and Steve wore body armour with heavy ballistic plates.

Gavin Oates produced the red painted 'enforcer'; the door ram used for locks during rapid entry to barricaded premises. He had the build and strength to swing the heavy metal tool and had plenty of experience in using it.

Shortly afterwards, three vehicles set off in convoy, with Jack and Dave leading followed by the two firearms officers in their marked patrol car. The other detectives from the squad taking up the rear.

The drive down to Bell's flat took less than fifteen minutes. During most of the journey Slade and Armstrong sat in silence. The atmosphere in the vehicle felt tense with everyone lost in their own private thoughts.

Would the arrest signal the beginning of the end for what had seemed an almost impossible enquiry? What would they find in the flat? Was it to be the remaining body parts of the three missing girls or would the whole search turn out to be fruitless?

It was only as they neared the address that Jack broke the silence.

'Take the next left Dave and pull up along the street. We'll walk from there so as to not alert him that we're coming.'

Armstrong did as instructed and the other two vehicles slid in behind. The small convoy had parked up a street away from the target premises and well out of sight of the windows.

Bell's flat was what is known in the North East as a Tyneside flat; where each house was split into two apartments, one on the ground floor and one on the first floor, each having a separate front door.

Their suspect's home was the upper apartment at the end of a terrace.

On Jack's command, two officers hurried to the rear to prevent anyone lowering themselves from one of the first-floor windows, whilst the remainder, including the Armed Response officers, went to the front door.

Dave Armstrong banged hard on the door. The sort of knock that criminals dread hearing early in the morning. He could hear movement inside but there was no sign of anyone coming to answer the door.

At a nod from Jack, Oates swung the 'enforcer' aiming for the mortise lock. With a loud crash the door, the frame and the lock surround all splintered and the cops piled in.

First through the door were the two ARV officers, tasers drawn, loudly announcing their presence as they quickly made their way up the stairs to the upper flat.

As they were half way up Bell appeared on the landing. Wearing only boxer shorts and a grubby grey vest which did little to restrain his sagging gut. Unshaven and with thinning hair that looked greasy and unkempt, he had clearly just awoken and looked shocked.

'Police! Stay where you are!' shouted Mike, his hands raised and the Taser pointed out in front of him.

Bell was not armed with any weapon but held his ground.

'What the fuck do you want?' he screamed at Mike who was cautiously, but steadily, making his way towards the top of the stairs.

'Step back!' ordered Mike and although Bell was spoiling for a fight, the sight of the bright yellow taser pointed at his chest gave him second thoughts. He began slowly backing away from the advancing cop.

'Where's your fucking warrant?'

Jack appeared at the bottom of the stairs and followed the two-armed officers as they advanced towards the target.

As soon as Bell saw Slade his face twisted into a malevolent expression.

'It's you!' he snarled. 'Is this another fit up?'

Steve Black produced a set of quick cuffs and in a practiced movement, secured Bell who put up little resistance.

As officers checked and secured the other rooms, Jack came face to face with the man they had come to arrest.

Bell made no attempt to disguise his hatred.

'Show me your fucking warrant!'

'Good morning John. It's nice to see you too. You've been watching too many television cop shows. Someone with as much form as you should know we don't need a warrant. I can search any person

119

who is arrested and search their premises …without a warrant. Well…
guess who's turn it is today to be arrested.'

'What for? I've done nowt?'

'It's a biggie today John. Murder.'

Bell couldn't cover the nervousness that suddenly appeared in
his voice.

'You're having a fucking joke!'

'When I joke, I smile. Do you see me smiling? No? Well in that
case you do not have to say anything…'

'I know the fucking caution!'

'… but it may harm your defence if you do not mention when
questioned something that you later rely on in court. Anything you say
may be given in evidence.'

Bell turned to look at his bedroom where Dave Armstrong was
already going through some drawers and pulling out several
pornographic magazines.

'That's all legal. Don't try to plant any kiddie porn charges on
me.'

When Bell realised that his bluster and protests were getting him
nowhere, he began to calm down and was led sullenly into his lounge,
where he dropped down onto a threadbare sofa. From his vantage
point he glared at the officers around him as they went about the
methodical task of checking every nook and cranny; searching for any
evidence that might link their suspect with the missing girls.

After about ten minutes Armstrong called across to Slade from
Bell's bedroom.

'Boss! You need to see this.'

Jack moved through and saw Armstrong standing next to a
wardrobe door. He was holding a cardboard box slightly larger than a
shoebox. He handed it to Jack.

Inside were several newspapers all relating to the current murder
investigation. Looking through them Jack gave a wide grin.

There was a missing section where an article had been cut out
from one of the pages.

Taking the box back through to the front room Slade found Bell
sitting glowering at him. When he spotted what Jack was holding, it
didn't improve his mood.

He began to go very pale and lowered his head avoiding Jack's
eyes. Slade stood directly in front of him, the hint of a smile playing on
his lips.

'Did you know that if we had the missing article that has been cut out from this newspaper, then forensics could match it up with one hundred percent certainty.'

All the colour had now drained from Bell's face and he looked about to keel over.

'Of course you do. Well John, would you like to guess where the missing piece from this newspaper is?'

Bell remained silent and Jack's smile was not reciprocated.

'John…I think you're screwed.'

Back at the nick Bell had lost any of his previous arrogance. Booked into the custody office on an offence of murder, he had very quickly realised that he was way out of his depth. He even declined his usual solicitor; he was so desperate to get his story out and to be believed.

In an unusual move, because of the seriousness of the charges against him, Bell was persuaded by the custody officer to get some legal advice and a solicitor was duly summoned.

After talking to his legal representative, Bell was still insistent on talking to the detectives and giving his side of the story and after a very brief consultation with the solicitor, he was taken to an interview room.

Slade and Armstrong were to conduct the recorded interview. In view of the nature of the offence it was to be remotely monitored by Jim Jackson, who had specialist training as an interview advisor. He would sit in a nearby office listening on headphones and making notes of anything that required further investigation.

As soon as the preliminary introductions were over Bell couldn't wait to get his story out.

'Look I admit it was me who sent the letter to that newspaper reporter, but honest to God I had nowt to do with that lass you lot found dead.'

'That's not what you said in your letter,' responded Jack, enjoying the other man's discomfort.

'I was only taking the piss. I swear on me mother's life I never done no murder.'

'Your mother's six feet under at the West Road Cemetery… and has been for ten years.'

'Aye, aye ah kna… but if she was alive, I'd swear on her life.'

'John, I know you of old. You're so bent you can't lie straight in bed. I think that you'd better start telling the whole story, and miss nothing out or you're looking at a room to yourself in Durham jail until they carry you out in a pine box.'

Bell told his story. He explained about cutting the article out of the paper and sending the letter to Liz Harmon, and told them how he couldn't wait for the paper the next day to see if they had printed it.

When asked by Armstrong to explain why he would do such a thing, he became a little reticent, before finally admitting that it was to get revenge on Slade for having him locked up for three years on the indecent assault charges. It had been a hard stretch and as a sex offender he had been isolated under Rule 45 as a vulnerable prisoner. The isolation had not prevented the frequent threats, fear of violence and constant checks of his food for any foreign matter. The stress had at times left him depressed and suicidal.

Bell needed to blame all of that on someone else. Who better than the detective who had put him away? Jack Slade.

When he had seen on the television and in the newspapers that Jack Slade was in charge of the murder enquiry Bell had spotted an opportunity. A chance to get his revenge by discrediting Slade and his investigation.

After the interview Jack and Dave sat in the Inspector's office sipping cups of coffee and mulling over the interrogation.

'Do you believe him Jack?'

'As much as I hate to say so… I do. Bell's not bright enough to lie that convincingly. If he had any less brains, you'd have to water him twice a week.'

'So! What do we do?'

'Bail him out. Speak to C.P.S. and see what they want to charge him with. We might get an attempt to pervert the course of Justice charge but I doubt it. A charge of wasting Police time is more hassle than it's worth with the restraints of time calculations and burden of proof. My guess is C.P.S. will take a plea to an obstruct police and give him a conditional discharge.'

'Chalk one up for the revolving justice system,' grumbled Armstrong bitterly.

At that there was a knock on the door and Mike Henderson came in. 'Sorry to be the bearer of bad news but I've been going through Bell's previous. It turns out that at the time of Jacqueline Marshall's disappearance he was banged up for a month on a Burglary charge. He couldn't possibly be our man.'

'Well whoopee shit!' exclaimed Armstrong with a shrug of the shoulders. And with that it's back to square one.'

Chapter 27

He had seen the article in the local newspaper and it had left him infuriated. Some jumped up nobody was claiming responsibility for all his work and planning.

The imposter's note had been reprinted in the newspaper. It had been written in red ink. Fucking amateur. Should have been in blood. He had a good mind to send that reporter a letter himself to let her know exactly who she was really dealing with.

And that Detective Inspector Slade. It just goes to show how stupid he really is. Fooled by some moron who couldn't even spell correctly? Slade was someone else who needed to be put in his place.

Wandering across to an old wooden sideboard he took out a bottle of whisky and poured himself a large glass. He took a large gulp. The amber liquid felt sharp on his throat but warm on his chest.

He looked down angrily at the open newspaper.

He would show them… he needed to show them.

It was no longer just about just getting rid of the bodies. It had become a battle of wits between him and the cops.

And in a battle of wits Inspector Slade was clearly ill equipped.

He was seriously pissed off that the journalist Harmon had tried to give credit for his work to some glory hunting nonentity. He took another large swig of whisky.

But stay calm. There was no need to go off halfcocked.

If you do things in temper that's when you make mistakes.

Remember. Plan, think, check and double check.

He tipped up his glass, draining it.

Only then do you act.

Crossing the room he refilled his glass.

He had hoped the whisky would relax him but instead, it had the opposite effect. The more he thought about someone trying to steal his glory, the more wound up he was becoming.

Then he had an idea. He thought of the contents of the freezer and it just seemed so obvious. He smiled to himself.

I'll give Harmon her front-page story. One that she won't forget in a hurry.

Chapter 28

As usual Jack was early into the office. He was determined to get a head start on the paperwork before the telephones began ringing off the hook and the bosses started mooching around.

Slade always kept his office drawers locked. Some senior officers had been known to root through drawers and cop's trays to see what was lying about. It wouldn't be the first time some police officer had dropped himself in it by putting a piece of evidence in a drawer and forgetting to log it into the property.

Those types of snooping supervisors he could well do without.

When he had been a young probationer, he had passed the open door of Chief Inspector Jim Milburn's office. Glancing in, Jack spotted him lying back in his chair, feet up on the desk, reading a newspaper.

Milburn was what Jack thought of as the real "old school". Just short of his thirty years' service, over six foot three and still well-built he had seen time in The Guards before joining the police in the late seventies. With his clipped moustache, pristine tunic and military bearing he looked every inch a relic from the past.

In these days of graduate entries, he would be regarded by many as a dinosaur.

Milburn however was as sharp as a tack and not much got past him.

On that day that was to include the young P.C. Slade.

Jack had hardly gone a few steps when he heard his name called and was summoned back into the office of his senior officer.

'I saw the look on your face as you walked past Slade. You obviously have the same level of respect for senior officers as your dad did.'

'I don't know what you mean sir.'

'Aye… and that same bloody look of offended innocence. You can ask your dad what sort of Chief inspector you should have. One who knows exactly what's going on in his nick… has his finger on the pulse but lets the troops get on and do their jobs…'

He sat back in his chair, obviously warming to a sermon that he'd probably recited many times before.

'…or maybe you would like the sort that hangs around the parade room and C.I.D. office looking for things to pick fault with? Then sends out memos 'til there's enough of them to decorate the downstairs netty.'

He sat forward suddenly, causing the young Jack to jump.

'Well, I'm the former and you should thank God for it. Now, clear off and if I see that look on your face again you'll be walking the beat in Scotswood 'til your hair turns grey.'

Milburn had picked up his newspaper and Jack was hurrying out the door when he was halted in his tracks.

'One more thing Slade.'

'Yes sir.'

'Tell your dad I was asking kindly after him.'

'Yes Sir. I will'.

Milburn had raised his paper again. 'Now bugger off.'

Milburn had died a few years back and Jack had gone to his funeral. It had been standing room only with many more clustered around outside the chapel door.

He had been a real "copper's copper" who had earned his fellow officers' respect from his wisdom, his personality and not just his rank.

The latest Home Office gimmick in the twenty first century Police Service, was to parachute in managers from industry to take over senior roles in the police service. Experienced cops regarded them as having no real idea of what police work entailed and thought that they wouldn't recognise an angry man if he ran up and bit them on their arse. Bankers were being brought in as supervisors to run the Police force like a business.

And you know what rhymes with "Bankers."

Please God, bring back the dinosaurs!

After checking his "In Tray", Jack strolled through to the Incident Room where he caught the whiff of freshly made coffee. It was no surprise to see Chris Tait in before him again.

As he entered Tait angrily ripped a piece of paper in two, before crumpling it up and throwing it in the bin.

Glancing up, he saw Slade had entered and gave a smile and a cheerful, if slightly forced, 'Good morning, sir.'

'Still getting up to speed?'

'Yes sir, I don't like to fall behind. Can I get you a coffee?'

'No, just get on with your paperwork. I'll help myself.'

Jack walked to the coffee machine and poured himself a cup. He called out over his shoulder. 'How are you fitting in with the squad?'

There was just the slightest pause before Tait answered.

'Good sir. I mean it'll take time to get to know everyone, but I'm sure I'll get on well as part of the team.'

Slade turned and peered at him over the rim of his cup, trying to pick up some clue as to what was really going through the young detective's mind.

'Good to hear. Any results on tracing the packaging tape yet?'

'Not a lot to go on. I've located the manufacturer. A firm based in Yorkshire. They have several distributors throughout the country including the North East. The brand and type are not very common, but it's not scarce either. It's a very heavy-duty woven filament tape, reinforced with strands running across and down.'

'Pretty strong then?'

'Very strong sir. It's used a lot in industry for the wrapping of pallets.'

'Good work Chris. Keep at it and keep me informed.'

'Will do.'

Jack glanced surreptitiously at the waste bin beside Tait's desk.

'Chris, you couldn't do me a quick favour? I can't remember if I checked the overnight message tray downstairs. Could you nip down and look for me. Just bring up anything relating to the enquiry?'

'Yes Boss. Not a problem,' Tait replied, eager to please and quickly getting to his feet.

As soon as Tait was outside the room Jack went across to the bin and retrieved the pieces of paper that Tait had torn up and discarded.

Opening them up, Slade put the pieces together. It was a health information leaflet aimed at giving advice to people suffering from A.I.D.S.

Someone had scrawled across it in heavy felt tipped pen, 'Faggot.'

From the way Tait had angrily torn it up Slade guessed that it had been placed in his "In Tray" overnight.

Slade realised that he was holding the real reason for Tait's early starts each morning. He was making sure that he intercepted any abusive messages before the rest of the crew got in and saw them.

When Tait returned a few minutes later, Jack was standing with the leaflet re-assembled like a jigsaw and placed carefully on the desk.

'Anything you want to tell me Chris?'

Tait looked at the torn pieces of paper but merely shrugged his shoulders.

'It's nothing. Just some stupid joke. I got a lot of it at the West End. I just ignored it.'

'Really? And how many such jokes have there been since you arrived on my team?'

Tait shifted uncomfortably on his feet.

'A couple…'

'Just a couple?'

'Well a few. I just bin them. It's no big deal.'

'Is that why you come in early each morning. To check your tray and see what today's abusive communication reads?'

Chris Tait remained silent.

'We're on a murder case. I can't afford distractions. I need my cops focused on the investigation.'

'Like I say, I just ignore it.'

'You might. I can't.'

Chris Tait was clearly becoming agitated.

'Are you saying that because of somebody's silly prank that I'm not focused on the case? Is that some excuse to use to kick me off the team and send me back to The West? Maybe the real reason is that you don't think I'm going to fit in?'

'If you feel you want to go back to your sector that's a decision for you and you alone. I won't force you either way,' said Jack, keeping his voice quiet and even.

There was a prolonged silence as they both appeared to be weighing each other up.

Jack drained his coffee. 'But I think it's more likely that the person that sent you this could be the one getting a move. Have you any idea who that might be?'

Tait sat down at his desk and made a show of shuffling some papers into order on his desk. 'How long have you got? Just because we're supposed to all sing from the same equal opportunities hymn book that doesn't mean we do. There's a whole load of bigots out there. Changes in discrimination law doesn't change attitudes… it just drives them underground.'

'What do you want to do about it?'

Tait avoided his eyes and stared down at the now neat pile of papers. 'Just let it rest boss.'

Jack wandered across to the filing cabinet and took out a clear plastic evidence bag and a plastic cable tie seal.

'Not an option!'

Then placing the ripped-up pieces of the leaflet in the bag, he pulled the tie tight and headed towards his office.

As he got to the Incident Room door he paused, and half turning, called over his shoulder.

'Nice work with the packing tape. You're doing a good job Chris. Keep me informed of any developments.'

Chapter 29

That morning the briefing lacked the usual boisterousness and banter of cops sparking off each other. It was clear that they were still reeling from the disappointment of the previous day.

Jack told the assembled detectives his theory that Bell would end up charged with a minor 'Obstruct Police'.

This was met with considerable grumbling.

'What about 'Wasting Police Time?'

'We all know that people getting charged with that is just a myth perpetuated by the media. It's more bother than it's worth. A file to the Director of Public Prosecutions for authority wastes far more time than the offender ever did. And then what? Probably a bloody Fixed Penalty Ticket. Let's try to draw a line under John Paul Bell. We have a murder to solve.'

Everyone was pleased that Bell was going to end up on a charge sheet and they could close down that particular dead-end alley. However, he was not the man that they were all hunting.

With their best suspect eliminated it would be the usual routine of gathering evidence until a new one emerged.

As the muttering subsided Slade turned to Chris Tait.

'Chris, you've got some information to give us about the tape used on the packages.'

'Yes boss.'

Chris Tait then provided a brief update for the room on the heavy-duty tape used to wrap the body parts and gave them details on a dozen or so outlets in the North East.

'I've got a list of suppliers but it's not the type of sealing tape that you can purchase in your average D.I.Y. store.'

He handed across to Slade an enlarged photograph showing the packaging of the body parts. He distributed copies around the room and then produced a roll of identical packing tape. This was also passed around so that everyone could examine it.

'As you can see it's quite distinctive with that unusual weave running through it.'

Jack waited until everyone else had checked out the tape before taking it and studying it closely.

'I'll leave it here for everyone to familiarise themselves with it. Chris will put the photo up on the wall and he will be continuing enquiries to trace any shops that stock it and may have sold some recently.'

One of the other detectives then gave the team the lab report results on the DNA tests on the recovered body parts.

'The familial DNA results positively identified the head and torso to be from the West End 'misper' Jacqueline Marshall.'

The room was subdued as Gavin Oates and Donna Shaw were allocated the unenviable task of informing her sister. Although she was probably expecting it, the news would still come as a shock.

The other arm was linked by DNA to hairs on a brush in the bedroom of the missing girl Elaine Robinson and by fingerprints recovered from the inside of her jewellery box. A familial sample taken from her mother confirmed the identification.

It would be a difficult one to break to the mother who had always prayed that her daughter would one day return. Her last hope was about to be shattered by a visit from a couple of the H.MET team. Gavin Oates did not look happy at being the one allocated to deliver the news but Donna volunteered to accompany him on what was one of the worst jobs in the Police service.

Death messages are one of the most distressing tasks that police officers have to undertake. Unlike on cheap television dramas they are never delivered over the phone but always in person. An officer can never be certain how the recipient might react and if they are not local, then the assistance of another force is always requested.

Jack's mind drifted back to one time when he was on the beat. He had been sent to inform the father of a seventeen-year-old boy, killed when struck by a bus after a night out and only identified the following morning after a press appeal. A passer-by who had witnessed the tragic accident heard the plea on local radio and had come forward with a name for the victim.

Slade's knock on the family home had been answered by the boy's father who was waiting, intending to berate his only son for being out all night.

As soon as he saw the uniform and the sombre look on Jack's face, the father's mood changed. In that instant he knew why the policeman was at his door. Without a word spoken he understood in his heart.

And it was news that he didn't want to hear.

He actually lunged at Jack and tried to cover the officer's mouth, as if by stopping him delivering the message he could somehow prevent his whole world from crashing down around him.

The experience had a profound effect on Slade who even now ten years later, could never get the incident out of his mind.

He shut the thought out and turned his mind back to the briefing.

Nothing new had come of plaster casts of footprints found beside the body parts in Jesmond Dene. Several came from the two young boys and others belonged to a parent of one of the children.

The lack of any relevant footprints seemed to back up Kirkby's theory that the torso and arms had been thrown in from above and rolled down to where they were found.

The briefing at an end, everyone was about to disperse when Jack held up his hand causing them all to stop in their tracks.

'Wait! There's just one other thing and I hope that it doesn't involve anyone in this room.'

Jack held up a clear plastic forensics bag.

Chris Tait averted his eyes but everyone else focused on the bag and contents, although nobody could actually read the leaflet or know exactly what it was about.

'It concerns this. A leaflet appeared in the in-tray of one of our squad. I'm sure it didn't come from anyone in this room but I need to make myself clear. H.MET is a team. Each and every one of us is a part of that team. I don't condone bullying… of any kind. If anyone knows who is responsible for this leaflet then come and see me in my office. I hope that it was nobody in this room but if it was then come and see me. It might be the only chance to save what's left of your career.'

'What is it Boss?' asked Oates.

'The person who left it knows exactly what it is.'

Jack turned to leave and signalled for Dave Armstrong to follow.

Once in his office Slade told Armstrong to close the door behind him.

'What was that all about Jack?'

'I think I now know why Tait would act strangely when I came in early. He's been getting some abusive homophobic notes and was trying to get rid of them before anyone saw them.'

'From who?'

'The office is locked at night but there will be spare keys in the custody office so it's anyone's guess. Obviously, it's got to be another cop.'

'Maybe it's a cleaner or one of the office staff.' Armstrong paused. 'You're not really considering that it's one of our team?'

'I'm keeping an open mind but I hope to God that it's not.'

Jack changed the subject.

'Anyway Dave, I've got a job for you. That damned reporter Liz Harmon. I want you to call and see her. Take Mike Henderson with you. Let Harmon know that the letter she was so quick to publicize was definitely a hoax. See if you can get her to give as many column inches to the rebuttal of the letter as she did to the initial article.

They both knew that was highly unlikely.

After Armstrong left Slade had hardly sat back down at his desk when there was a loud knock on the door. It opened and framed in the doorway was Mike Henderson, his face set in a scowl.

'Can I come in boss?'

Jack nodded and the detective entered, pulling the door closed behind him.

'Closing the door? Frowning? It must be serious. What's bothering you, Mike?'

'Can I look at that leaflet?'

Jack unlocked his drawer and, reaching in, produced the leaflet, still enclosed in the clear polythene evidence bag. He handed it to Henderson who studied it carefully.'

'I saw you glance at me when you were asking if anyone recognised it.'

'Did I? Nothing was intended.'

'I take it that this was sent to our new team member D.C. Tait.'

'Who mentioned Tait?'

'Come off it boss. I can see it's about gays. That's his gang isn't it. I wouldn't have to be a murder squad polis to work that one out.'

'Give that man a coconut.'

'And you think that I might have left it?'

Jack shrugged. 'To be honest the thought had crossed my mind. You were quite clear that you didn't want him on the team. You've made your thoughts about gay people clear many times in the past.'

'Listen boss, I admit he wouldn't have been my first choice for the team, but he's here so we just get on with it. Besides, leaving daft bloody leaflets isn't my style. I say what I think. I might be a lot of things but I'm not noted for being subtle.'

'I can't dispute that. And you've never seen it before?'

'Never!'

Jack held out a hand for the property bag but Henderson kept hold of it.

'Boss, we both know that a simple forensic test will show up any latent prints on the paper. I'm telling you now… my prints will not be on it.'

131

'You're saying you've never touched it?'

'I'm saying if I had sent it, I wouldn't be so bloody stupid as to leave my prints all over it. Give me some credit for being a detective.'

He threw the bag down onto the desk.

'If you don't believe me, have it checked by the lab.'

Jack picked up the bag and scrutinised it for some moments before looking back at Henderson who was clearly annoyed.

'I believe you', Slade said, throwing the bag back to Henderson. 'I've asked Dave to go back and speak to that crime reporter Harmon down at the newspaper offices. I want you to go with him. Afterwards stick that leaflet on your 'to do' list. Have it checked out for prints. Don't waste too much time on it though. I'm trying to run a murder investigation here... but I don't want any distractions that might undermine the team. Find out who sent it. Report back to me... and only me. Got that?'

'So, you now no longer think that I sent it?

'If I did then I've just handed the keys of the chicken coop to the fox'.

Slade paused and gave a smile. 'Besides, as you say yourself ...you've never been that subtle.'

Henderson nodded and picking up the property bag, turned and left.

Chapter 30

The newspaper offices were situated in a large complex above a commercial centre in the city. Access was via a lift but only after being questioned by a disembodied voice over an external intercom.

Armstrong identified himself and explained that they were there to see Liz Harmon. There was a loud buzz and the door mechanism was released.

Leaving the lift on the first floor they entered a large open plan reception area which managed to give the space a bright feel to it with light flooding in from floor to ceiling windows. It all felt very clean and professional.

There was some limited seating and behind a long reception counter a young woman in her early twenties was sitting answering a telephone switchboard. Clearly more at home taking orders for advertisements than dealing with two dour-faced murder squad detectives, she put the phone down and cautiously appraised the two officers.

Dave Armstrong produced his warrant card, introducing himself and Mike Henderson. The receptionist made a pretence of studying the identification for a few seconds as if to be sure that it was genuine. In reality she had probably never seen one before so wouldn't know a Police warrant card from a bus pass.

Confident that she was not being subjected to a prank by one of the junior reporters, she nodded and telephoned through to the newsroom.

After a brief whispered conversation and several surreptitious glances across at the detectives, she hung up and gave her best receptionist's smile. With a wave of the arm she indicated to the row of seats. 'Please take a seat. Ms. Harmon will be down to see you presently.'

Five minutes later Harmon appeared and gave a welcoming smile which was just as fake as the Cartier watch on her wrist.

Armstrong and Henderson were shown through to a cramped side office which contained a small table and three metal framed chairs. Dave began by telling her that an arrest had been made following the letter that she had received.

Before he could say anything further the barrage of questions began.

'Is he being named? Has he admitted involvement in the murders? Will the newspaper be given an exclusive in recognition of the help they had provided?'

Armstrong quickly shut her down, explaining that enquiries had revealed the letter sent to her had been a crude attempt at a hoax; intended to mislead the enquiry.

'A Hoax? How can you be so sure?'

'We are sure and are liaising with C.P.S. to decide on what charges he might face.'

'Can you tell me his name?'

'Not until he is actually charged.'

'So, why are you here then?'

'Two reasons. Firstly, out of courtesy. Since you contacted us, I'm obliged to keep you informed of the result of your report.'

'And secondly?'

'Inspector Slade wants you to run a story stating that the whole letter was a hoax. He feels that failure to do so at the earliest opportunity, might cloud the investigation in the eyes of the public. If they believe that it was genuine, they might feel that any little clue or suspicion that they have may be irrelevant. It might even prevent someone from coming forward with real information.'

Harmon thought about this for a moment.

'Are you sure it's not Inspector Slade wanting to gloat and make me look stupid for getting it wrong?'

Armstrong shook his head.

'I can assure you it's nothing of the sort. If we let you stick with the story and later you were shown to be totally wrong it would make you look worse in the long run. Playing it our way helps keep the enquiry on track and saves you future embarrassment.'

'And you're absolutely positive that it's a hoax?'

'There's no doubt.'

Harmon stayed silent for a few moments considering her options.

'OK. I'll do as you ask... but I hope you remember this in the future when I'm looking for a bit of inside information.'

Armstrong couldn't help but smile.

'You never give up do you?'

Harmon returned the smile.

'It's what keeps me at the top of my game. I get the impression your boss is of a similar mentality.'

She held out her hand and Dave took it.

'I'll show you out detectives.'

As they walked to the exit Armstrong was starting to realise how Liz Harmon was able to turn on the charm and although he didn't find her physically attractive, he still understood how some men might find her alluring.

They returned to the reception and were just summoning the lift when the receptionist called across.

'Miss Harmon when you're finished there's been a courier delivery for you.'

Armstrong heard the steady hum of the lift approaching and casually glanced across at the reception desk. On top was a parcel about eighteen inches tall and about the same width. It was wrapped tightly in brown paper and sealed with tape.

It was the tape that caught Dave's eye. 'Don't touch it!'

Harmon, who was already reaching out for it, stopped abruptly.

Even from several feet away Dave recognised the tape around the package.

He had handled the very same type of seal that morning at the briefing.

Jack took the call from Dave Armstrong in his office and wasted no time in getting one of the uniform officers to 'blue light' him through the city centre traffic and drop him off at the newspaper offices. Armstrong was waiting there with Harmon hovering behind him like a vulture.

The package, addressed to Harmon, had been taken from the receptionist and placed in the small side office out of sight of anyone. Armstrong had wanted to take it away with him to the station but Harmon had created a scene, pointing out that it was addressed to her and until it was actually opened, he had no reason to believe that it was anything to do with his case.

Armstrong didn't want to mention that the packing tape was his confirmation. That was something known only to the investigating team and there was no way that he was going to reveal the significance to the reporter.

Eventually they had come to a compromise. The container could be opened at the newspaper offices after a press photographer had taken a couple of shots of it.

'I lifted it by the corners using gloves, so as not to disturb any prints,' said Armstrong, as Slade stood back scrutinising the box and the distinctive wrapping tape. 'Forensics are on their way but I suspect that there won't be any prints... not if it's come from our man.'

Armstrong nodded towards the tape. 'That's a bit much of a coincidence if it isn't from our man.'

'What's a coincidence?' demanded Harmon who was ignored.

Just at that moment the lift door opened and the smiling figure of Ged Kirkby strolled out carrying a large black case and already wearing his white forensic suit.

He glanced across at the box on a table and immediately his eyes were drawn to the wrapping. Glancing across at the reporter straining to get a closer look at the package, he wisely chose not to mention the tape.

'Somebody's birthday then? Will I get a slice of the cake?'

'Aye Ged. If you can find a label giving the return address. We want to send a thank you card.'

'You always want the easy solutions Jack.' Kirkby grinned, pulling on a pair of blue forensic gloves. 'You want this taken to the lab?'

Slade shook his head. 'Not just yet. Miss Harmon here is quoting "The Postal Services Act" and feels we don't have any reasonable excuse to open it. She says that it was sent to her and could be private or personal.'

Kirkby shook his head and his face turned serious.

'From what I see I'm pretty certain it's going to be our man.'

'What do you see?' said Harmon, straining forward to get a better look at the package.

'I don't think that "pretty certain" is going to swing it for Miss Harmon,' said Jack. 'Can you just open it up here and check it out? If it is from our man we'll seize it as evidence…' He turned towards Harmon, '… no matter what she has to say. If it's nothing we can just leave it and sod off back to the nick.'

Kirkby seemed to consider this for a second or two.

'OK. Give me a moment.'

He laid out the black case and opened it, selecting some small tools, forensic bags, seals and a large piece of thick brown paper.

Placing the brown paper on the table he took a sharp blade and sliced along the packaging, keeping to the very edges so as not to obliterate any area that might possibly hold a fingerprint.

Kirkby then gingerly prised open the packet and looked inside. With a pair of tweezers, he extricated a single page of paper upon which he could see writing. He put it down carefully where Slade could view it.

'Is that written in red ink?'

Kirkby frowned. 'If I'm not mistaken Jack… it's blood.'

'Human?'

'There's no way to tell without a forensic test.' He looked concerned. 'What I can say is that it looks fresh.'

Everyone was quiet as the implication sank in.

Placing the note into a forensic bag, Kirkby turned again to the parcel.

There was a large amount of half inch long polystyrene pieces, acting as packaging to prevent the contents being damaged in transit and he began to remove them carefully to see what they were covering up.

As Kirkby cleared away the protective packaging Slade and Armstrong huddled closer, with Harmon attempting to peer over their shoulders.

Suddenly Kirkby let out an exclamation. 'Oh shit!'

Staring up at them from inside the box was the severed head of a young girl.

Chapter 31

Liz Harmon was unceremoniously shuffled out of the room, although not without a lot of resistance and argument. She became very irate when Slade told her that the package and contents were being seized as evidence and demanded a closer look at what was inside. Jack remained resolute, refusing to allow her anywhere near it, citing the danger of cross contamination.

When he also refused all pleas for the photographer to be allowed to get some images Harmon was almost spitting blood.

With Harmon safely removed from the room, Kirkby photographed the head in situ. The box, packaging, note and the macabre contents were placed in evidence bags for transportation to the forensic lab.

Harmon was not about to give up. Even as the officers were leaving the newspaper offices, a photographer continued snapping away, following them into the street as far as their vehicle.

Slade didn't bother asking Harmon to hold back on the story. It would have been pointless. She had been handed a scoop and nothing would prevent her making the most of the situation. Jack knew that this was going to be the front page of the next edition.

Back at the nick, Jack asked Kirkby if he could again see the note that had accompanied the body part. He hadn't wanted to inspect it too closely whilst they had been in the side office with Liz Harmon stretching and pushing to get a closer look.

The forensic officer handed over a clear plastic bag and Jack read the message on the single sheet of paper. Written in crude block capitals it certainly looked to him as if it had been written in blood. In a couple of places the blood had run giving it an evil aspect; conjuring up an image of fresh gore.

Armstrong looked over Jack's shoulder and they both read through the message.

> *Dear Ms. Harmon,*
> *You disappoint me being so easily taken in by an illiterate hoaxer.*
> *Be assured that I am not a hoaxer.*
> *Should you doubt me, look inside the box.*

Jack placed the polythene evidence bag carefully down on a desk so as not to smudge any of the writing. Kirkby took several photographs, before placing it aside with the other exhibits.

Dave had arranged with one of the team to take a statement from the receptionist, along with elimination prints from anyone who had been in any contact with the parcel. However, everyone was fairly certain that if anything was to be found, it would prove to be yet another false trail, set by the killer to mislead the investigators. The person that they were dealing with had already proven himself very forensically aware.

Leaving Kirkby to get on with forensically packaging the exhibits, Slade and Armstrong made their way to Jack's office.

'Did you see the grey discolouration on the head around the extremities?'

Jack nodded. 'The same freezer damage as on the head of Jackie Marshall.'

'Harmon's not daft and made sure she managed to get a look at what was inside the package before she was kicked out of the room. After the first head was found in the river, she must have had a bloody good idea what we might find inside that box.'

'Well. She certainly has her lead story tonight.'

'The lab should tell us which of our other outstanding 'mispers' the head belongs to. Our guy's getting busy Jack.'

'Yes he is. There's someone I want to speak to about that. Sooner rather than later.' replied Slade. 'Can you grab some keys. We're off out again.'

Twenty-five minutes later Slade and Armstrong were sitting in a wood paneled room at Newcastle University, surrounded on three sides by heavily laden bookcases. The chairs that they were sitting on were upholstered in a worn dark brown leather and were not particularly comfortable

Opposite them was a large mahogany wood Victorian writing desk strewn with papers. The desk exuded age and Jack was certain that it was no reproduction piece. The musty smell of old books and a faint aroma of pipe smoke leant itself to the atmosphere of stuffy academia.

Behind the desk, relaxing in a high-backed chair in the same worn brown leather, was Professor McNaughton.

McNaughton was sipping tea from a China tea cup which had a mosaic design on it. Jack recognised the design as similar to some found on a recent archaeological dig of Roman remains in nearby Corbridge.

The professor had offered them a sherry but they had both settled for coffee

'Thanks for seeing us at short notice Professor. I'm sure you must be very busy.'

'Any excuse to put off wading through these undergraduate essays,' he replied, sweeping a hand in the direction of a large stack of papers. 'You know I've always believed that a university academic life would be simply perfect… if it wasn't for all those damned students getting in the way.'

'I feel the same about police work and the public,' smiled Slade.

'Well Inspector Slade, in view of what you've said I'm sure that you are well aware that you are dealing with what researchers classify as an 'Organised Sociopathic Offender. Your offender's crimes are well thought out and carefully planned. He will be methodical in the ways he finds his victims and will avoid leaving any evidence at the crime scene.'

'He dumped Jackie Marshall in the Tyne. Why is there now such a total change in M.O.' asked Slade. 'There was no attempt to conceal the body parts in Jesmond Dene… and now he is actually sending a second head to a reporter?'

'Perhaps, at first, he simply wanted to dispose of the body parts but then things changed. The media became involved. An organised offender will follow his crimes in the press. He or she often comes to revel in the coverage that they get. Leaving a body… or in this case a head… where it can easily be found is symptomatic of this type of criminal. He is to put it simply… attention seeking.'

'Well, the bastard has got my attention all right,' said Slade, leaning forward in his chair. 'And he'll keep getting it right up until I see his face behind bars in a prison cell.'

McNaughton smiled. 'He's wanting you to get angry.'

'He scores on that one too. This guy is as mad as a box of frogs.'

'On the contrary, he is clearly of above average intelligence and likes to think of himself as such. More importantly he will want to portray himself as more intelligent than the police officers who are trying to catch him. He will take a lot of pride in his ability to thwart and confuse your investigation. Going so far as to taunt law enforcement. He's saying, "Here I am… catch me if you can".'

McNaughton paused and looked down at his desk. The brief smile now replaced with a concerned look.

'Is there something that you're not saying, professor?'

'I'm worried that with this third disposal he's getting more brazen. He has become much more confident. I believe that he's building up to something.'

'Building up to what?'

'What else could he do to get even more attention than he already has? What would shock not only the police, but also all the people reading about him in the papers and on the news? What would panic them even more than they already are?'

Jack's heart began to race as he realised what Professor McNaughton was alluding to.

He's getting ready to commit another murder.

Chapter 32

That night, despite Slade's attempts to thwart her, Liz Harmon made sure that she had her story on the front page.

She hadn't been allowed by the police to examine the contents of the package but it was obvious from their demeanour and the way the parcel was being handled that it was another body part. When the forensic officer had recoiled back, she had managed to push forward and had caught a glimpse of the head of a female before she was quickly pushed from the room.

The detectives had refused to confirm that the package had contained the severed head from one of the missing girls... but crucially no-one denied it.

That was as good as an admission in her book.

From the little she had seen and the shocked reactions of the police officers she was certain that it was a real head and not some kind of stupid student prank... or another hoax.

If this was a second decapitation it was to some extent a confirmation that more than one body was involved. It would give her a great angle for her story.

The article in that night's newspaper asked questions that would no doubt cause some consternation in the team dealing with the murder... or murders.

Were the Police covering up the fact that a serial killer was on the loose?

Did the police have parts from more than one body?

Are the other missing girls being treated as potential murder victims?

She might not have all of the answers but just asking the questions would allow her readers to fill in the blanks and make their own minds up. Liz Harmon had never been one to allow a lack of facts to get in the way of a good headline.

The only photographs she managed to obtain were of the detectives, both inside and outside of the offices, and of the white garbed forensic officer carrying his exhibits. Every picture tells a story. She had been careful to ensure that the photographer angled a few of his outside the office shots to include the signage of the newspaper offices. That kept the paper and of course by association, the chief crime reporter Liz Harmon, at the centre of the story.

The parcel being addressed personally to her was a dream come true. If she played her cards right, she could end up as a sort of intermediary between the killer and the cops. She could be seen to be at the very heart of the investigation.

Her editorial concluded with an appeal for the killer to contact her directly to give his side of the story. She knew that was highly unlikely but if it did happen that would be the icing on the cake. She had even included an unregistered mobile number where she could be contacted if he wanted to talk.

Harmon was relishing the amount of front-page coverage she would be afforded if she were to be regarded as a direct line of communication from the killer to the police. She was already envisaging the prospect of a book deal and already had her title. It was the one she had finally persuaded the editor to use.

"The Jackie in the Box Murders".

This could be her big break. It might propel her career forward, allowing her to leave the local rag behind for a job with one of the nationals. Maybe there would be a slot on television appearing in one of those investigative documentaries.

She even dared fantasise about what it would be like if she managed to identify the killer before the police did.

In particular before that arrogant bastard Slade.

Now that would guarantee the book deal.

Chapter 33

The following morning the mood in the Murder Incident Room was sombre.

'Did Professor McNaughton actually say that the killer was about to embark on another kidnap and murder spree?' asked Gavin Oates when Slade began the briefing.

'As good as. He said that it was his considered opinion that the disposal of the body parts suggested that the killer was building up to a resurgence of attacks on young girls. He couldn't have been clearer.'

'But why now after nearly forty years? It doesn't make any sense.'

'He didn't have an answer to that but sending a body part to a newspaper reporter certainly suggests a steep escalation of behaviour.'

Everyone turned to the latest photographs to be added to the Murder Wall, which included a particularly grisly shot of the severed head.

Slade looked out across a sea of downcast faces, all of whom had their own theories about the direction that the investigation was moving. If McNaughton was right the urgency to trace the killer had been ratcheted up considerably.

A fresh wave of murders of young girls would be the nightmare scenario.

'Right, listen in. Is everyone fully up to speed with yesterday's developments.'

'How could we not be? Harmon ensured that it was plastered all over last night's bloody paper,' muttered Henderson.

The newspaper was now calling it "The Jackie in the Box Murders" which Slade thought very irreverent and lurid but had enough of a ring about it for it to catch on with the 'red top' readers.

'Well, we have CSI and the forensics lab working at full speed on this one. The latest is that both the packaging and the box that the head came in, have been thoroughly examined. There are a couple of prints on the outside of the packaging but these are likely to be from the parcel delivery staff. There's an action raised to track down anyone in the firm that may have handled the box during transit.'

Jack indicated a photo on the Murder Wall.

'The interior of the package has undergone tests for fingerprints, fibres, stray hairs, DNA and any damned thing that might lead us to our killer.'

'The letter that came with the parcel is also with the lab but no fingerprints or DNA has been found so far. Bearing in mind the previous lack of any forensics and taking into account the comments of Professor McNaughton, our man has already demonstrated an appreciation of police procedure. He is not going to be stupid enough to leave any obvious clues.'

Jack looked around at the glum faces in front of him.

'We have however, been given a result on the blood used to write the letter. Although it's fresh you'll be relieved to know that it's not human. It's cat's blood. So thankfully there is no evidence that we're looking at any further victims… at this time.'

'I don't think the cat will see it that way,' said Henderson sardonically.

Jack ignored the comment. 'The writing has been done in block capitals. Quite probably stenciled to disguise it.'

Jack pointed behind him.

'A photographic copy of the letter is up there on the murder wall. I don't want any of the facts leaking out to the press. I particularly don't want anyone to even speak to Liz Harmon unless I tell them to. She is seriously pissed off at losing out on any photos of the evidence and feels that we've robbed her of a scoop. She's baying for blood and wouldn't think twice about causing the enquiry maximum embarrassment. From now on no cops other than the H.MET get access to the incident room and the room is to be locked and secure each night and if left unattended at any time. I have taken the spare keys. Try to keep the place tidy because even cleaners are banned for the minute.'

Jack pointed to the photograph of the dismembered head.

'The pathologist Paul Clifford has confirmed that the head was removed post mortem and like other items that have been recovered it shows signs of freezer burn consistent with long term storage in a deep freeze.'

Everyone remained silent, their eyes fixed on Slade as he continued.

'Professor McNaughton is of the opinion that our killer is building up to another murder. If anyone was planning on taking leave or days off you can forget it for a while. We're going flat out until we get this lunatic. The priority now is to stop him before he kills again.'

Jack paused. 'Any questions?'

Chris Tait raised his hand and Slade nodded in his direction.

'Boss, the forty-year gap really bothers me.'

'McNaughton has said that a serial killer does occasionally leave long gaps between his victims. However, he does not know of any where the inactive period has been as long as this. His only suggestion was that perhaps the killer may have been carrying on with his spree somewhere else other than Tyneside... perhaps abroad. Now it looks like he is back on his home territory. At this minute, I'm open to any suggestion that might help us get to him before he kills again.'

'What about the victims? With them all being of a very similar description. Does Professor McNaughton have any theory about that?' asked Donna.

'It might be that our killer was at one time rejected by someone who looked similar to our victims. Perhaps he was even convicted in the past of an offence involving such a girl and bears a grudge. It may be that it just happens to be the type of girl he is attracted to. We need to check out anything and everything.'

Slade paused. 'One thing Professor McNaughton stressed was that the killer wants to portray himself as more intelligent and educated than those hunting him.'

There was a muted silence.

'So come on! Let's get out there, get focused... and prove this bastard wrong.'

Chapter 34

It was still very early in the morning but the sun had already risen on a sunny spring day as he stood in the rear garden scraping the excess soil off the spade onto the edge of the path. He had dug down quite a way to prevent foxes digging up the remains.

On the internet he had read about how to dispose of dead bodies. Once he had overcome his surprise that there were so many pages on the subject, he had found it all very interesting.

Apparently the most recommended route was dissolving a body in acid but as barrels of sulphuric acid had never featured on his weekly shopping list, that seemed a bit impractical. There was also the added problem of what to put the acid in. It wasn't only great for dissolving dead bodies but also managed to melt a large variety of other things. Including, in many cases, whatever you poured it into. Chemistry had never been his strong point.

Other helpful suggestions on the internet had been feeding the body to pigs, bribing someone at a crematorium to put it in a furnace and even disposing of a weighted down corpse from a fishing boat out at sea. None of these methods were particularly convenient... or necessary in this particular case. He had no need to worry too much about the disposal of today's dead body. The corpse of a cat was hardly likely to cause much of a hue and cry... unless of course it was your cat.

It had been easy to find some fresh road kill. He had collected some of the blood but had been taken aback at how quickly it had begun to congeal.

Shame ...he would have liked to have written a longer letter.

Chapter 35

Slade was sitting in his office facing three of his detectives, each of whom were holding a bundle of assorted papers. The meeting had been arranged to review the stages that they were at with the three missing persons.

Donna Shaw who had been allocated the case of Jacqueline Marshall, began her summation of where she was at in the enquiry.

'The head recovered from the Tyne has been positively identified as that of Jacqueline, as has the torso and one of the arms recovered from Jesmond Dene. The familial DNA confirmed it and the family are fully aware.'

Jack nodded. 'Where are we with the old 'misper' forms? Did you find anything that we need to revisit?'

'At the time of her disappearance there had been quite wide-ranging enquiries including extensive house to house in the area and a leaflet drop at the bars in town that she had visited. There was plenty of media coverage in both the press and on local television and her photograph had been widely distributed. A few suspects had been brought in for questioning. They seemed to check out with alibis but there were a couple that the detectives at the time weren't happy with.'

'Not happy? In what way?'

'One of a number of school friends she had been out with that night was named Alan Hall. He was known to have had a bit of an infatuation with Jacqueline and had sent her Valentine cards. It seems his feelings weren't being reciprocated. On a couple of occasions, he had been noticed following her home from school and hanging around her home in the evenings. These days we would be calling it 'stalking', but forty years ago there were no such harassment laws.'

'What did he have to say for himself?'

'After Jackie disappeared Hall was brought in and questioned. He admitted being with her and some others on the night she went missing but claimed that when Jacqueline left for home, he had stayed with the group to get burgers. He never saw Jacqueline again. He stuck to his story. It was confirmed by the group and the detectives became convinced that he was just a kid with a teenage crush. They sweated him in the cells for a few hours but in the end kicked him out.'

Slade jotted down a reminder to himself and went on.

'What about the other one?'

'There was a neighbour, Ian Paxton. Considered by people in the area to be a bit strange. He was known to hang around children's play parks and was often seen outside the nearby secondary school when the kids were leaving for the day. He had been stopped on a couple of occasions by the local beat cops after they had found him snooping around late at night. They suspected that he might have been a 'peeping tom'. He was given an early morning call and his house turned over. Nothing was found to link him with any of the girls and he was ruled out as a suspect.

Jack had been taking notes and when Donna finished he looked up.

'Right Donna. Give Alan Hall another shot. I think he might be due a further interview. Also, I want you to track down all the other kids that were out with Jacqueline that night. Let's see if we can have another crack at them. Double check that their stories haven't altered and they're still giving Hall an alibi. In forty years loyalties can change. Check Alan Hall out on C.I.S. and P.N.C. for details of any offences before or since Jacqueline's disappearance… particularly anything sexual.'

He glanced down at his notes. Also, let's also see if we can track down the creepy neighbour Paxton. Find out whether he knew or ever spoke with Jackie. You can also run him through C.I.S. and P.N.C.'

Donna made notes of her allocated enquiries and then it was Chris Tait's turn to speak.

He had been allocated the Elizabeth Mortimer enquiry.

'Elizabeth was the first to go missing in January. At the time she was considered just another teenage runaway and the initial enquiries had been cursory to say the least. A missing person report was filled in but the investigation had been limited to friends and family connections. She was an only child and living with her parents in the Walker area.

'Suspects?'

'None to speak of. Initially nobody was being questioned in depth. It was only after the third young lass went missing that anyone began linking the three cases.'

'And once they were linked?'

'The case was reviewed and the detectives focused in on Elizabeth's boyfriend… a boy called Craig Nelson. He was dragged in and given the third degree. He was questioned for several hours and according to the report… "had become emotional".'

Jack smiled.

That was a police euphemism for crying his bloody eyes out.

149

'Although he admitted being in a relationship with the missing girl there had been no evidence of any violence in the relationship and the alibi he gave checked out. There was never anything additional to connect him to her disappearance and nothing at the time to link him with the other two girls. He was ruled out.'

Tait flicked through some pages and continued with his update.

'Several years after the disappearance the parents moved away up to the Borders area just outside of Berwick. Apparently, in the years after the disappearance there was a bit of a whispering campaign against them. It turned out that the father had previously been interviewed by social services after some report from a school. Elizabeth had turned up one day with some unexplained injuries. In the end nothing had come of it and the father was NFA'd.'

'OK Chris,' said Slade, 'track down the boyfriend Craig Nelson. Get him into an interview room and see how he reacts. Was he crying because he was intimidated by two big hairy arsed detectives… or was he crying because he was responsible for Elizabeth's disappearance?'

Chris Tait nodded and made some notes.

'Also, I want you to take a trip up to Berwick and see what the parents have to say. I'm not happy with the suggestion the father may have at one time physically abused Elizabeth. Had that been the reason Elizabeth did a runner… or did dad maybe give her a smacking that went too far? It seems odd that they moved out of the area with their daughter still missing. Did they already know that Elizabeth wasn't coming back? Put both parents through the usual checks. Also, see if you can dig up full details of any social services enquiry and how much involvement the police had. I need to know if there was anything that they didn't mention at the time or wasn't recorded in the initial report?'

The last to give their résumé was Simon Walters who had been looking into the Elaine Robinson case. The second head recovered at the newspaper office had been linked to her by DNA, as had one of the left arms abandoned in the Jesmond Dene.

'Well Boss, at first the uniform cops who attended back in the eighties had been blasé about Elaine leaving home. It was the usual half-baked enquiries that often happened in those days.'

'Yeah. The past is a foreign country. They do things differently there,' muttered Slade.

'However, the parents had been friendly with a senior police officer and following some judicious name dropping the officers were given a kick up the arse which seems to have spurred them into action. To be fair by the time C.I.D. took over the enquiry everything that could be done had already been done.'

Walters glanced down at his notes. 'Enquiries had been quite extensive and recorded on the missing person report but there had been no real suspects. Elaine had been cosseted by her parents, rarely mixed with people out of school hours, had no boyfriend and few close friends. The tragedy was, that on the night she went missing, it was very much a one-off special occasion to mark her birthday, and she was supposed to get a taxi home.'

'Who was she with?'

'Two girls from her school. She wasn't used to drinking and the lasses she was with tried to put her in a taxi but she insisted on walking. She wanted to sober up before being seen by her parents. The walk from the city centre was less than two miles along a straight road and would have taken about thirty minutes. Back then walking home was a lot more common than today.'

'Any sightings after her two friends left her?'

Walters shook his head. 'She walked off into the night and was never seen again. As you know, her mother never came to terms with her disappearance and kept her bedroom as a shrine hoping she would return.'

Jack jotted down some points in his policy booklet.

'I want the two girlfriends traced and re-interviewed. Elaine hid her drinking from her parents. Was she keeping any other secrets? Did the girls know something else that the parents didn't? Was there a secret boyfriend? Was she off to see him when she went missing? I don't believe she spent every night sitting alone in her room. I want to know everything about her.'

Slade closed up his Policy Booklet. The review was at an end.

As the three detectives left, Jack had the distinctive feeling that the current investigators knew nothing more than the cops that had looked into the reports back in the eighties.

Four decades later he wasn't sure that they were ever going to uncover anything new.

Chapter 36

Donna Shaw ran Alan Hall, the "wannabe" boyfriend come stalker of Jackie Marshall through the system. She quickly found nine Alan Halls in the force area but only one that matched the age range, and at the time had been residing in the West End of the city.

Inputting the code PH on the record threw up an old photograph of a teenage male with an acne complexion and short lank greasy looking dark hair. A later photograph taken in the late eighties showed that, in a short time, he had filled out considerably, the hair was now shaven and there was the addition of several tattoos.

The historic screen of the record made for interesting reading.

As a thirteen-year-old Alan had been caught in the rear garden of a neighbour's house in the late evening following a report of a prowler. When questioned he claimed that he had accidently kicked his football into the garden and had only gone in to retrieve it. He had a football in his possession but the officer attending had felt this didn't so much corroborate his story… as show a little forward planning.

The householder suspected that Alan might be the same 'Peeping Tom' who had been disturbed outside his twelve-year-old daughter's bedroom two weeks before. However, with no evidence to back up that theory there had been no further action.

What was even more interesting was that Hall had been arrested not long after Jackie had gone missing. The offence was an alleged indecent assault that had occurred in a bar in the city centre. Tracy Doherty, a girl who he had met in the bar, made an allegation that after buying her a couple of drinks Hall had led her to a yard at the rear of the pub where he had pushed her against a wall and put his hand under her skirt.

Hall had strenuously denied any offence stating that what had occurred had been entirely consensual and they had just been 'messing about'.

When the victim sobered up, although she maintained that she had been indecently assaulted, she refused to make a statement or take the incident any further. It was put down as drunken behaviour from both of them and Hall walked away without charge.

Policing back in the eighties often left a lot to be desired and Donna knew that today such a complaint would undoubtedly end very differently. She made a note to trace the victim of the alleged indecent assault and see what she had to say about the incident all these years later.

Donna was having some serious misgivings about Alan Hall who fitted the profile of a stalker and a possible sexual predator. Gathering together the file she had compiled she took her findings to Slade.

Jack listened to what she had to say and carefully read through the assembled paperwork.

'Our Mister Hall seems to have led a charmed life. A number of complaints but no convictions.'

Donna nodded. 'Looks like the officer dealing with the indecent assault allegation in the city centre believed him at the time. Apparently, the girl involved had a bit of reputation amongst the male staff workers and on the night was shown to have consumed a large amount of vodka. Also witnesses said that she had been seen kissing Hall inside the pub before they went to the rear yard. Add to that her refusal to make a statement and back in those days her complaint was going nowhere.'

'What do you think of the actual allegation?'

'Truthfully? I really don't know. It's all a bit he said… she said.'

'You're not sold on this Alan Hall being our man?'

'I wouldn't say that. He fits the profile. He was a friend of the missing girl. He had an obsession with her. He had 'means, opportunity and motive'. He ticks all the right boxes. He has got to be a good suspect.'

'Any connection with the other missing girls?'

'Not really. There's one sighting on C.I.S of him confirming that he was known to drink in the same bar that Elaine Robinson visited on the night she disappeared. I guess that might give him an opportunity. But then again, how many hundreds of others drank in the same bar. The link is very tenuous.'

'Anything else?'

'Well, I checked with the friends that he was with on the night Jackie went missing. He did go with them for a burger as he said but then left shortly afterwards. He could easily have caught up with Jackie if she was walking home.'

Jack nodded and handed the sheaf of papers back to Donna.

'He's definitely worth a visit, Boss.'

'I agree', said Slade. 'Do we have a current address?'

Donna nodded. 'He's living in a flat in Sandyford.'

'Right, take Chris Tait and have a bit of a chat with Mister Hall. See if he passes the "attitude test". If not, see if you can find something to bring him in on. Let's have a crack at him on our turf.'

A twenty-minute drive through the town traffic brought Donna Shaw and Chris Tait to the Sandyford area about a mile to the East of the city. The neighbourhood was similar to Jesmond; a mix of permanent residents and students who rented during term time, but returned to their homes in the summer and over the Christmas period.

Consisting of Victorian terraced housing and Tyneside flats, the area provided affordable housing within a short walking distance of the city centre.

Alan Hall lived in the upstairs flat of a narrow terraced house that had been converted. The front garden was only slightly bigger than a flower planter… minus any flowers.

Before approaching the apartment, Donna took a final look at Hall's photo from the C.I.S. A face glowered out at them. 'He's going to be a lot older but should still be easy to pick out.'

Chris glanced down at the photograph. 'He looks like he's had more tattoos than Edinburgh Castle.'

After knocking at the door a couple of times, the Detectives could see through the beveled glass a thick set figure making his way down the stairs.

Now in his mid-fifties, Alan Hall sported a goatee with his hair cut very short to disguise a rapidly balding head. Standing at over six feet tall and with a muscled build he looked as if he knew how to use his size to intimidate others when required.

'Mr. Hall?' asked Donna, clearly not daunted by the towering figure.

'Who are you?' he asked, but it was evident from the shifty look on his face that he knew exactly who they were.

'D.C. Shaw from Northumbria Police and this is my colleague Detective Constable Tait. Can we come in and have a chat?'

Hall's eyes flickered from one to another but he remained blocking the door.

'What about?'

'We're investigating a cold case file of a missing girl from the nineteen eighties. Jacqueline Marshall. I believe that she was a friend of yours?'

Hall seemed to relax a little. 'I knew her but it was a long time ago'.

'Can we come in?'

Hall hesitated. He appeared to be weighing up his options but after a few moments, grunted and began to make his way back up the stairs.

Taking the grunt as acquiescence they followed. The steep and narrow staircase led to a landing and onto a corridor with several doors leading off.

Hall indicated to the farthest of the doors and they followed him into an untidy lounge which had a stale smell and a general air of neglect. On the floor a discarded half-eaten pizza lay in an open box next to some empty cider cans. Looking around Donna spotted an off the shelf pornographic magazine lying by the side of the scuffed leather sofa.

Hall noticed Donna's glance at the magazine and gave a smirk but made no attempt to move it.

The flat wasn't exactly the place where you would feel the urge to wipe your shoes when you leave... but it wasn't far off. The detectives remained standing, declining the invitation to sit down on the cracked and stained leather couch.

Donna wasted no time in getting to the point.

'We understand that you went to school with Jacqueline Marshall and were in her class in sixth form?'

'Yeah, Jackie was a canny lass.'

'You got on alright with her then?'

Hall gave a little smirk. 'I think she fancied me but we were never actually going out.'

'You were with her on the night she disappeared?'

'Aye. We'd just got our exam results. I nearly didn't go 'cause I got shit grades and I didn't want to listen to the rest of them boasting about how well they'd done.'

'But you did meet up with them?'

'Yeah. A piss up is a piss up and besides I was hoping to get lucky.' Nicotine-stained teeth smiled at Donna. 'If you know what I mean.'

'With Jackie?'

'Not just her. There were a couple of other bonny lasses in our year.'

'And did you?'

'What?'

'Get lucky with one of the girls.'

The smile retreated behind the goatee. 'You can't get lucky all the time.'

'Am I right that Jackie left early?' asked Chris.

Hall turned away from Donna as if noticing Chris for the first time.

'A few of us wanted to go on to a club but there wasn't much choice in those days and what there was didn't come cheap. We all decided to go for some food to the Haymarket. Jackie said she had to go home so she left.'

'And you stayed with the others?'

'I've told the bizzies all this years ago. Yes. I went with the rest of them and we got burgers at one of the hotdog carts that used to be around the town back in the day.'

Chris's face twisted. He had heard stories about the old hot dog trolleys and the dubious characters that used to serve food from them. To say that they had a reputation for a lack of cleanliness did not do justice to the grime encrusted carts they pushed before them. They were little more than salmonella on wheels. Thankfully, with the increased licensing and hygiene laws they had rapidly faded out of existence.

'Did you see Jackie again after she left to head home?'

Hall was becoming more wary and glanced from one detective to the other.

'No. I did not. Where are you going with this?'

Donna was studying him, checking for his body language and reactions.

She continued. 'You see Alan, I've asked the others that were there that night. They say you left soon after you had bought your burger. You didn't stop with them.'

'What's this about? We're talking about forty years ago.'

'You weren't tempted to follow Jackie? Walk home with her? Maybe… get lucky?' she added with a trace of sarcasm.

'No,' replied Hall a little too sharply.

'Because you'd walked her home in the past. I'm told that you had a bit of a crush on her. Is that true?'

'Who been saying all this crap?' Hall snapped, now no longer bothering to hide his irritation.

'The people that were with you and Jackie on the night she went missing.'

'No. I didn't follow her.'

'You're sure about that?'

It was clear that Hall didn't like the way the questioning was going and he folded his heavily tattooed arms across his chest. 'I told some bizzies at the time everything I knew.'

'We're just trying to get a picture of the events that night.'

156

'Well, I've told you everything. I don't know what you're trying to suggest but I need to get some rest. I'm late shift security tonight at work.'

He stepped to one side and nodded towards the door, 'So if you don't mind…'

It was apparent that the conversation was over and that Donna and Chris were no longer welcome… not that they had ever felt otherwise.

At the bottom of the stairs Hall held the door open for them and they were ushered outside.

As they turned to speak to him the door was slammed in their faces.

'Well…' muttered Chris, 'I don't think that registers as a pass on the attitude test.'

Chapter 37

The team was gathered in the Incident Room and Slade waited until the chatter died down and he had their full attention.

'At the time she went missing the boyfriend of Elizabeth Mortimer was a lad called Craig Nelson. He has been brought in and interviewed. At the moment he is not considered a suspect. Mortimer's parents have also been traced to Berwick and spoken to. Despite the rumours, the injuries to Elizabeth were nothing to do with her parents. There is also no evidence whatsoever that they were involved in Elizabeth's disappearance. They've been spoken to at length and say that they moved because the address they were in held too many painful memories.'

Turning to the Murder Wall he pointed to a new photograph alongside those of the victims.

'However, let me introduce you to Alan Hall.'

The face of Hall glared out at them from an enlarged C.I.S. photograph.

'This photo is not recent but is from a previous arrest for indecent assault. Hall was one of the last people to see Jacqueline Marshall alive on the night that she went missing. Donna and Chris gave him a visit and he was, let's say… less than fully co-operative.'

'He was not exactly pro-police,' Chris agreed.

'Bit creepy,' added Donna. 'We did a bit of house to house after we left his flat. According to neighbours he's a strange character… and keeps very odd hours. A bit nocturnal. He works late shifts but even on days that he's not working he goes out and about at all hours of the night.'

Jack pointed at the photograph.

'I want a full background check on this guy. All the usual computer checks plus anything else you can find. He's in the system but doesn't have any arrest records since the early eighties. A couple of very old previous cautions for minor stuff. Petty theft and assault. Let's look a bit deeper into him. In particular I want to know if there is any connection between him and any of the other victims.'

Slade looked around the room at the assembled detectives. 'Now I know we're looking into what amounts to a cold case, but out there will be something that the original investigators missed. Find it and we could find our killer.'

He turned to Donna. 'How are you getting on with tracing any transits that fit the description of the one seen near Jesmond Dene?'

'Slowly but surely. It's not exactly a short list.'

'Keep at it… but for now Hall is the priority. I want to know where he goes every night when he's not working. I'll try to get authority for "directed surveillance" but I first need to have a bit more on him to convince the bosses.'

Slade looked around at the rest of the Murder Incident Team. 'Has anyone any other updates?'

Simon Walters raised a hand and Slade gave a nod.

'Around the time that the three girls went missing there were numerous reports of indecent exposure in the West End area. Analysis of the descriptions provided by the victims suggest that there were possibly three offenders. Only one of whom was ever arrested. If he were still alive now he'd be in his seventies. The other two offenders were never traced.'

'Flashing was a popular hobby back in the eighties.' Henderson muttered, prompting a few chuckles around the room.

'With no sex offenders register back then,' continued Walters, 'tracing offenders means checking through all the old arrests and crime statistics.'

'OK. Just look into it Simon', replied Jack, 'and check out our septuagenarian flasher. See if he's fit and capable of disposing of our body parts, although I'm not holding my breath on that one.'

When the briefing was over and everyone was up to speed, Slade signalled to Donna Shaw and Chris Tait to follow him to his office.

Once inside Slade closed the door. 'This Hall character. What's your gut instinct?'

'I can see why he's been described by other women as creepy'. Donna said grimacing. 'And there's something seedy about his flat with all the porn lying about'.

'I agree with the creepy bit,' added Chris, 'but I'm not so sure that he's our killer.'

'Why not?'

'We're looking at nearly forty years ago when he was just a teenager. Hall didn't have access to a vehicle… not many kids his age did. The M.O. points towards the victims having been picked up in a vehicle. They were all walking home from town and probably on a main traffic route. Not many buses at that time of night and taxis were too expensive for kids still just out of school. Back in those days people thought nothing of "thumbing" a lift. They weren't so wary about accepting rides from strangers as they are these days.'

Jack nodded. 'Or Hall could have followed her. Offered to walk her home. We haven't got an actual primary scene for where the murder took place, so he could still be in the frame? Do we have his DNA?'

'No. When he was arrested in the mid-eighties we didn't take DNA as a routine.'

Jack was thoughtful. 'Well at the minute he's all we've got. I'm thinking we could try to get authorisation for Directed Surveillance'.

'I don't think we've enough to approach T.C.P. with what we have so far,' volunteered Donna, who realised that she had, without thinking, used Superintendent's Parker's nickname.

Jack raised his eyebrows and Donna felt herself going red.

'Who's T.C.P.?' asked a bemused Chris Tait.

Donna blushed. 'Err…I'll tell you later,' she stammered, eager to change the subject.

Jack suppressed a smile and let it go.

'OK. Both of you keep digging and a visit to his previous accuser would be a good start. In the meantime, I'll try to persuade the Boss to get us the necessary authorisation.'

Donna began her background research on Hall by looking at the allegation of indecent assault that was dropped against him some years earlier.

The alleged victim in that case was a Tracy Doherty who had worked at the same video rental shop as Hall back in the mid-nineties. DVDs were not released until late nineteen ninety-six and prior to that movies were available for sale or hire in the VHS video format.

Before going to interview Doherty, Donna decided to put her name through C.I.S. to see if there was any information on her, in particular a current address.

It turned out that Doherty herself was not so squeaky clean. Shortly before her allegation against Hall she had been given an adult caution for an offence of drunk and disorderly in Newcastle's Bigg Market. A vibrant if rather down-market haunt of the young drinking crowd in the eighties and nineties, it had a reputation for drunkenness and violence back then. A reputation not much diminished in the present day.

There was one further arrest of Doherty in 2010, for an offence of shoplifting for which she was also given a caution. At that time, she had changed her surname to Knight and was living in the Westerhope area of the city. Donna assumed that she must be now married, and decided to give the address shown on the last arrest a visit.

With Chris driving, they headed across to the west of the city and to Doherty's last known address.

Newbiggin Hall Estate was a major Housing project built in the very early sixties to the West of the city. Eastgarth was one of the sections of the sprawling urban development. Accessed by a steep downhill road it had been built primarily as a council estate and although a few of the houses had been purchased by the current owners under the right to buy scheme, most remained with the Local Authority. The majority of the houses were clean and well-kept but there was the occasional one that had a scrap car or piles of discarded rubbish on the driveway.

The road looped around in a semicircle, with several cul-de-sacs leading off in different directions. Chris cruised along, whilst Donna tried to make sense of the haphazard numbering system to locate the house of Doherty or Knight as she was now calling herself.

Eventually they found the number that they were seeking and parked up in a small dead end side street. The house had a well-kept garden and looked generally in good order.

When Donna knocked on the door it was answered by an overweight woman in her early fifties, wearing black trousers and a blue short sleeved shirt. She had the burnt orange look of someone sporting fake tan and her hair was tied back with a pink-coloured band.

As soon as she saw the two people at the door, she sensed that they were police officers. Cops were not amongst her favourite callers. It was written all over her face in the undisguised scowl. She glanced behind them, to the left and right. To her and to her nosey neighbours, any house call from the polis spelled trouble.

'Tracy Doherty?' asked Donna.

'Tracy Knight now.' she replied. 'What's it about?'

Donna explained that it was concerning a missing person enquiry. Sharon stared back but there was no invitation to go inside.

'What has that to do with me?'

'Is it alright if we come in and talk?' asked Donna, forcing a smile.

Tracy hesitated a moment, and it was with some obvious reluctance that she stepped aside allowing them entry.

Once inside they were shown to a lounge with plain cream walls and light blue carpet. There was a well-defined track worn from the door to the dark blue leather settee placed directly in front of an over-large flat screen television.

Donna noticed that one of the seat cushions on the worn leather settee was considerably lower than the other two, where the springs had obviously given up the ghost.

A small girl of about four was sitting on the carpet playing with some brightly coloured toy, whilst a smaller child in a nappy crawled around attempting to grab at it.

Doherty noticed where Donna was looking.

'Grandkids. I'm the free babysitter.'

The child in the nappy was reaching for the toy and began to scream.

'Sophie, take your Liam into the garden,' barked their reluctant host, clearing some women's magazines to allow access to the battered sofa.

The two detectives sat down, both careful to avoid the sinking cushion.

'So, who's missing,' asked Doherty reaching for a packet of cigarettes and flicking a yellowed thumb against a plastic lighter.

'Well, the missing person was a friend of someone that you knew. It's really about him that we want to speak to you?' Donna said with the friendliest smile she could muster.

The smile was not returned and Doherty's eyes narrowed.

'Who?'

'Alan Hall.'

Hardly were the words out of Donna's mouth before Tracy snapped. 'That bastard. I hope he rots in Hell.' She lit her cigarette and inhaled deeply. 'So what's this about? Has he raped some lass? I always knew that he would do that one day.'

'Why do you say that?'

'There's just something really weird about him. You know what I mean?'

Donna nodded. Having met Alan Hall she knew exactly what she meant.

'I understand that some years ago you made an allegation against him of indecent assault.'

'And a fat lot of bloody good it did. The bizzies did nowt about it.' She took a long drag from her cigarette which set off a short coughing fit.

'Can you tell me about what happened?'

'We worked at City Videos in town and the slimy git was always trying to chat up the lasses that come into the shop as customers. Thought he was the bee's knees he did. Most of the girls thought he was a bit strange. Well this night it was the staff do and we were doing the pubs down the Bigg Market. Hall kept asking me if I wanted a drink. He was offering to pay so I thought well why not.'

She took another drag and blew out a large cloud of smoke.

'I reckoned he must have spiked my drink 'cause all of a sudden I got really pissed. He said he'd walk me somewhere so I could get some fresh air and we went out in the delivery yard out back of the bar. So then he starts trying to snog me and next thing I know his hands were all over me. I thought he was going to rape me.'

'Then what happened?'

'Well Lisa who just lived down the street from me comes out. I'm not sure if she was looking for me or just wanted some fresh air. She saw what was going on. Well she knew I wouldn't do nowt with Hall 'cause she knew my boyfriend, so I pushed him off and says to her 'This dirty bastard is trying to shag me' So she says I should tell the polis. So that's what I did.'

'And you say he may have put something in your drink?'

'Whey Aye! He must have done. The polis tried to say it was just the vodka 'cause I had a half litre bottle in my bag… you kna the prices they charge for spirits in pubs.'

'I understand that the following morning, when Police officers tried to take a statement you refused to make any complaint?'

'Well what's the point? They kept asking how much I'd had to drink and why I had gone with him to the back yard. They'd already made their bloody minds up.'

'So Hall was released.'

'Aye, but when I told my boyfriend he said I should pack the job in and if he ever saw Hall he'd kill the bastard.'

'And has your boyfriend seen him since.'

'I wouldn't know. It was about twenty five years ago and my lad pissed off with that Lisa about four weeks later.'

'So have you seen Alan Hall since then.'

'I've seen him in pubs a couple of times but he never speaks. I always thought he was a bit scary. I says to Lisa one time, I said he'll kill some lass one day.'

Chris and Donna exchanged glances.

What they were both thinking didn't need to be spoken.

Jack sat in Parker's office and gave him an update on their enquiries so far. He included what Donna had gleaned from Tracy Doherty

'Do you fancy this Alan Hall as our man Jack?'

'He fits the profile. He knew the first victim and Donna did a bit of house to house. He's out most nights sometimes well into the early hours. We can't afford not to put him in the frame.'

'I'm happy to get you surveillance authority but I'm already getting grief from Headquarters about the overtime budget. Could we handle it in house?'

'We need to do it properly, boss. Get in a proper surveillance team,' protested Slade, who often got frustrated about how modern police work was run like a business; dictated by costs.

'The budget Jack. Let's get real. If somebody turns the spotlight on why we brought in a full surveillance team on just your gut feeling, it might not stand the scrutiny. Let's keep it low key and 'in house' for the minute. Your team is surveillance trained. Cover it for a couple of days. If it starts impacting the investigation then we'll look at getting support in.'

Slade was unhappy but reluctantly nodded his agreement.

Returning to the Incident Room he updated the squad on the new plan of action and that Hall had now become the latest focus of their enquiry.

I just hope to God that he isn't yet another dead end that will keep us from getting to the real murderer.

Chapter 38

He watched the local television news and was becoming annoyed and a little frustrated. It was less than a week since sending the little surprise to that reporter Harmon and already his exploits had been put back to the fourth item on local news… and didn't even get a mention on the national channels.

There was a small piece in the local newspaper but even that was downgraded to an inside story. Harmon had just thrown together a rehash of the case so far, padding it out using some comments from a couple of so-called 'experts' in criminal psychology.

It was pissing him off that they didn't seem to realise the planning and effort that he was putting into his plan, and how it was making the cops look more incompetent as time went on. He was running rings around the whole of Northumbria Police.

And yet he was now relegated to a few columns on page four. It was time to really start to stir things up. He needed something to get everyone's attention.

Something so spectacular that he would make the front page of every newspaper and be the lead story of all the channels.

And he knew exactly what to do.

Chapter 39

At nine o'clock that night Jack briefed the team. There was a buzz of excitement in the room.

'Thank you for agreeing to change your shifts at such short notice. As you know we have authority for a mobile surveillance on our suspect Alan Hall. According to neighbours he is known to leave his house late at night and often doesn't return until the early hours. Where does he go? What does he do? Answer those questions and we might find our murderer.'

Dave Armstrong raised his hand. 'Do we know if he has any knowledge of anti-surveillance techniques?'

'There's nothing to suggest that he does but everyone and his granny watches cop programmes and documentaries. He's bound to have some awareness. Add to the mix the recent visit by Donna and Chris, which I'm sure will have spooked him and he's likely to be extra cautious.'

Chris Tait cut in. 'Control room has allocated us a designated back-to-back channel for the length of tonight's surveillance.

'Thanks Chris.' Jack pointed to a photo of Hall on the Murder Wall. 'Now, tonight Hall is due to finish his shift at ten. According to neighbours he always arrives home about ten thirty, gets changed and heads back out in his car. A black Fiesta. Make a note of the registration number. I want someone to follow him from leaving work but I want everyone else to plot up around his flat. As soon as he goes mobile, I want him to be eyeballed at all times. Everyone happy?'

As one, the cops all nodded.

'Right! Let's find out what Mr. Hall gets up to in his spare time.'

Chapter 40

By nine thirty Dave Armstrong and Simon Walters were parked outside the twenty-four-hour supermarket where Hall worked. At five past ten as expected he came out of the staff entrance and headed towards his black Ford Fiesta.

With the two detectives following from three cars back they trailed him back to the Sandyford address. He drove a direct route and gave no indications that he was aware that he was being tailed.

As Hall pulled up outside his home Dave Armstrong drove past in the unmarked vehicle. There were no signs of the other detectives but Dave knew that they would be somewhere nearby, in the shadows, watching and waiting.

Simon Walters spoke into his radio. 'Target is back at home address.'

He turned to Dave. 'If he decides to stop in with a bottle of wine and Netflix this is going to be a hell of a waste of resources.'

Despite his misgivings, after twenty minutes the detectives' patience was rewarded when Hall appeared at the front door. He had changed into dark clothing and after quickly glancing up and down the street, headed to his Fiesta.

'Target out of home address and approaching his vehicle', Oates whispered into the radio.

Armstrong sat up straight and alert. 'It looks like he's on the move again.'

Seconds later the Fiesta passed Armstrong and Walters who were parked up a side street and drove off, merging with the late-night traffic.

Armstrong followed, keeping some distance between him and Hall. They passed through Jesmond onto the Central motorway and headed west out of the city.

'Where the hell is he going?' muttered Armstrong.

The surveillance vehicles had to leapfrog several times to avoid being recognised by their quarry and on several occasions were forced to drop behind on the less busy roads outside the city, where there was more danger of being spotted.

After several miles Hall drove down into Ponteland village, where his pursuers and his surveillance had to close up the gap to ensure that they didn't lose him.

In the village, the Fiesta passed a few shops and a couple of pubs before turning into a shopping area car park and coming to a halt.

It was a dead end with one way in and one way out.

Mike Henderson, who was now the lead vehicle, drove past the car park and pulled up out of sight of the parked Fiesta.

'Target is stationary and exiting his vehicle. Chris! Donna! Can you get an eyeball?'

Chris Tait, who had been some distance behind as 'Vehicle Two', pulled short of the entrance to the car park and getting out, made his way on foot followed by Donna. As Donna kept pace with Chris she was continually updating the others via the back-to-back channel.

'He's out on foot and moving west towards a row of houses. Chris and I are following.'

Mike Henderson started up the vehicle and he and Oates drove around the estate, trying to anticipate where Hall might emerge.

Chris and Donna stalked Hall on foot through a housing estate, where after several hundred yards, he came to an open stretch of land leading to the rear of a number of semi-detached houses. Donna kept the others informed as she watched Hall make his way across a grassed area to a small copse of trees behind the houses.

In his dark clothing Hall was almost invisible against the dark foliage.

Chris hissed across to Donna, 'Stay here. I'm going to get a closer look.'

Keeping low to avoid being seen, Chris edged forward.

Hall was crouched down in the shadows behind a large bush, from where he had a view of the back of the houses.

An upstairs light was on in one of the bedrooms.

Come on you creep. What are you up to?

A young girl of about sixteen appeared at the window and suddenly Chris understood the reason for Hall's frequent nocturnal wanderings.

He spoke to Dave Armstrong on the back-to-back whispering, 'Sarge, he's just a damned peeper. What do you want me to do?'

'Don't blow our cover just to nick him for peeping. We can't rule him out as a suspect yet. Let's keep an eye on him and see what he does next.'

As Chris watched he saw Hall pull on a ski mask and begin to climb over the fence into the garden of the house.

What the hell are you doing now?

Chris could feel his heart thumping in his chest. Was Hall going to be content with just spying on his quarry… or did he have much darker intentions?

As he watched Hall removed a small jemmy from inside his jacket and placed it against the window jamb by the lock.

'I think he's going to force entry. All units move closer in case we have to call a strike.'

Chris edged nearer to the fence to get a better vantage point.

A dog began loudly barking.

Whirling around he saw a middle-aged man crossing the field and holding the lead of a large black Labrador dog. The man had stopped and was staring across in Chris' direction.

A voice called out shattering the night time silence.

'Hey you there! What are you doing?'

On hearing the shout, Hall, who had been forcing the window frame, spun around in a panic. Then running back to the garden fence, with one quick movement he hauled himself over, landing with a thump on the other side.

It was as he was getting to his feet that he caught sight of Chris Tait running towards him and without hesitation set off at a fast pace in the opposite direction.

Chris followed shouting breathless directions into his radio. He was losing the pursuit, when Hall stumbled on a section of uneven ground and Chris was upon him.

Out of breath and struggling to keep hold of his radio, Chris managed with his free hand to grab the collar on Hall's jacket, yanking him backwards.

With both hands occupied Chris was now at a disadvantage as the larger man swung around, fists flailing.

The detective felt a heavy blow to his left cheek and his head felt like it had exploded as he tumbled backwards crashing to the ground.

In an instant Hall was up on his feet and off again, rapidly putting distance between himself and his pursuer.

Chris, head throbbing, staggered back to his feet.

Hall could feel his lungs straining and a burning sensation in the back of his calf muscles, as he crossed the last bit of grassland and onto pavement, heading for the quickest route back to his car.

Taking a deep breath he charged on.

Just when he thought he was almost home and dry, he turned a corner and came face to face with Mike Henderson.

'Stop there lad!'

Hall stood his ground regaining his breath. Then, reaching into the pocket of his camouflage jacket, he withdrew a knife, the blade glinting in the streetlights.

He began waving the knife menacingly. 'Get out my fucking way.'

Henderson reached behind him, taking a small black cylinder from the harness on his belt. Giving it a sharp flick with his wrist, there were the ominous rapid clicks, as the ratchet allowed the expandable baton to reach full length.

In the stillness of the night the noise sounded like the racking of a pump action shotgun.

They were at a standoff.

'Put it down lad. We're police. You're going to make a bad situation worse.'

Hall was like a trapped animal and suddenly letting out a loud roar, charged towards the officer, the knife held out in front of him.

Henderson lashed out with the baton aiming for Hall's arm… but was a fraction of a second too late.

The younger fitter Hall was on him, knocking him backwards and sending him crashing heavily to the pavement.

With the wind knocked out of him, Henderson had dropped his baton and was using both hands to grasp Hall's arm, desperately trying to wrestle the knife from his attacker.

His adversary was younger, fitter and stronger. The years of drinking had taken their toll on Mike Henderson who was no match for his attacker.

Pinned against the hard pavement, arms burning with the effort, the knife inching closer, Mike realised that he was now in a fight for his life.

He felt his arms weakening as Hall pushed down; the knife only inches from his chest.

Just as he felt the blade against his chest, the weight was released from him and he saw his attacker being dragged backwards.

Gasping to get some air in his lungs, Henderson watched as Chris Tait put Hall into a choke hold with one arm, whilst with the other he attempted to restrain the arm holding the knife.

Hall was not giving up, and as much as Chris pulled him back, he used his weight to heave forward.

Hall was strong and it was proving impossible for the slim officer to restrain him.

Henderson gulped in the cold night air and struggled to get back to his feet and assist.

Unexpectedly Chris changed tack.

Instead of pulling back, Chris went with Hall's weight, dropping forward. The combined mass of the larger man and himself sent Hall crashing down and into the pavement. There was a sickening crunch as his nose smashed into the concrete.

Hall cried out in pain through a face streaming with blood but released his grip on the knife, which fell with a loud clatter. Arms twisted behind his back, Hall both heard and felt the ratchet of the quick cuffs tighten around his wrists.

Donna appeared and on seeing the knife and a large pool of blood looked horrified.

'It's alright. It's all his,' said a breathless Tait forcing a smile.

Shaken, but relieved that both cops appeared to have escaped any serious injury, Donna radioed in their location to the other units.

Henderson, still gasping for air, hobbled on unsteady feet to where Chris stood above Hall.

'I didn't think that choke holds were allowed these days, young un,' gasped Henderson.

'They're in the manual... on the same page as how to smack your suspect's nose into the pavement.'

Henderson pretended to consider this. 'Hmm! I'm not sure. That doesn't sound like the same police manual that I've read. I'm going to make sure I get the updated version.'

As Chris dragged his prisoner to his feet, another spray of blood from Hall's nose splashed onto the pavement.

'Yeah! Well in the meantime... I'll not tell anyone if you don't.'

171

Chapter 41

Slade had been dozing in front of the television when the telephone burst into life. He hadn't even tried to go to bed as he knew any sleep would elude him so long as his thoughts kept returning to what was happening with the surveillance.

He had considered being part of the op himself but knew that was just wanting to be close to the action. It would be safe in Dave Armstrong's hands. Jack's proper place should be at the hub during the day, coordinating the enquiry from the Incident Room.

When he took the call from the Control room informing him that one of his officers had been injured and was being transferred to casualty, he had immediately snatched up his keys, jumped into his car and headed across town to the hospital.

On arrival at the Royal Victoria Infirmary in the city centre, he had found Chris Tait sitting up in a treatment room, nursing a swollen cheekbone and the rapid onset of what was going to prove the beauty of a black eye.

Chris being a cop and unlike most of the other ragtag of casualty visitors, being sober, the nursing staff had moved him up the list to be seen.

He had just been examined by an overworked junior doctor, who looked in need of some decent sleep. The doctor was assuring him that despite how it looked, the cheek didn't appear to be broken.

'Come back in a couple of days when the swelling goes down. We can get a better look and maybe do an x-ray if we need to.'

Satisfied that the officer had only minor injuries, the overworked A&E medic abandoned him to attend to three bloodied drunks who had been involved in an altercation outside a city centre pub.

Reassured and satisfied that his injured cop was "walking wounded", Slade suggested that Chris should go home.

Still running on adrenaline and not wanting to miss out on how the investigation progressed Chris tried to refuse, but Jack was insistent.

'Come in tomorrow if you feel up to it but tonight's paperwork can wait. Your shift is over. I'll run you home.'

A young nurse came across and handed Chris a "Head Injuries Information Card" containing instructions of what to do if he felt unwell.

Along with the card came a big smile. Slade wondered if the nurse was flirting with the handsome young cop.

If only she knew.

After dropping Tait off, Slade headed back across town to the police station Custody Office where Hall was being processed through the arrest procedure.

An examination by the police surgeon had declared him fit for interview, despite his bloodied nose and grazed face. The doctor had assured the cops that their prisoner was going to have two black eyes as compared with Chris Tait's one.

That gave Slade some degree of satisfaction.

Hall had initially demanded to go to hospital, until the Custody Officer pointed out that any time spent at hospital stopped the 'Detention Clock.' In effect it would automatically extend the maximum detention time he could be kept at the station. At that point Hall had changed his mind.

A search of his flat was authorised by the night shift uniform Inspector, so Dave Armstrong and Simon Walters took Hall's house keys and headed across town to Sandyford.

The search revealed the expected pornographic magazines and DVDs lying underneath the bed. Armstrong grimaced at the sheets, which looked like they hadn't seen the inside of a washing machine since they were taken out of their wrappers.

In a drawer by his bedside table there were magazines of a more specialised nature depicting women tied up and bound by leather straps. Hall clearly had a strong interest in some of the more deviant sexual practices.

The most important find was a well-thumbed A-Z map of the Tyneside area where several locations had been circled, including the area in which he had been arrested.

The cops became even more convinced that Hall was a serial voyeur which explained his regular night time sojourns. They had no doubt that each of the ringed locations would be one of his regular haunts.

There was nothing however, to connect Hall with any of the missing girls. No old newspapers, no photographs or letters and most importantly no recent newspaper cuttings from the current investigation.

At the police station Slade and Armstrong prepared an interview plan, but were acutely aware that all the best that they really had on their suspect was a possible attempted burglary. There was a chance they might be able to prove an additional offence of voyeurism but that would be up to the Crown Prosecutions Service.

Hall had elected to have a solicitor present during the interview, so it came as no surprise that he refused to answer any questions, repeating 'No reply' to everything put to him. Though frustrating for the cops, it was the usual tactic employed by solicitors, who often advise their clients to say nothing when they know that they're dead to rights for an offence.

It was only when Slade questioned Hall about the knife and what he had intended to do with it if he had entered the house, that their suspect became agitated. Despite the warnings of his legal representative, he couldn't stop himself launching into a tirade of abuse against the police officers.

'It was for self defence. I didn't know they were coppers. It's them that attacked me for no reason. Look at my face. I've got a tooth loose at the front. They assaulted me. I'll be suing them.'

'The officer you tried to stab identified himself and you met and spoke to DC Tait just a couple of days ago at your flat. How did you not recognise him?'

'It was dark wasn't it?'

'Yes, it was dark. Can you tell me what you were doing in the dark at the window of a young girl's bedroom?'

At the sharp glance from his solicitor, Hall once more lapsed into a sullen silence, before returning to his usual response.

'No reply!'

'You're claiming that DC Tait attacked you. At the time of your arrest you were in possession of a knife.' Slade placed a large clear plastic cylinder containing a knife on the table. 'I am showing Mr Bell a knife exhibit number CT1. Is this your knife?'

'No reply.'

All questions concerning the A to Z street map recovered from his flat met with the same stock response.

The interview continued, but despite everything that was put to him, the answer was always the same.

'No reply.'

Jack turned the interview towards the missing girls and Hall's connection with Jacqueline Marshall.

The solicitor immediately objected, demanding to know where the line of questioning was headed.

'I must insist that you either further arrest my client and provide full disclosure on the grounds for arrest, or restrict your questioning to the offence for which he is currently detained.'

174

They had no disclosure. There was no evidence to arrest him for Jacqueline's murder.

In the cramped interview room Jack and Dave's frustration was almost tangible.

After the interview Armstrong followed Slade up to his office.

'Donna has spoken with the young girl at the house. There have been several reports of a prowler in the area recently. The girl was in the house alone as her parents had just gone on holiday. Did Hall know that? Has he been watching the family's movements?'

'It wouldn't surprise me Dave. From the way he went straight there there's no way it was his first visit to the house. I don't believe that we're so lucky that the first night that we put surveillance on him he goes straight there. He's clearly been peeping on a regular basis. Probably nightly. I hope to God that the magistrates see that as well and bang him up until the court case.'

'The area was definitely circled in the A to Z that was recovered. That convinces me that Hall has been stalking the young lass for some time.'

Jack nodded. 'Tomorrow I'll generate an action for every street ringed in the map book to be checked out.'

'I'll be interested to see what that throws up.'

Jack looked pensive. 'It's been a good result Dave but we've still got absolutely nothing to connect him with the missing girls other than a little circumstantial.'

'I'm sorry to say this Jack. I'm getting an awful feeling that he's not going to turn out to be our man. Nobody starts with murder and downgrades to peeping. It's always the other way around.'

'The knife and mask suggest he intended more than just looking.'

Slade looked at his watch and considered his options.

'It's coming up to three o'clock. Give him his eight hours lie down and in the morning at first light, I want a thorough search of the garden and the surrounding area where he was arrested. He had a mask with him so check out if he ditched anything else. I'm thinking rape kit. Tape, rope, ties... we already have his knife.'

'I'll ask the night shift Inspector to organise it.'

'There's also some jemmy damage to the window frame. Get Henderson and Tait to write up statements covering their injuries. We'll go for attempted burglary, offensive weapon, voyeurism and chuck in two assaults on police just for good measure. Get everything we can gather to put before the C.P.S. I want Hall on a charge sheet before his twenty-four hours detention runs out. And I want an application for refusal of bail on the grounds of the potential interference with witnesses.'

'Will do Boss.'

As Dave Armstrong left the room Slade felt some measure of satisfaction that Hall was off the streets but for how long. So far they hadn't been able to find any evidence to link him to the cold case murders.

And he had that sinking feeling that they weren't going to.

Chapter 42

The following morning was a sunny spring day. With hardly a breath of wind the River Tyne was like a millpond reflecting the azure blue sky.

The call out the previous night had led to a restless sleep, so fresh coffee in hand Slade stood on the balcony and looked out across the river. On the north side he spotted a lone jogger pounding the pavement past the front of the Crown Court building and watched as she made her way over the Millennium Bridge to the south side of the river where she was lost to sight.

After a slice of toast and a second strong coffee Jack grabbed his jacket. Deciding that the crisp early morning air would be just what was needed to clear his head, he set off to walk along the Tyne and up Forth Bank to the nick.

As soon as he crossed the river dark thoughts seeped into his brain.

What if Dave Armstrong was right and Hall wasn't their killer? Where would we go from there? For the moment he was the only possible solid lead.

There was the dull realisation that the case might be destined to remain unsolved and eventually filed away in the archives with the many other cold cases. The black dog of depression had begun scratching at his door and Slade was determined to keep it locked out.

Arriving at the station, he made a conscious effort to be more positive, so as to be ready to face whatever the day held.

If he had expected to be first into the Incident Room, he was sadly mistaken. Despite his injuries Chris Tait had again beaten him in.

As Chris glanced up from his desk Jack could see the left side of the young detective's face was still swollen, and had now turned a strange mixture of red black and yellow from the bruising.

'That's one hell of a black eye you've got there Chris.'
'Yeah, well you should see the other bloke,' he replied wincing. 'Ouch! It hurts when I smile.'

'Any developments since we left?'

'I think you're going to like this Boss.'

Chris passed a handwritten note to Jack.

'It's from the night shift Inspector. At first light he had arranged for some of his cops to meet up with their counterparts from Ponteland and together they conducted a search over the route that Hall had run before his arrest.'

Slade read through the note.

'Bloody good work. A roll of black tape found dumped along with a packet of unopened condoms. Where are they now?'

'In the exhibits store. Packaged up for C.S.I. We're looking at good prints from the cellophane wrapper on the condom packet.'

'I don't suppose…'

'No. I thought the same and checked. The tape is nothing like that used to wrap the body parts.'

'We're never that lucky are we. It's not like on the television. Vera would have had it all sorted by now. We could do with her at Forth Banks.'

'True. Anyway, following the recovery it gives us something to have another go at Hall about. But no doubt his brief will advise him to say nowt.'

The phone began ringing and Jack picked it up. After a few seconds a smile spread over his face. When he hung up Chris was staring at him expectantly.

'More good news?'

'You could say that. It was Crime Intelligence. They wanted to let us know that Hall's M.O. is similar to that of three undetected rapes in the Berwick and Scottish Borders areas. The offender description matches Hall and a vehicle similar to his black Fiesta was seen parked up near the scene of one of the attacks.'

'Berwick is about an hour away.'

'It turns out that all of their offences are within reach of the main A1 which had led the local detectives to believe that they had a travelling criminal… either from Scotland or from Tyneside.' Jack smiled', Hall's Sandyford flat would fit the bill.'

Slade's day was improving by the minute.

As predicted, later that morning when Hall was further interviewed, having consulted with his solicitor, he refused to respond to any questions. It didn't matter. With the mounting evidence the Crown Prosecution Service authorised a charge for the attempted burglary and two assaults on police officers.

The rest of the day was taken up with obtaining statements and preparing a remand file for the following day.

There were also several long conversations with Berwick C.I.D concerning their rape offences and trying to tie Hall into dates on which they had occurred.

Nothing had been mentioned to Hall or his solicitor about the Berwick enquiry.

His fingerprints and DNA would be taken when he was charged with the current offences. If there was a subsequent DNA match for the rapes that would be a bonus.

Although Jack was sure Hall wouldn't see it that way.

When the paperwork was completed and Hall was charged, he continued to be his usual uncooperative and belligerent self.

It was only when he was informed by the Custody Officer that bail was to be refused and there was to be an application for a remand in custody, that he suddenly flew into a violent rage. He had to be led struggling and screaming to his cell by uniform cops.

'Someone has a nasty temper there Jack,' said Dave Armstrong smiling.

'Just wait and see if his DNA comes back positive for the Berwick and Scottish rapes. Then he really will have a temper tantrum,' replied Slade.

'I wonder how many women and girls have been on the receiving end of his temper in the past.'

'Aye. And I wonder if Jackie Marshall was one of them.'

'So, there's nowt more to do until the court gets him tomorrow and hopefully remands him to Durham.

Jack gave a smile. 'Get the troops together. The drinks are on me.'

Chapter 43

On entering the door of the Police Club, a booming voice called across from a corner of the bar; a pastiche of some cinema screen villain. 'We meet again, Mister Slade!'

Glancing across Jack was pleased to see Mike Robson sitting at a table, grinning and raising a full pint of beer. Next to him was his firearms partner, Steve Black.

'Thanks for your help the other morning Mike. I'll put a couple of pints behind the bar for you both.'

'Cheers my man.'

'You're welcome.'

'But hey Jack, I understand that all did not go well. I've heard on the grapevine that you're having a bad time with the press over this historic enquiry you're on.'

'It appears that my favourite journalist Liz Harmon is intent on highlighting any failings in the enquiry.' Jack gave a broad smile. 'Seems I must have upset her in the past.'

'Want me to shoot her for you?' said Mike, the familiar grin spreading across his face.

'Not just yet Mike… but I'll bear it in mind if she really begins to piss me off.'

'Ah well! Just a thought. Let me know if you change your mind.'

Smiling and shaking his head at Robson's black humour, Slade joined the rest of the team at the bar.

Behind the bar Paul Brunton was his usual ebullient self as the H.MET team stood patiently at the counter ordering their drinks.

'You lot look happy. And since 'The Toon' hasn't had a game today, I'm guessing you lot have either won the lottery or you've had a good result?'

'The latter!,' smiled Armstrong half draining his glass as soon as Brunton had placed it in front of him. 'A bloody good one.'

'Don't count your chickens,' cautioned Slade as they grabbed their drinks and headed for the far room, where they pulled tables together, and huddled down out of earshot of the other customers.

'We've got Hall dead to rights for our offences last night and he's looking in the frame for the rapes up north. I'm sure before long we can get him for ours,' said Gavin Oates.

'But unfortunately there's still nothing to positively link him to our missing girls,' countered Slade.

'Boss, there's plenty of circumstantial. If we keep digging, we'll find the evidence to link him.'

There was lots of nodding from several of the other detectives.

Slade was being more circumspect.

'One of the worst mistakes a cop can make is deciding too early that a suspect is guilty. Once you do that you only start to look for evidence that fits your theory and end up dismissing anything that contradicts your belief. Pretty soon you have plenty of circumstantial evidence to back up your case but ignore anything to the contrary. Professor McNaughton calls it confirmation bias.'

'I think that's being a bit negative boss,' protested Henderson, taking a swig from his frothing pint.

'It's how miscarriages of justice happen,' responded Slade. 'Let's just wait and see what we get back from his DNA sample and keep digging deep into his past. We'll know better then how he shapes up as our murderer.'

'I'll put money on him being our man,' Gavin said, swallowing a large swig of beer.

'So go out tomorrow and find me the proof,' said Slade. 'And if you do then tomorrow night all the drinks will be on me.'

Everyone raised their glasses and appeared cheerful except for Slade.

He had a deepening suspicion that his money was going to stay safe in his wallet.

Chapter 44

It was after midnight. The dark blue van was standing in a line of vehicles on a quiet leafy side street of Jesmond to the East side of the Great North Road. He had parked it so as not to draw any attention. It was well out of sight of any CCTV and unlikely to be distinguished from those of any of the residents.

Getting out the driver glanced around. Although several of the nearby houses were in complete darkness, light still leaked out from behind the curtains of a few.

He wondered if he should have left it until later but lone cars driving through darkened streets in the early hours of the morning drew too much police attention. At this time of the night the roads were still relatively busy with cars, backwards and forwards, into and away from the city.

He paused to listen; checking around for sounds of any movement.

He could hear the steady hum of traffic on the nearby dual carriageway. The constant flow of traffic could afford him some anonymity when he had finished his task and was making his way to the safety of home.

Apart from vehicles, there were no noises of any drunken late-night stragglers heading back from town to disturb him.

Silently he went to the side door of the van. He attempted to slide it open as slowly and quietly as possible but in the silence, it sounded to him as loud as dragging a set of chains.

He paused and listened. No sounds of windows opening. No signs of curtains being drawn back.

Just silence and darkness.

The two large black canvas bags on the floor inside the van were partly hidden in the shadows. With a last nervous glance around he began to drag the largest of them along the metal floor of the van and hauled it out onto the pavement.

The heavy weight was a strain on his back but it wasn't too far a walk down through the gloomy underpass and under the main road to emerge at the entrance to the Exhibition Park.

The park was a section of the Newcastle Town Moor that had been developed as a recreational area in the late nineteenth century. Though it could be very busy during the day, at this time of night it was almost always deserted.

On entering the eerie silence of the park he stopped, panting from the exertion. Concealed in the shadows of trees he paused to catch his breath.

Scanning the area for any signs of life and satisfied that there was nobody to distract him, he ventured deeper into the darkened grounds. He felt confident that whatever Police were out and about, they would be too busy with pubs and drunken disorder to stray this far from the city centre.

After a further stop to redistribute the weight of the pack, he finally arrived at the edge of the trees. Ahead he could see the restored bandstand which was the only remaining feature of the Jubilee Exhibition of 1887, after which the park had been named. Before that it had been known as The Bull Park because that was where the city's prized stud bull was penned.

Keeping to the right of the bandstand, a large domed building, once the old Science Museum, loomed up beside the still waters of the deserted boating lake. It was now a microbrewery and wary of any possible security cameras, he kept his head down and face concealed.

There was a patch of open ground where he felt very exposed but within seconds he was up to the water's edge.

The lake was black and motionless and the area around shrouded in darkness from the cloudy moonless sky.

Putting the heavy burden down, he gave one further glance around to ensure that there were no sounds of teenagers getting drunk, sniffing glue, taking drugs or doing any of the other pursuits that young people got up to in darkened parks at midnight.

Then, satisfied, he shuffled forward dragging the bag behind him. The area was better lit than expected, so wasting no time, he quickly opened the bag and tipped the contents out onto the hard cobbled stone surround of the lake.

The torso tumbled over and over, rolling down towards the black water and entering the lake with a loud splash. The sudden noise shattered the stillness of the night and a bird took off from a nearby tree.

Then once again…silence.

A cautious glance around. Nothing stirred.

Turning he retraced his steps, hurrying through the trees and underpass back to the parked van. The street was still deserted as the second less bulky sack was dragged from the van. Nowhere near as heavy as the torso it took far less time to carry it over to the lakeside.

Fearing further loud splashes, he resisted the urge to just fling the arms and legs as far as possible into the centre of the lake. Instead, he silently slipped them into the onyx black water where they disappeared from sight.

The last piece of the macabre jigsaw was the head. He considered rolling it like a bowling ball into the lake and smiled at the thought, but then had another better idea.

Striding across to one of the benches around the park he removed the head from the bag and placed it down carefully, as if looking out over the lake.

Pleased with the staged scenario, he grabbed the canvas bag and headed away through the darkened trees and back to the waiting van. During all this time there had been neither sight nor sound of any other person.

Starting up the engine there was the sudden wave of relief at a job well done. It was impossible to suppress a smile.

I can't wait to switch on the news in the morning.

Chapter 45

The following morning was yet another crisp clear spring day and Slade was woken by birdsong. Walking to the balcony he looked across the river to the city. To his left he could see The Keep, all that remained from the twelfth century castle from which the city had derived its name.

Showered and dressed Slade decided to walk into work along the Quayside arriving at the nick just before seven o'clock.

The coffee pot was hot and Chris was as usual seated at his desk.

'You should wear dark glasses to cover up that eye of yours.'

'Today is the day for sunglasses, Boss. There's not a cloud in the sky. I think that we're in for a really beautiful day.'

The beautiful day was about to turn very dark.

From the street outside the office came the loud screech of tyres and the strident wail of two-tone horns, as a police vehicle shot out of the yard and accelerated away towards the city centre.

Slade and Tait looked out the window in time to see a second car following and as they watched, both vehicles disappeared from sight.

'Looks like the early shift are late for their breakfast,' joked Chris returning to his desk.

At that moment the office phone began ringing and they exchanged worried glances. As Jack picked it up, he was already feeling that familiar sinking feeling in the pit of his stomach.

On the other end the Control Room operator sounded ominous. 'Inspector, we've received a report of a body found in Exhibition Park by the boating lake.' There was a slight hesitation. 'When I say body… actually sir… it's just a head.'

Hanging up, Jack snatched up the keys to one of the H.MET unmarked vehicles and shouting for Chris to follow, headed for the door.

The drive across town at that time in the morning took longer than he had hoped and even with the blue lights fitted behind the grill and a two-tone claxon yelping out a warning, vehicles carrying early morning commuters kept blocking their way.

Arriving at Exhibition Park several marked vehicles were already parked up and a number of uniformed officers had started to section off an area. Stretches of blue and white tape fluttered in the morning breeze.

Jack hurried across and spoke to a uniform Sergeant. 'Can you make this the inner cordon but if possible, get some guys to the park entrances and set up a much wider outer secure area.'

'I'll try Inspector but you're talking about a hell of an outer cordon. It'll take some cops.'

'Just see what you can do for me'

The Sergeant nodded and went to speak to a couple of the uniformed officers. Keeping such a large sterile area was not going to be easy. During the day a steady procession of walkers and children would make their way through the park to stroll around the boating lake, or linger on one of the many benches dotted around it. It was a very busy public place and only a few minutes' stroll from the centre of the city.

An incredibly brazen place in which to dump a body part.

Slade quickly established that the severed head had been found by one of the medical students from the nearby university who had been out for his regular early morning jog.

The witness had been more than a little shocked to see the head propped up on a park bench as if admiring the view over the lake. Being a third-year medical student himself, he had at first thought it was some kind of sick prank using a dummy head. However, when he got near and took a closer look, he soon realised that this was no joke by any of his fellow students. It was very much the real thing.

As a doctor in the making, he was no stranger to severed body parts but more used to seeing them in a pathology lab… not taking in the early morning view in his local park.

When Slade spoke to him, he said that the head was not wrapped in anything but had been placed upright and in clear view.

'I run here every morning and again in the evening and it's not what you expect to find.'

Were you out running last night?'

'Yes, around about nine o'clock. I do a circuit around the park and finish up at that bench to do my cool down. I can say for definite that it wasn't here then.'

As the student was escorted away by a uniform cop to provide a written statement Jack turned to Chris Tait.

'Shit! That confirms it. Hall can't be our man! He's been kept in police custody all last night for court.'

'Maybe he has an accomplice who knows about his arrest and is hoping to get him in the clear by leaving us a body part.'

'Everyone we've spoken to says Hall is a loner. There's not going to be an accomplice.'

Jack looked across at the surreal image of the severed head balanced on the park bench. It was that of a young fair-haired girl and even from a distance Jack could see evidence of the same freezer burns that had been found on the others.

This was the work of their man. Of that he had no doubt.

And he was now almost certain. Alan Hall was not their killer.

Deflated, Slade studied the cordoned off bench surrounded by Police tape and hoped that someone from C.S.I. would arrive soon to erect a forensic tent to keep out the prying eyes of the public and media.

As he studied the head something was niggling at him.

Jack turned to Chris. 'The head is unwrapped… not like all the other dumped body parts. It's a complete change of Modus Operandi regarding deposition of the body parts.'

'There's definitely no longer any attempt to conceal the body,' agreed Tait, looking down at the gruesome body part.

'No. Quite the opposite. He wanted it to be found very soon. His primary aim is no longer the disposal of the bodies. He's moved on. This has all been carefully staged. It's just as McNaughton said. He wants to taunt us… show how clever he is compared to the Police.'

As they were speaking a forensic van pulled up and the familiar figure of Ged Kirkby climbed out and began donning his usual coveralls.

Jack walked across to speak to him and received a broad smile.

'We're going to have to stop meeting like this, Jack. People are beginning to talk.'

'I'm pretty certain that this is our same guy Ged.'

'I bloody well hope so. We don't want more than one "nutter" leaving severed heads around the city. It could be bad for the tourist trade.'

Kirkby indicated to the rear of his van.

'Grab some gloves and shoe coverings. Let's set up a forensic tent and I'll take a closer look.'

A few minutes later the three officers were inside a white tent, shielding the body part from the sight of the public and their ever-present mobile phone cameras.

They stared down at the severed head of a young girl.

Kirkby already had his camera out and was taking several photographs.

'The same mummified appearance and what appears to be freezer burns. I notice that he didn't bother wrapping her up this time, Jack. Exhibition Park is a bit public for dumping a body, isn't it?'

187

'I'm guessing the clue is in the location. Exhibition Park! He wants them found and seen. He's enjoying the thought of us struggling.'

'I'll take photographs in situ and dust the bench and general area for prints, if you can arrange for the usual TSG fingertip search. I'll have the head packaged and delivered to the pathologist but I'm expecting a zero result on forensics just like the others.'

Jack stepped out of the tent and looked around at the vastness of the park.

'Chris, arrange for uniform to seize any CCTV from the university and any other buildings on Claremont Road at the edge of the park. Before that can you check with the micro-brewery to see if they have any cameras installed.'

Kirkby looked around at the moor stretching off into the distance. 'If you take into account the extent of the Town Moor then he could have accessed the park from anywhere.'

'The Great North Road is only a hundred yards away. That's probably the closest,' replied Jack.

'Or he could come in from Claremont Road past the skate park or even have cut across the Moor from Gosforth.'

'You're right. It's a massive area to cover. For now, we'll have to concentrate on the inner cordon and the immediate area. Maybe seal off the underpass through to Jesmond. Even then it's going to be a bloody logistical nightmare. I'll ask T.C.P to arrange for another press appeal for anyone seen in the park last night or the early hours of this morning.'

Jack turned again to Chris Tait. 'After you've checked the micro-brewery for CCTV can you also start pulling together a possible release for me to run past the press office.'

'Will do.'

Slade crossed behind the bench being careful not to cause any disturbance to the scene. The head had been placed overlooking the lake. He re-entered the tent and lowered himself down to the same height as the head.

'Spotted something on the back of the head?' asked Kirkby.

'No. Nothing on the head itself. It just strikes me the angle at which it was placed. It's as if it had been posed looking at the ducks and the lake.'

'What are you thinking Jack?'

'Our murderer is pretty thorough so I'm wondering whether the positioning of the head is significant? Maybe it's one of his little cryptic clues? Is he telling us to look in the lake?'

Slade and Kirkby left the tent and stopping at the edge of the lake followed the direction that the head was facing. Several ducks glided across the water leaving ever expanding wakes on the still surface and occasionally bobbing their heads under the water in search of food.

'It would just fit his M.O. to dispose of the body in a way that would cause us maximum embarrassment,' said Slade quietly.

He turned to one of the uniform cops guarding the cordon.

'Can you get on to control and ask them to have Inspector Maitland from Marine section attend with a couple of his divers. I want them to search the lake. Tell them we're looking for a possible weapon... or maybe a body.'

'Wouldn't a body float sir... unless it was weighed down with something?'

Kirkby smiled. 'Only if this was a cheap TV programme. In real life fresh bodies don't float... they sink. It's only when they start to decompose that the gases gather inside and they pop up to say hello. And believe me when they do you don't want to be around. I've smelled it.'

The young cop blanched and walked off to do as Slade had requested.

Kirkby finished his photographs and carefully placed the head into a large plastic circular box. 'You'll want to know the time for the P.M. Jack?'

'Just keep me in the loop Ged. You can get me on my mobile.'

There seemed little else to do at the scene. The jungle drums had been beating far and wide and press and photo-journalists were already gathering. The uniform cops were struggling to stop them breaching the cordon.

As soon as Chris had finished making enquiries at the Micro-Brewery, Jack went with him back to their car to return to the nick. He would have to organise searches and update the rest of the team who would have turned in for duty by now.

At the Police Station Jack went off to update Parker whilst Chris made a start on a media release for the press department.

After speaking with Parker, Slade returned to the H.MET office. It was clear from his face that the discovery of the head had not gone down well with the Detective Superintendent.

When the rest of the team gathered, the morning briefing lacked the previous night's lively atmosphere following Hall being charged and kept for court.

It was beginning to dawn on everyone that, despite the evidence against him, it was now very unlikely that he was their killer.

The situation was summed up by a sullen Mike Henderson. 'Bloody Hell Boss. This sodding enquiry has seen more twists than a sixties dance floor.'

A couple of hours later as Jack was reviewing some of the action returns, the call came in from the underwater search advisor Steve Maitland.

'I'm giving you the heads up … if you pardon the pun. You were spot on to suggest there might be something in the lake. One of the divers located something else in just a few feet of water and is busy dragging it out now if you want to come down.'

'What is it?'

'The torso of a young female… minus the head.'

Chapter 46

Twenty minutes later and for the second time that day Jack found himself standing by the side of the Exhibition Park boating lake staring out across the still water.

The torso of a female body had been dragged from the lake by two Marine Department divers and now contained in a black heavy duty body bag, it was being loaded into a van for the journey to Lemington mortuary.

That morning there had been relatively few people about when the head had been first discovered. Now it was very different. The location had become a press frenzy, with television cameras from not only local stations, but also a large outdoor broadcasting unit parked on Claremont Road. The word Sky was emblazoned across the side of the vehicle in letters six foot high and above them the clatter of blades announced the presence of a press helicopter.

Tait scowled. 'It's become a bloody media circus.'

If it could be described as a media circus then in the distance Slade spotted the elephant arriving.

Liz Harmon stomped up just behind the police tape and began talking to one of the young cops who was trying to keep the 'rubberneckers' back. Slade hoped that he would have the good sense not to be persuaded into making an unguarded comment to her.

Jack used to seethe when he heard that frequent phrase in press reports, 'A police spokesman said…'

What it meant was that some fool was now praying that he will never be identified, after making an offhand comment to a reporter and unwittingly providing an angle for a story that was never there in the first place.

Even from a distance away Jack could hear the clicking of digital cameras as the torso remains were placed into the van for transportation. Photographers with lenses like cannon barrels were pointing across in his direction.

The press vultures had their photographs. They've got their story. Now just go away! There's nothing else for you here.

Slade was wrong.

He turned again to look at the lake. On pleasant sunny days it would be dotted with small boats and excited children being ferried around by their parents. Today despite the clear skies any visitors were being held back and the boats lay tied up; empty and forlorn.

Two Marine Unit divers were standing in shallow water and deep in conversation. They looked across in his direction just as Slade spotted the figure of Steve Maitland striding towards him.

From his face Jack could tell this wasn't going to be good news.

'Jack, I've just heard from one of the divers. He's located some more.'

'Body parts?'

Steve nodded. 'Aye. He's found a leg and what he believes is an arm. They are wrapped in packaging and are some distance from where the torso was found. He's moved them to the side of the lake but with all the press around he hasn't brought them out yet. We're going to get a body bag in the water to prevent the media ghouls getting their gory snaps. He's still searching around to see if there's more.'

'The killer hasn't disposed of all that in one go... unless he had help.'

'Or he made more than one trip. It would have taken at least one trip for the torso and a second for the limbs. Maybe even a third for the head which is very heavy by itself.'

Maitland frowned. 'You know I've seen some sights in my time Jack, the usual decomposing river stuff... but this... just what kind of nut job are you dealing with?'

'I wish I knew. He's some sick bastard.'

'When we're finished, we'll place the other limbs into separate bags and have it all taken down to Lemington mortuary for the pathologist.'

'Thanks Steve, I'm going to head back to the nick. I spoke to T.C.P. this morning about the head. He'll have a bloody seizure when he hears about this lot. He's already got the Command Block screaming in his ear about the crap press coverage we're getting. The fact that this is likely to rule Hall out as our suspect won't help his mood. Pissed off is an understatement.'

Jack looked beyond Maitland to where a diver stood knee deep in water apparently moving something just below the surface. A further black body bag was lying open at the edge of the lake awaiting the macabre remains.

Behind him Slade could hear the cameras once again clicking.

'Why don't they just piss off and let us get on with our job?'

'I suppose they think that they're just doing theirs. But they can certainly make ours more difficult.'

'Well, I appreciate all your assistance Steve. Keep me informed on the mobile if you find anything else.'

Leaving Maitland standing beside the edge of the lake, Jack ducked back under the police cordon tape and began making his way with Chris towards the unmarked car.

On seeing him Harmon hurried over and began firing off a barrage of questions.

She was the last person he wanted to deal with but within seconds the other reporters, alerted by her raised voice, joined in the melee. Slade found himself surrounded and being assailed by cameras and microphones. All the while people were shouting out questions at him.

'Can you confirm that more body parts have been found?'

'Do they correspond with the body part found early this morning?'

'Is it connected to the others found around the city?'

'Do you know the identity of the latest victim?'

He caught the shrill voice of Harmon. 'Are you anywhere near identifying who is responsible?'

Jack was brought to a halt. Not that he wanted to speak but because he couldn't get through the throng. He was conscious that it didn't look good on television to be seen pushing over camera operators and reporters to make your exit. Politicians and celebrities might get away with it but cops can't.

He knew that he wouldn't escape without answering at least some of their demands.

Holding up his arms to calm down the baying journalists, Jack began to speak. Someone with a large shoulder mounted television camera pressed in closer until it was only a couple of feet from his face.

'I can confirm that the body of a female has been found this morning in Exhibition Park. At this time, she remains unidentified and enquiries are underway in that regard. I would ask that anybody who was in Exhibition Park from about six o'clock last night to contact the Incident Room at Forth Banks Police Station and give your details. In particular anyone who may have seen anything suspicious, or noticed a person carrying a weighty package. We need to hear from you. Now if you'll excuse me, I have to get back and get on with my enquiries.'

As Jack threaded his way through the throng with difficulty, a few more questions were screamed out but the majority of those present had their "soundbite". Some were already dispersing in order to transmit their film to the studio, or to email in a written copy to their news desk.

When he finally reached his car, he couldn't wait to get back to the relative calm of his office and it was with some relief that he pulled away from the scoop of reporters and escaped into the rush hour traffic.

Back at the office the earlier elation the team had felt from the connection between Hall and the Berwick rapes had long receded. It might be good news for Berwick C.I.D. but Hall being in custody overnight undermined any links with Slade's murder enquiry. Whilst locked up in the Police cells he couldn't have been in two places at the same time.

There was a knock on his door and Donna entered. 'Just an update on the visits to registered sex offenders.'

So far Donna had drawn a blank but was by no means near working through the complete list. Several had alibis for one, or in some cases all of the dates when body parts had been dumped. Fifteen of them would have been in junior school or younger when the original murders occurred. Twenty-two hadn't even been born.'

'Anything else?'

'One of the possible suspects on the list had served ten years for a series of rapes and was actually looking good for a while until I called at the address.'

'I'm waiting for the "but".'

'But... for the past twelve months he has had one of the better views from the top of the Westgate Hill cemetery. He died of cancer last year.'

Donna glanced down at her notes.

'There's still quite a few on the list. You could be forgiven for thinking that half the West End is on the sex offenders register for one thing or another.'

'Thanks Donna. Just keep on working through the list. Hopefully our man is on it.'

'Will do Boss.'

'What about the actions for owners of blue transit van owners?'

'I've split the list with Mike Henderson whilst I've been checking into sex offenders but I'll be back on it shortly.'

As she left Dave Armstrong appeared at the door of Slade's office. 'That's a hell of a busy start to the day. Obviously, it can't have been Hall dumping the body parts. I take it there's no doubt that they're connected with our enquiry.'

'We'll have to await DNA confirmation but I'm almost certain that this will turn out to be the third victim, Elizabeth Mortimer.'

Slade reached for his coffee. 'We're still short of several pieces if we want to complete the three bodies.'

'That's assuming he hadn't already disposed of them some time earlier, maybe in the Tyne and we haven't found them yet,' said Armstrong. 'How's T.C.P. taking the latest press coverage?'

'He's not saying a lot but I can tell he's ready to explode. He's like an earthquake building up. You don't know when he's going to blow but you'd better make sure you're far away when he does.'

'Any word coming down from Headquarters?'

'Parker says that the A.C.C. Crime was on the phone earlier giving him earache. Apparently Harmon has submitted a Freedom of Information request asking for details of all missing females that are unaccounted for since nineteen eighty.'

'She never gives up!' sighed Armstrong. 'If Mike Robson is still offering to shoot her, I'll organise the whip round.'

Chapter 47

That evening all the news channels had broadcast the scenes of frenetic groups of reporters swarming around Slade, demanding answers to their questions.

A stroke of genius putting the head there.

The report showed press, like sharks, circling the detective, as he ducked under the Police tape and tried to push through the crowd to get to a parked car.

Like flies around shite.

He had recorded all the press coverage onto a digital recorder so that it was available to watch over and over again. It was a real entertainment; watching all the confusion and that stupid Jack Slade and his not so merry men wandering around like headless chickens.

Headless chickens. Now that was an amusing analogy.

Slade had been featured in various footage several times now. You could clearly see the utter frustration in the detective's face.

Knowing that I'm personally responsible for all of his grief is as good as it gets.

It had definitely put both the police and that newspaper reporter Harmon in their places. Hopefully the timing was right for the next phase. If so, Harmon would receive the letter the next day.

Keeping the pressure up was all about timing.

Lying on the table was Liz Harmon's latest article detailing that morning's recovery in Exhibition Park. It concentrated on all the macabre aspects; mentioning the head being positioned overlooking the lake. With Harmon on the case, it was like having your own personal publicity officer.

The tired clichés in her editorials were running thick and fast. He laughed out loud at her phrase, "Tyneside in the grip of fear". Harmon seemed to be stealing her dialogue from nineteen twenties Raymond Chandler novels.

Then there were the cops. Reassuring the public that patrols had been stepped up all around the city and that the Police were, 'confident of tracing the perpetrator of these horrific crimes'.

That was never going to happen.

Reaching for the remote he cut the BBC news and did some channel hopping. It confirmed that the other news outlets were all carrying the same story.

The dumping of the bodies had caught the attention of the Nationals and he was now being compared in the press to people like Neilson and Sutcliffe.

I'm not worthy of that comparison but there is one aspect in which I rise above them.

I'm never going to get caught.

Chapter 48

That night at home after a takeaway pizza and several glasses of Merlot, Slade sat alone going over everything in his head when his mobile burst into life.

Picking it up he saw from the display that it was Elaine.

Shit! I was supposed to be having Dale down for a couple of days as a birthday treat.

He hesitated and considered whether to avoid answering. He didn't want some kind of long-distance domestic dispute.

Guilt got the better of him and he reluctantly took the call.

Elaine sounded angry but Jack had no energy for an argument.

'I've spoken to your dad. He says you're talking about not having Dale down for his birthday. Is that right?'

'I was going to call you.'

'When? Aren't you leaving it a bit bloody late? He's supposed to be coming down in a couple of days.'

'It's just that I've been very busy. I'm up to my neck in…'

'Not the usual work excuse again. After all this time don't you think it's wearing a bit thin? I'm telling you. The train tickets are booked and paid for and he's been looking forward to it for ages. I'm not going to be the one to disappoint him.'

'I'll sort something out.'

'You bloody well better. You know what it is, Jack? When it comes down to it you always put the job above your family.'

'Come on Elaine… you know that's not true.'

'Jack, regarding your priorities you are, and always have been, an arsehole!'

Before he could reply the phone went dead.

She had hung up.

The call had done nothing to lift his mood.

Everything was falling apart.

The enquiry had gone off at a tangent on several occasions, causing it to be bogged down in the multitude of actions and subsequent dead ends. It was becoming difficult to get back on track.

Hall was off the street but had diverted resources that left them no further forward. Any forensics found turned out to be false trails left deliberately by the killer to send them off in the wrong direction. All the actions were fizzling out and it was as if the whole enquiry was becoming atrophied.

He looked at his empty glass and reaching for the bottle poured in the remains of the wine. He was starting to drink too much. He needed to cut down and to try to get more sleep.

Tomorrow was another day.

Raising the glass heavenwards he made a silent prayer.

Please God. Give me a bloody break!

Chapter 49

The letter landed on Harmon's desk just after mid-day as she was putting the finishing touches to the afternoon's lead story. It would be a rerun of the body parts story from the beginning complete with illustrations. One of the sketch artists had put together a diagram showing which body parts had been recovered to date and which might still be outstanding.

She had entitled it "The Jigsaw of Death".

It was a bit ghoulish but catchy.

Just what her readers loved.

It was sure to sell more papers and keep her name up there on the front page.

There was another thing that was cheering her on and keeping her as the editor's 'pet'. The Nationals had now picked up on the name she had first come up with and were labelling the killer as 'The Jackie in the Box Murderer'.

She had saved all the articles from the newspapers in a blue box file. They would, in time, be rehashed, re-edited and eventually become the kernel of the book she was planning to write.

With that in mind she had made a great show of cosying up to the press photographer who had been attending the scenes of crime. She might need his help later when it came to photos for the book.

She picked up one of the sugar free cookies and washed it down with a large cup of coffee. It tasted like cardboard but she was determined to make an effort to cut down on the chocolate and junk food.

The day before she had seen her doctor who had suggested that she was becoming very overweight and perhaps borderline diabetic. He had suggested that she could do with cutting down on sweet food in order to lose some pounds. She had lost interest long before he began droning on about the value of a low fat, low carbohydrate diet and the evils of sugar.

The Doctor had given her a small booklet entitled, "The Way to Healthy Weight Loss". She had accepted it with good grace... and her very best fake smile.

A smile that she switched off as soon as the doctor looked away.

He had tentatively suggested that "the first step" would be to cut down on her alcohol intake.

For Liz Harmon that first step... was a step too far.

As she left the surgery Harmon managed to get the leaflet in the bin at the first throw before making a beeline to the nearby 'City Tavern.'

After all the lecturing about her diet she was in need of a large Vodka and Tonic.

Sitting back at her desk in the newspaper offices absorbed in writing the article, she almost didn't notice the office junior slip an envelope onto her desk.

Peeking across she saw that the front bore the now familiar block capital writing. Her heart began to beat a little faster.

Detective Inspector Slade had told her that if any further correspondence arrived, she should immediately call the Police and not open it or handle it unnecessarily.

Well sod him!

Holding it by the corners in the way she had seen the forensic officer do with other evidence, she took her steel dagger shaped letter opener and slipped it under the flap of the envelope.

Slicing it open and carefully removing the contents, she laid the single page letter down on the desk. Ensuring that she didn't touch anything except the very tips of the corners she began to read.

Dear Ms. Harmon,

Thank you for taking such an interest in my work.

You inspire me to greater things.

I think I'll go out and find myself something much fresher for you to write about.

That should be fun.

Chapter 50

In the Incident room Dave Armstrong looked up from a report to see Slade approaching.

'Boss, I heard from a mate up at Headquarters that yesterday Harmon was ringing the press office. She's demanding an interview with a senior officer. When she got fobbed off, she started ringing around various extensions and somehow managed to get through to the Chief Constable's office. Thankfully her call was intercepted by his Staff officer and she got nowhere.'

'Harmon's a persistent bitch… isn't she?' smiled Slade.

'I wish she would just piss off and leave us to get on with the investigation.' Armstrong got up and strolled across to the coffee machine to pour himself a cup from the freshly brewed pot. 'I'm starting to hate the name Harmon.'

As he walked back to his desk the telephone rang and Chris picked it up. After a couple of seconds he covered the receiver and called across to Slade.

'Boss, I swear she's like Beetlejuice. You mention her name three times and she bloody well appears. Harmon's downstairs. She's claiming to have had another letter from our murderer.'

Slade sat in the cramped interview room with Armstrong and Harmon. The letter was now sealed in an evidence bag with the envelope packaged separately.

'You were told not to open any letters that looked like they came from our suspect.'

The cold tone of Slade's voice betrayed his anger that evidence may have been compromised.

'I get lots of letters… fan mail and such. Do you not get fan mail Inspector Slade?'

Slade glared at her but didn't respond.

'Anyway, I'd opened it before I realised what it was.'

Jack scowled. She was lying like a cheap watch.

He knew it… and she knew that he knew it.

But there was no way he could prove it.

The letter was addressed with the usual block capitals but appeared this time to be written in red ink instead of blood.

The suggestion contained within the phrase, 'I think I'll go out and find myself something much fresher for you to write about,' unsettled Jack more than he wanted to let on.

Was the killer threatening to start up killing again?

That had always been the thing that Jack had most feared.

Could Dave Armstrong's prediction be right?

Was the killer making room for more victims?

And what should he do about the letter?

Harmon had obviously read it and no doubt had her photographer record it on film. The contents were likely to spread panic but Slade knew that he couldn't just sit on it.

What if the writer did kill again and the Police hadn't warned the public? He was already being lined up as the scapegoat!

The decision was taken away from him.

'I've discussed it with my editor. We've got a photograph of the note and we're running the story tomorrow. We just wanted to know if you have anything to add?'

'You're running it? What if it's another hoax?'

Harmon shook her head. 'You've seen the writing. It's the same as the last time. We both know it's not a hoax. We just needed to give you an opportunity to comment. So do you have any comment?'

Inside Jack was seething but didn't reply.

Harmon gave a twisted smile. 'No change there then. Well, I'd better be going. I've got an article to write.'

With that she stood up and gave a smile before heading for the door.

The last line of the letter kept running through Slade's head. It was generating a deep sense of dread.

'I think I'll go out and find myself something much fresher for you to write about.'

Chapter 51

It was late that afternoon when Slade drove through the wrought iron gates of the almost deserted cemetery and pulled up outside the mortuary building. Inside he found the Home Office pathologist Paul Clifford already dressed in green surgical robes and standing next to him, ready to package any exhibits, was Jim Jackson.

'Good afternoon, Jack,' said Clifford. 'You've arrived just in time for the show. The 'main feature' is just about to start.'

Clifford indicated the dismembered body parts. 'This is becoming a bit of a habit.'

'I'm starting to recognise the signs myself. Freezer burn?'

'The M.O. is the same as in the other cases. They have been in long term cold storage for some considerable time. Shall we begin?'

Jack looked down at the various body parts and nodded.

'Having been out of any freezer for several hours the arms, legs and head were fully defrosted but the torso may still be a little frozen in the middle. I intend to examine each part as if it comes from a different cadaver so as to avoid any cross contamination.'

Clifford went through the post mortem in his usual professional way starting with the limbs and saving the torso until last.

D.C. Jackson was always at hand with the appropriate plastic containers for any exhibits that were passed to him.

Throughout the P.M. Samples were taken for a detailed forensic examination.

Nail clippings, hair, swabs from every orifice, stomach contents from the torso and DNA to establish which of the missing girls the parts belonged to.

Jack was praying that it wasn't a fourth as yet unknown victim.

Once again it was impossible to give any conclusive cause or time of death but the damage to the ends of the limbs suggested that the body had been dismembered prior to any long-term storage.

That evening the late briefing was going to be sombre. With more body parts and their main suspect eliminated, each and every one would be aware that the enquiry was losing momentum.

They were no further forward tracing their murderer than on the day the Tyne gave up the head of Jackie Marshall.

Chapter 52

It was dark and cruising around the outskirts of the city was proving fruitless. Regarding tonight's plan Newcastle city centre itself was a no-go area. Twenty years ago there were hardly any CCTV cameras but now a person couldn't walk through town without leaving a digital data trail on any number of hard drives.

Before he had set out, he had read the late edition newspaper and had been elated to see that Harmon had not only printed his letter in full but had a colour photograph to accompany the article. The image showed the writing had been done in blood red ink.

When Harmon had ranked him with some of the great murderers like Sutcliffe and Neilson it was embarrassing. He knew that up until now it wasn't true.

But after tonight it would be different.

His growing notoriety was providing him with quite a confidence boost. He was feeling more powerful with every article he read or television feature he watched.

However, he knew that it was dangerous to become over confident.

Because of that, cruising the City Centre just wasn't worth the risk.

With that in mind he had headed out of the city and away from the ever-present prying CCTV cameras. It had turned out to be a fortuitous move.

It was as he was driving along Grandstand Road circulating the Newcastle Town Moor that he spotted her.

About seventeen with flowing blonde hair and a slim figure she fitted the profile perfectly.

Imagine what it would be like to keep her chained up like a slave and have her as a plaything for a few weeks or so.

It would be just like in one of his True Crime magazines. A long-held fantasy coming true.

And once he began to be bored… just get rid of her and seek out a change of victim.

The girl was walking alone on the opposite side of the road. He was forced to do a full circle of the roundabout and returned behind her. Stealing a quick sideways look he passed her a second time and slowed to a halt against the kerb.

He was now a couple of hundred yards ahead and waiting and watching her in his rear-view mirror. Closer and closer she got.

205

He shuffled nervously in his seat and could feel the knife concealed up the sleeve of his lightweight jacket.

Heart now racing as the blood coursed through veins.

Thump! Thump!

Closer and closer.

His hand tightened on the knife handle.

He began to imagine holding the blade against her throat.

He would move close to her. He would feel…even smell her fear.

Becoming high on her terror as if it were a drug.

Then, back at the house she would be a prisoner. Submissive, compliant, passive… obedient.

To use in whatever way I desire. Whenever I desire

He was becoming aroused.

Closer and closer.

Then the girl turned, looking behind her as a vehicle approached.

No! No! No!

She put out her hand and the taxi glided to a stop next to the kerb.

After a brief conversation she climbed in behind the driver and seconds later the taxi was disappearing into the distance.

Angry and annoyed he began cursing loudly.

Then, in his rear-view mirror he spotted some lights as a marked police car approached. His heart was still thumping. This time for a different reason.

As it passed a uniformed cop in the passenger seat glanced across and for a split second their eyes met, before the policeman looked away and the police car continued on. Suddenly the brake lights of the police vehicle flashed on.

Heart thumping! Holding his breath.

Then without indicating, the police car turned left, disappearing away down a side street.

That cop looking across was a bad omen.

Frustrated and enraged, it was nevertheless lucky that the Police vehicle hadn't appeared just as he was dragging the girl into the side door of his van. He started the engine, made a U- turn and headed towards home.

Fulfilling my fantasy would have to wait for another night.

Chapter 53

Jack woke up early in the morning just after four o'clock from a disturbed sleep. Frustrating, disjointed nightmares of dismembered limbs turning up in the strangest of places.

At one point in his dream, he had gone to get some milk and on opening the refrigerator door was confronted by the disembodied head of a teenage girl glaring accusingly at him.

He had awoken with a start, heart thumping and bathed in sweat.

The words of the latest communication with Harmon were flashing through his mind.

'I think I'll go out and find myself something much fresher for you to write about.'

The clock showed four thirty. He didn't even try to get back to sleep.

Leaving quite a bit earlier for the office, Slade used the walking time to formulate a plan of action for the day. Once at his desk he began to scroll the computer incident logs for every Area Command, searching for any missing persons that fitted the description of previous victims.

There were two girls from a local authority care home in the East End and a thirty-eight-year-old woman from North Kenton who had left after a domestic dispute with her boyfriend.

The North Kenton 'misper' was too old and didn't fit the profile.

The two young girls had been missing from the care home six times previously in the past four weeks. They had always turned up safe and well when they got hungry.

The results of his checks eased his mind a little but what if someone was missing and simply hadn't yet been reported? They might live alone or not have been missed by family, neighbours or workmates.

Chris Tait was the first to arrive in the office at half seven. Jack gave a cheery greeting, secretly pleased that for once he had beaten him in. Fifteen minutes later the others began to file in and head for their desks.

Jack saw Mike Henderson sifting through paperwork and called him over.

'Mike! Get on to the control room. I want any 'mispers' in the force area that fit the description of our victims to be immediately forwarded to H.MET.'

'Will do Boss.' Henderson paused and Jack saw him glance around to see if anyone was listening.

'There's something that I need to speak to you about,' he said, nodding in the direction of Jack's office.

Once inside and with the door shut Henderson pulled up a chair and sat facing Slade.

'Boss, about what you asked me…'

'Mike, I know that you're up to your nuts in missing persons reports but I just want...'

'That's not it Boss,' interrupted Henderson. 'I'll sort out the Control Room. That's easy… it's the other thing. The Tait problem.'

'What have you got for me?'

'How about a present, neatly wrapped in a forensic bag.'

Henderson withdrew from his inside jacket pocket a clear plastic bag containing the torn leaflet that Jack had given him, along with a closely typed sheet of A4 paper. 'It's the results of the test on the leaflet found in DC Tait's tray.'

Jack took the sheet of paper from him and looked through it.

Henderson smiled. 'They found a partial and two full fingerprints.'

'You've identified them?'

'Aye Boss… a positive result… but you're not going to like it.'

Jack scrolled down through the report and immediately recognised the person named in it.

All police officers are required to provide their fingerprints and DNA on joining the force. This made it easier to eliminate them from samples found at crime scenes. Cynics within the job claimed that the real reason was in case something happened to them… and what was left made any visual identification impossible.

Slade looked back at Henderson, his face hard and serious. He nodded down at the paperwork.

'There's no doubt?'

The detective shook his head. 'No doubt about it Boss.'

'I'm going to fill in the duty Inspector. Meanwhile you go find our leaflet writer and collar him. I don't care what he's doing. I want him in this office in half an hour… after I've spoken to supervision.'

Henderson had hardly left the office before Jack snatched up the phone and punched in the number for the Control Room.

'Can you get the Newcastle duty inspector to give me a call.'

Jack kept the briefing short that morning and with everyone allocated their Actions, hurried back to his office.

Ten minutes later the duty Inspector Peter Worthing was sitting in Slade's office when there was a rap on the door and Mike Henderson came in.

He was accompanied by Police Constable James Dalton.

Looking around Dalton spotted his inspector sitting on a chair in the corner of the office. Silent, eyes cold and jaw clenched, he looked ready to explode.

Before entering the office Dalton had been all smiles, anticipating that he was about to be offered a more long-term attachment to the team. The look on the two senior officer's faces and the curt tone of Jack Slade suggested otherwise.

'Come in!' snapped Slade as the officer entered with growing trepidation.

Dalton nodded, 'Sir,' and cautiously walked towards the chair in front of Slade's desk.

'Don't bother sitting down PC Dalton,' Jack growled trying to control his growing anger. 'I was wondering if you recognised this.'

He threw the bag containing the leaflet down on his desk in front of the now very nervous officer.

It did not go unnoticed that the leaflet was contained in a forensic laboratory bag and had obviously come from the testing centre.

Dalton blanched.

When he spoke, his voice sounded different as his mouth had gone very dry. His eyes were flickering from Slade to the evidence bag and to the Duty Inspector.

He knew instinctively that this was no time to dig a deeper hole by lying.

'It was just a joke sir.'

Slade glanced around the room.

'Do you see anyone laughing?'

Dalton looked across to his Inspector sitting immobile and glaring back at him.

Slade continued. 'Are you aware of the current force policy on bullying in the workplace? Particularly the section on Equality and Diversity.'

Dalton managed to get out a 'Yes Sir,' but it sounded croaky and strangled.

'You do know that it's a sackable offence to send crap like that to anyone... let alone another cop?'

This time Dalton could only manage a nod, apparently having temporarily lost the power of speech.

'If it was up to me, you'd be suspended, disciplined and hopefully sacked. After the references you would get from headquarters, you'd be hard pressed to get a job working security at Tesco.'

James Dalton seemed to be a little unsteady on his feet but Jack still did not suggest he sit down.

'Unfortunately, I have to take account of the victim in this case. DC Tait has asked that it doesn't proceed any further. Personally, I think he's wrong! I think people like you are little better than the bullies we deal with out on the street!'

Dalton seemed to sag a little but remained silent.

'You'll find me not so forgiving,' continued Slade, his eyes narrowing. 'Now, I want you to listen very carefully and understand me. In my book this is a hair breadth from criminal harassment. If I hear of anything like this again, I'm coming looking for you and I won't give a toss what anyone says, you'll be in the dole queue quicker than you can sign your resignation papers. Do I make myself clear?'

'Yes Sir. Thank you, sir.'

'It's not me you need to thank. It's Detective Constable Tait who is clearly more of a man than you'll ever be. If it were down to me, I would have thrown you under the bus. Clear your desk! I want you out of my Incident Room. Now get out before I change my mind!'

After he had gone out Jack turned to Inspector Worthen.

'What a pathetic little shit.'

'He's not a bad cop, Jack. He's just a throwback to the old culture. He's not the only one who has views stuck in a different century. I'm sure that lots think that way. It's just he's been stupid enough to say it.'

'Yes, well he's been yet another distraction and I've got a murder or three to solve.'

Later that afternoon the results came in from the lab confirming that the body parts recovered from the park had all belonged to the missing girl Elizabeth Mortimer. It would allow her family to have some closure but the lack of progress in the case was becoming more and more frustrating for Jack and the rest of the team.

Clutching his empty coffee cup Jack walked through to the Incident Room to grab a refill and to check whether there had been any messages left that could generate actions. The room was empty except for Chris Tait who was sitting at his desk going through some paperwork.

'I see your bruised face is coming along nicely Chris.'

'It's become a bit of a talking point.'

'You know that Hall has made a complaint against you for assault. Claims that you smashed his face into the pavement.'

Tait shrugged. 'Complaints are par for the course.'

Jack gave a smile. 'My dad is ex-job. He used to say that if you weren't getting complaints then you weren't working.'

'I'm not bothered too much about Hall's complaint. He seems to be a bit selective with his recollections of that night. Appears to have forgotten that he was attempting to stick a blade into Mike Henderson at the time.'

'A point that has not gone unnoticed by DC Henderson. You won't be aware but DC Henderson has been doing a little side enquiry for me the last few days. He came up with a result this morning.'

'Oh yeah.'

'Involving a certain abusive leaflet.'

Chris did not reply.

'Have you and James Dalton had any run-ins in the past?'

Tait went silent for a few moments before answering.

'Dalton? He was at training school at the same time as me so I guess it figures.'

'Which means?'

'Let's just say he has made his feelings clear about gay people on more than one occasion in the past.'

'If you had decided to clear off back to the West End C.I.D. then I'm guessing that he was hoping to be next in line for your job.'

Chris Tait looked thoughtful but didn't reply and it was Jack who broke the silence.

'P.C. Dalton and I have had words.'

'I said I didn't want anything done,' responded Chris a little too sharply.

'I took what you wanted into account and nothing is going down on paper… unless you've changed your mind and want it to.'

Tait shook his head.

'Well, I can guarantee he'll be giving you a wide berth in future and there'll be no more abusive leaflets appearing.'

'Thanks Boss.'

'Don't thank me. Thank Mike Henderson. He did all the graft.'

Chris Tait's face registered surprise. 'Henderson? I thought that…' His voice trailed off.

'You thought that he was the one most likely to have sent it?'

Tait shrugged his shoulders, 'He's not exactly enamoured with a gay detective being seconded to the squad.'

'Well, let's say his attitude might have changed since it was a gay detective prevented him getting disemboweled.'

Just at that moment the phone next to Jack began ringing. He reached out and picked it up.

'Inspector Slade. H.MET.'

He heard the familiar voice of Ged Kirby on the other end of the line.

'Jack, I wanted to be the first to let you know. Some good news and some bad news.'

'I could do with a bit of good news. Fire away'.

'The good news is that some DNA has been recovered from the torso in the Leases Park boating lake.'

Slade's hand tightened on the receiver until it felt that he might snap it.

'That's brilliant. Have you a match?'

'Not yet but we're working on it.'

He paused and Jack waited for the bad news.

'It's not all good Jack. The pathologist's findings mention two deep parallel lines on each of the wrists.'

Jack had seen marks like that numerous times on prisoners brought into the station.

'She was handcuffed so tightly that it bit into the flesh,' muttered Jack softly.

'Yes, but it gets worse. The DNA that was recovered was found internally. She'd been raped and sodomised. Christ alone knows what that poor young lass went through before she was killed. From the marks on the body, she may have been kept prisoner for a while. The only saving grace is that we've got more than enough DNA to get a full profile on our killer. We might not have him yet Jack but the bastard's soon going to be in the cells.'

Jack was silent and thoughtful.

'I'm sorry Ged. That doesn't make sense. Up to now our killer had demonstrated that he is very forensically aware. Why the sudden change?'

'There was no such thing as a DNA database and no mitochondrial DNA back in 1985 when the girls went missing. Offenders never considered DNA because nobody had even heard of it. Cops relied on blood matches to get a conviction. A common group like 'O' meant that forty-eight per cent of the population matched. Even if half of those were women, we were still looking at fifteen million suspects. It wasn't until the Colin Pitchfork case in 1987 that DNA was used in a prosecution.'

'That's not what I meant,' Slade responded. 'Everyone knows about DNA now! Did it slip our killer's mind that he'd left a sample inside our victim when he raped her? And then he just goes and hands the evidence to us.'

'He made a mistake,' suggested the forensic officer. 'It happens. Be thankful for it.'

Slade was not convinced. 'I don't buy it. Our man doesn't make stupid mistakes.'

'Well, he has this time and the fact that the body was frozen has helped preserve the samples. Why won't you just accept that he's screwed up big style?'

Jack smiled. 'Maybe because recently I've been invited to far too many parties to find there was no cake when I arrived. He could be pissing us about again. Planting more false evidence.'

'Well identification of the DNA samples will tell us for sure.'

'Can you fix the usual 'hurry up' on the profile Ged. Put this rapidly ageing detective out of his misery.'

'Would you expect anything less?'

That night at the evening briefing Jack gave the good news to the team and it took some time for the whoops and self-congratulation to calm down.

'Listen in! I don't want us to get ahead of ourselves so it's business as usual until we have a positive identification and a name on the top of a charge sheet. This guy has laid so many false trails for us we can't be sure he isn't laying just one more to send us off in the wrong direction. Let's focus. Check and double check. Let's nail this bastard once and for all.'

The noise died down but everyone was finding it difficult to suppress their smiles.

'So, with that in mind what updates have we got?'

Jackson gave an update on the growing list of exhibits and the preliminary update on the results of the recent Post Mortem.

Donna gave an update on her enquiries so far concerning visits to registered Sex offenders who fitted the profile and age range. In relation to the Blue Transit van 'action' her list was now down to thirty-four people yet to visit. At four addresses she had not been able to get a reply so they were down for repeat visits.

'Any you're concerned with please ensure that you go double crewed.'

'Will do Boss but I'm a big girl now.'

Henderson looked about to make a sexist comment but thought better of it and kept his thoughts to himself.

Chris produced a late edition of the local paper and quoted details that Harmon had included. As expected, she had highlighted the implied threat that the killer may be looking to take another victim. It was all press hype but guaranteed to spread fear and increase her newspaper sales.

'Right. Let's keep on with the routine stuff until we get the lab results.'

As Slade left the incident room Dave Armstrong followed him out. 'You think the supposed forensic mistake is just another wind up by the murderer?'

'He goes from the super-efficient forensically aware mastermind... to a murderer muppet in one move. It doesn't ring true.'

'Could our victim have had sex with someone prior to being picked up and murdered by our killer?'

'It's possible but from what we know of our victims none of them were too free and easy with their favours. I think any sexual contact would have been non-consensual.'

'That means once we get the DNA test back we've got him?'

'Let's not open the champagne just yet. However we're further forward than we were this time yesterday. As I said for now it's business as usual.'

Jack glanced around to see that nobody was within earshot.

'Talking about business, I need your help. I need to go out for a while. Will you hold the fort and cover for me?'

'No problem Jack. Everyone's cracking on with their enquiries.'

'I'll be away for a couple of hours but I'll have a radio and if I'm out of range you can get me on my mobile.'

'Do you not need any back up?'

'No. It's personal business. There's something I have to sort out.'

At Newcastle Central Station Slade didn't have a platform ticket to get him through the barriers but flashing his warrant card worked just as well.

The train arrived on time at platform three and Jack picked out Dale straight away. As all their recent contact had been over the telephone, he was a little taken aback at how tall his little boy had grown.

Elaine appeared behind him carrying two small cases.

As soon as Dale spotted his dad he ran across and hugged him tightly.

Elaine was considerably less enthusiastic.

'I've packed his case. He's got enough changes of clothes for five days. I'm visiting a friend in Carlisle but can meet you back here on Tuesday and Dale and I can head back up to Scotland.'

A friend in Carlisle?

Jack wondered if that was the new boyfriend.

If asked Elaine would get defensive and it was sure to end in an argument. He wisely stayed silent.

As Elaine disappeared to get the Northern Rail train to Carlisle, Jack picked up the small black case and led Dale through the barriers and out to the car park.

Dale let out a whoop when he saw the BMW and as Jack had bought the car over a year ago it brought home to him how long it had been since he had last seen his boy.

'Are we going for a drive?'

'Yes, there's someone who is really excited to see you.'

Dale was talking nonstop on the journey in the way eleven-year-old boys do; recounting to his dad the adventure of his trip down on the train. Jack realised just how much he had missed his son since the divorce.

Pulling up in front of the stone-built cottage the young boy knew exactly where they were and if anything became more excited.

'Grandad's house!'

Jack gave a knock and after a couple of minutes his dad opened the door.

Jack hadn't telephoned ahead but if Charlie Slade was shocked to see his grandson arrive so unexpectedly, he gave nothing away and hugged him so tightly that Dale protested.

'I can't breathe grandad.'

Whilst Dale ran around the back garden exploring his former playground, Jack sat watching from the kitchen whilst Slade senior made some coffee.

'It's so good to see the bairn,' said Charlie, keeping his back to Jack who thought he had spotted his dad's eyes becoming watery. 'Are you stopping for your tea? We can head across to the Swan again.'

'Sorry dad. I have to get back.' Jack hesitated. 'Actually, I was going to ask you a favour.'

Jack felt guilty on the drive back to Forth Bank. The accusing glare of his father was bad enough but the look in Dale's eyes when he told him that he had to get back to work, had really upset the tough detective.

Elaine was maybe right.

'Regarding priorities I am, and always have been an arsehole.'

Chapter 54

Back at the nick, following the late briefing, Slade got the summons to see Parker. The Superintendent had his best grumpy face on, as if he'd just finished his coffee and found a dead slug at the bottom.

Jack noticed a copy of the previous evening's newspaper on his desk.

'Sit down Jack. I've had Headquarters on. I've passed the DNA breakthrough on to the ACC. He's pleased that we're making progress and hopes that you have a result soon.'

'I'm hoping so.'

'However, he did comment on the recent newspaper coverage from that reporter Harmon. It's becoming a concern to the Command Block. Her articles are very critical of the police suggesting that we're stumbling about and haven't got a clue. She is particularly scathing about you Jack suggesting that your enquiry is stalling and you've made no progress since day one when the head was pulled from the river.'

Parker leaned forward and tapped the copy of the newspaper. 'In her latest article she's saying that if the killer strikes again then the blame should be placed at the door of the investigating team. You even get a mention by name. Harmon is a dangerous woman, Jack. What have you done to piss her off so much?'

'My job. She's just spitting her dummy out and blaming me because, since she lost that prick Spence from Crime Intelligence she no longer has an inside line on Police enquiries.'

'Well just watch her Jack. She can be a vindictive bitch and seems intent on causing you trouble.'

'She's just stirring the shit to get herself a good headline.'

'It's obvious that she has it in for you and the ACC thinks it might reflect badly on the force if the enquiry goes tits up and we end up with another murder on our hands. Command Block are looking very carefully at what she's saying. They don't want any further loss of confidence in the Police. It might have passed you by but we're not exactly top of the popularity charts with the public these days.'

'I'm not in the popularity business. I'm in the locking up the 'scrotes' and villains business. The public losing confidence in the Police has more to do with political cuts to resources, than a lack of enthusiasm to do the job by street cops.'

'Well tread carefully Jack. You've made a dangerous enemy there. If this mad man takes another victim, Harmon will be scenting blood… your blood.'

217

Parker stared across the desk at Slade.

'Always remember Jack. Nobody's irreplaceable…. not even Jack Slade.'

Chapter 55

He'd followed her for quite a while as she had strolled along the main road out of the city passing the wide deserted expanse of the Town Moor.

The inner city area of grassland stretched for almost three hundred and fifty acres to the North of the city. Freeman of the city are afforded the right to graze their cattle on the Moor and once a year at the end of Jun, it is the site of Europe's largest travelling fair known as 'The Newcastle Hoppings.'

The traffic to the eastern end is the busiest of the surrounding roads and even though it was now well past midnight, many cars were passing; returning their occupants home after a night out in the city.

There are too many potential witnesses.

The frequent traffic did have an advantage. Although he had driven past the girl several times already, he easily blended into the dozens of other vehicles and had remained unnoticed. Monitoring her progress, he saw her reach the landmark Blue House Roundabout and turn left, walking along Grandstand Road on the Northern edge of the Moor.

Although not as busy with traffic, Grandstand Road was still well lit at that point and overlooked by several houses and apartments. It was not the best location for what he had in mind. Thankfully a small copse of trees provided him some cover and the side door of his van was on the nearside facing the expanse of the moor. Driving past her once again he put some distance between them, before pulling into a layby and waiting for her to approach.

Watching her in the rear-view mirror she was clearly a little unsteady on her feet, probably from alcohol.

That might prove to be an advantage.

He could see in the distance the distinctive Blue House owned by the Freemen of Newcastle upon Tyne and traditionally the home of one of the Moor caretakers. It was a busy junction which meant that he would have to be fast.

As he watched the girl she stumbled a couple of times, either from her heels or more likely the drink.

His heart had already begun beating faster in anticipation.

Thump. Thump, Thump.

Excitement was causing adrenaline to surge through his veins.

Taunting the police had been enjoyable but this was moving him into a whole new area of exhilaration.

Traffic had thinned out considerably on this section of the road and she was getting nearer… seemingly oblivious to the parked van.

He gave one last look around. Apart from his lone prey the street was deserted and other than the very occasional taxi on the far-off main road, traffic had almost petered out.

It was now or never.

Climbing through into the cargo area he slid open the nearside door and waited for her to pass. It was only when she was almost upon him that she looked up and became aware of his presence.

By then it was too late.

In one swift movement he reached out, had his hand over her mouth and dragged her backwards into the van.

He pressed the sharp blade of the knife against her throat.

'Scream and I'll kill you.'

She froze, rapidly sobering up and whimpering with fear allowed herself to be pushed onto the cold metal floor.

He quickly twisted her arms behind her back, securing her wrists with a plastic cable tie that he pulled tight. Some tape was wrapped across her mouth and more around her ankles. She lay on the floor in the back of the van, trussed up and unable to move. Her muffled snivelling pitiful through the makeshift gag.

Climbing through into the cab he started up the engine and quickly accelerated away.

It had taken only seconds.

He began to relax. The only sound was the clatter of the diesel engine and the whimpers coming from the girl in the rear cargo bay.

'Stop making a noise! Don't try to escape or I'll kill you. Do what I want and I'll let you go.'

Desperate to believe she would emerge from her ordeal alive the girl sobbed quietly, as the van was driven along the deserted night time streets, the driver putting as much distance as possible from them and the scene of the abduction.

He hadn't bothered to conceal his face. Nor had he disguised his voice or made any attempt to avoid her seeing his van.

He did not need to. Despite what he had told her when he was finished with her, she wouldn't be alive to identify him.

Chapter 56

The following morning Jack awoke early after another disturbed sleep.

Unrelenting rain rattled against the windows and a wind was howling outside his bedroom window. Today was definitely not going to be a day to walk to work.

Opening the blinds and looking out the dark brooding skies did little to raise his sombre mood. He knew that he should be happy that they had a viable DNA sample; it would surely lead to the killer. However, the blunt warning from T.C.P. was gnawing away at him.

'Always remember Jack. Nobody's irreplaceable…. not even Jack Slade.'

Trying to put any worries out of his head he snatched up the car keys and headed for the door. He hoped that today would bring some good news.

He was about to be sadly disappointed.

The message he had always dreaded was delivered before the morning's briefing had even started.

Inspector Peter Worthen arrived at Slade's office looking very dour and was clearly going to be the bearer of bad tidings.

'I've had the control room on. You asked that the team be informed of any missing from homes that might fit in with your three unsolved murders. One has popped up. It looks to have happened overnight but was reported just over an hour ago. A nineteen-year-old Theresa Harvey. As soon as I heard the description, I asked the cop at the scene to email me a recent photo. You're not going to like it, Jack.'

Worthen handed over a photograph of a young girl. Late teens, blonde and blue-eyed. Jack's heart sank. She was the image of any one of the previously murdered girls.

'Jack, I've already asked my Sergeant to attend the initial report and ensure that everything that can be done is covered. He's been asking all the right questions. There's no reason for her to have gone missing and there's been no indication of any problems either at home or at work that would prompt her disappearance.'

'When was she last seen?'

'Theresa went out with friends last night and wasn't expected back until late. She was only discovered missing when her mother went into her room this morning to make sure that she got up for work.'

Jack looked again at the photograph and felt a tight feeling in his gut.

Theresa Harvey could have been a sister to any one of his three murder victims.

That morning the briefing was fraught. The team was brought up to date with the latest development, which left everyone tense and apprehensive. There was a distinct lack of any of the usual Police banter.

Jack tried to remain calm in the face of what could turn out to be devastating news and tried his best to try to put a positive spin on it.

'You're all now aware of the misper. Further details are on the day's log. As you have seen from the photograph the missing girl fits our victim profile. It's troubling but I need to stress that so far we have nothing to positively link her with our enquiry. She may, like ninety nine percent of other missing persons, just turn up in a few hours.'

He wasn't convincing himself let alone the rest of the H.MET team.

'What is concerning me is that the M.O. could also fit that of our offender. Theresa was walking back along the Great North Road towards Gosforth after a night on the town.'

Slade looked around at the room of sullen faces.

'Until we have further information either way, the misper enquiry is being handled by uniform. Inspector Worthen is supervising so it's in safe hands and he will be providing regular updates to H.MET. We will be continually kept in the loop. It will be up to us to carry on our allocated 'actions' until such time we can establish a firm link. Let's keep focused.'

Following the briefing Dave Armstrong knocked on the open door of Slade's office and entered carrying two cups of freshly brewed coffee. He put one down in front of Slade.

'I thought you could do with a pick me up. With a bit of luck Inspector Worthen will come through that door in five minutes to tell you that Theresa Harvey is back home safe and well.'

Jack shook his head. 'We both know that's not going to happen. This is the news that I've been afraid of from the start. Just yesterday T.C.P. called me in and gave me the gypsy's warning. He's getting flak from Middle Earth and is making sure that he keeps his own back covered. If all goes well and we nail our man he will be the one taking the bow and applause. If the case turns to crap it will be me that gets the bullet.'

'That's the law of the jungle Jack. You've been in this game long enough to know that.'

'That doesn't stop me getting pissed off about it.'

222

'I'll chase up the lab this morning. Look on the bright side, it just takes one good break and the DNA recovery from the body of Elizabeth Mortimer could be the break that we've been waiting for.'

'Providing that the offender's DNA is in the system.'

'That psychologist bloke McNaughton told us, 'You don't start a criminal career with murder.' Our man will be in the system somewhere.'

'Well Dave…. Let's hope that you're right. For the minute, I'm just praying that this morning's misper turns up safe and well.'

'We don't know for sure yet that she has been abducted.'

'If she is another victim the bosses will be running for cover and looking for someone to throw to the media as a sacrificial lamb.'

Jack took a large swig of his coffee.

'Just you watch Dave. If Theresa Harvey turns up dead… when the music stops it will be me left holding this parcel of shit.

Chapter 57

He stood in the dingy cellar looking down at Theresa Harvey. She lay huddled in a foetal position, on a grey blanket spread out on the concrete floor. He had allowed her to get dressed afterwards and then secured her wrists to the leg of the heavy workbench by cable ties. He replaced the gag but in reality, there was no chance of anyone hearing her.

He had earlier removed it. Not hearing her screams would have spoiled some of the fun.

The girl had been compliant and done everything that he had demanded. It was surprising just what someone was prepared to do to save their life. It had been one of the most intense feelings he had known. A fantasy come true. A feeling of absolute dominance over his slave.

The feeling of power had been even more of a turn on than the sex.

Afterwards, through tears, she begged him to let her go. She said her parents would be worried and desperate to know that she was alright.

What concern was that of his?

He felt no empathy for her. It only added to his feeling of superiority to hear her pleading for her life... imploring him to release her.

She would stay alive so long as he didn't get bored of her and she satisfied his needs. He didn't know how long he would keep her captive before he got restless and would have to dispose of her to make room for another.

He closed his eyes and wondered what it would feel like to listen to her piteous appeals as he slowly tightened his grip around her throat, squeezing the last breathless words from her mouth.

Maybe he would do it one last time as he strangled her... feel her fear as he exploded inside her.

He opened his eyes and his heart was thumping.

This was the ultimate power.

The power over life and death.

He was becoming aroused again but before he could do anything he heard the noise of a diesel engine.

His eyes flashed to the cellar stairs.

A car was pulling up outside the house.

Donna drove the car onto the driveway of Stannington Grange, a stone-built detached building several miles outside of the city. Splitting the workload with Mike Henderson was definitely allowing them to plough through the lists quicker.

After this one it would leave only nineteen more Blue Transit owners left on her list.

Henderson had told Donna she should thank God it was a dark coloured Transit and not a white one or they might be following leads until the day of their retirement.

Donna had been a little annoyed when he had said, 'Mind you if there's anything on your list that you're wary of, or get a funny feeling about let me know and we can both attend.'

It sounded a little sexist and she didn't like any suggestion that she couldn't manage without some male detective by her side.

'I think I can manage but thanks anyway. I'll bear that in mind.'

The driveway of Stannington Grange was little more than a dirt track. Parking up and switching off the ignition Donna glanced down at her file.

Running a finger down the list she stopped at George Smith who was registered at this address as being the keeper of a dark blue Transit.

If so, it wasn't on the drive.

She looked up at the building which exuded an air of neglect; garden overgrown and paint peeling from wooden window frames. It had clearly seen better days and at one time would have been impressive. Stone steps up the front door had been adapted with a ramp, suggesting that the occupant had mobility issues. The place looked abandoned and Donna hoped that the DVLA record was up to date otherwise the visit would turn into yet another dead end.

Walking up the ramp she gave a rattle on a rusting imitation brass door knocker.

There was no answer and no signs of life from inside.

Going to the rear the house appeared as neglected from the back as the front. All the windows had a film of dust suggesting that they hadn't been cleaned in a long time.

An old rickety wooden garage stood in the garden but tattered curtains and some boxes piled up by the window prevented her looking inside. A mass of overgrown stinging nettles several feet high blocked access to the rear of it.

Returning to the front Donna took out a pad and scribbled a note requesting that Smith contact her at Forth Banks Police Station.

Pushing it through the letterbox, she gave a last look at the semi derelict building and made her way back to her car.

Climbing inside she glanced down at the next address on her list.

As Donna started up and reversed off the drive she didn't notice the greying net curtain at the upstairs window twitch slightly. Nor did she spot the figure peering down at her whilst she manoeuvred her way past the crumbling stone gate posts.

As she accelerated away the curtain dropped back down and once again all became still.

Chapter 58

It was mid-day and detectives were in the Incident Room shuffling paperwork when suddenly the door was thrown open and Dave Armstrong burst in. He was clearly out of breath having run up the stairs from the front office.

'Boss, the lab has come up with a match on the DNA.'

Everyone looked up and stopped what they were doing.

Jack felt his heart beating faster, an involuntary reaction to the rush of adrenaline coursing through his veins. 'Our killer is in the system?'

'Not only in the system but he's got several prior arrests for indecent assault.'

The room became a cacophony of noise as the whole team began talking at once and a few started clapping.

After all the false trails and dead ends finally a piece of good luck.

Jack tried desperately not to appear too excited.

He failed!

He couldn't help breaking into a wide grin and slapping the sergeant's shoulder.

'That's brilliant news, Dave. Give me a name.'

'He's local. Edward John Reed in his late sixties. Originally from the Cambois area. Apart from the last indecent assault arrest three years ago he's been clean since the early eighties. If it wasn't for the recent arrest his DNA wouldn't even be on file.'

'What form has he got?'

'A couple of previous for flashing as a teenager and then in 1981 he went to prison and did a full three years for indecent assault on a couple of young lasses. When he got out it appears that he kept his head down until just over three years ago and another arrest for another indecent assault, when he was accused of groping a woman carer.'

'Old habits die hard,' said Jack.

'Well, the latest one was dropped for lack of evidence. Reed claimed he had accidently stumbled and the carer refused to give a statement.'

Everyone began talking at once.

Jack held up his hand. 'Right! Quiet! Listen in! Let's not go off halfcocked. I want everything we can find on Edward John Reed. As much background on this guy as we can get. Previous convictions and

M.O. I want the full circumstances of any offences that he's been brought in for... whether charged or not. Get me his family background and all current and past addresses. I want to know more about this guy than his mother does!'

The next twenty minutes was an explosion of activity. Any shift finishing time was forgotten as each of the squad was allocated a piece of the suspect's life to delve into and research.

Edward John Reed had been born in 1954 and was just into his thirties at the time the girls went missing. He lived in Cambois, a small mining village in south east Northumberland on the north side of the River Blyth estuary.

Jack knew Cambois. Folk that weren't familiar with the area pronounced it 'Cam- Bwar' like the French but the locals called it 'Cam-Us'.

Originally a coal mining village, the area declined after the closure of the colliery in the late sixties. It was revived in the late seventies with the opening of a nearby international aluminium smelter site but that too closed in 2012.

As a juvenile Reed had a couple of cautions for minor thefts which included a theft of washing which caught Jack's eye. Could he have been stealing women's clothing... maybe as trophies?

There were two offences of indecent exposure, one of which he was cautioned for, and one which went to court resulting in him being given a conditional discharge.

'He's had more than his fair share of cautions,' grumbled Henderson.

Jack nodded. 'It was a bit different back in those days. Clear up rates were the Detective Inspector's God and cautions helped to detect offences when the evidence was a bit thin. The 'prigs' were much more ready to cough to an offence if they were offered the chance of a caution instead of going to court.'

Dave Armstrong checked through Reed's arrest records and updated the squad.

'For the first indecent assault offence as a juvenile there was little evidence and Reed wouldn't admit it even with the offer of a caution. In the end it was 'No Further Action'... although it appears that the cop dealing with it thought he was as guilty as sin.'

'Thinking it and proving it are two different things,' said Jack.

'Well, what was of more significance were two convictions for indecent assault in 1980. Two local girls in their early teens living in Cambois had made the complaints and Reed was arrested and questioned. Although he denied the allegations the Jury didn't believe him and he went down for a three-year stretch. I think the judge was pissed off that he pleaded not guilty and both girls were forced to give evidence.'

'There were no remote video evidence facilities available in those days Dave.'

Slade noted that the Cambois address was a Dune Side Cottage but between arrest and conviction there had been a change of address to the Newcastle area. Clearly the good folk of Cambois had made Reed less than welcome and he had moved away to somewhere he could be more anonymous.

The address in Newcastle had been in Moulton Place to the West of the city. Jack recalled it from a previous murder enquiry he had worked on. They were architect designed deck access flats. Built in 1969 they rapidly became an eyesore and were demolished around 2009. There was no chance of making any enquiries there.

Armstrong went on to say that there had been no more dealings with the Police, until three years ago when there had been a further allegation of indecent assault.

'Unfortunately, that offence was also referenced as 'No Further Action'. After that there was nothing else.'

'What did you find out about the last arrest?'

'At the time Edward Reed was living at The Northumberland Hills Residential Care Home in Cramlington. One of the young female carers alleged that he had grabbed her breasts as she was attending to him. Reed was arrested and interviewed but denied the offence claiming that he had stumbled. Looks like C.P.S wouldn't run with it. Despite his previous convictions they felt there was insufficient evidence to get a conviction.'

'I take it that, although there was no further action, his DNA was taken and that's what links him to the semen sample recovered from Elizabeth Mortimer?'

'Got it in one.'

'Dave, can you get on to the victim from the last offence. Arrange a visit and let's see what she can tell us about Edward Reed. I want as much background as we can before we make our move on him.'

He looked across the room. 'Mike, whilst Dave and I visit the last victim I want you to go with Gavin across to Cambois and make enquiries with the locals. Don't let him know that we're on to him but find out everything you can. OK. Let's get on with it.'

Jack smiled. 'This could be the break that we've been waiting for.'

Chapter 59

The victim of the last indecent assault allegation, Susan Dodd lived in Bedlington several miles north of the city. After telephoning ahead Dave Armstrong and Chris drove across to the address.

At the time of the incident she had been employed at Northumberland Hills Residential Care Home in Cramlington, where Reed had been admitted.

As she began to talk Slade was struck by how much younger she looked than her twenty-three years and thought she could easily pass for nineteen. Slender and wearing figure hugging pale blue jeans, her shoulder length blonde hair framed an unlined face of peaches and cream complexion and piercing blue eyes.

He shot a glance across at Dave who was clearly thinking exactly the same thing.

Susan Dodd was a ringer for the other girls who had gone missing.

If Reed was their man then he certainly had consistency in the type of victim he preyed upon.

Dodd was pleasant and polite but appeared reluctant to talk about the incident.

'I told the police at the time. I thought that this was all over with.'

'We're just following up something and it would be really helpful if you could go through what happened one more time for us.'

Susan told her story. It didn't vary from the statement in the file that Jack had already read through. She was adamant that the touching had not been accidental.

'That's what he claimed but he smiled as he did it. Not smiled… it was more of a leer. I can see his face now. He was a right creep.'

'So why did it not go to court?'

'There was talk of the onset of early dementia and he could hardly walk. He was actually in the home because of a fall so his stumbling excuse seemed to ring true.' She hesitated. 'Besides it was his word against mine and well… someone said it might be better for the care home company if I just let it go. They didn't want any bad publicity.'

She shrugged. 'At the time I needed the job so I just dropped it, and that was the end of it. I made sure I avoided the bastard after that. As soon as I could I left Northumberland Hills and got a job at a different care home. Edward was only there for temporary respite so I heard he went home shortly after I left. If I never see the dirty pervert again it'll be too soon.'

Jack knew instinctively that she was telling the truth about the assault.

'You know that a court would almost certainly have believed you.'

'At the time I was a twenty-year-old girl. My word against some poor old pensioner who has dementia, can hardly stand on his own feet and spends most of his time in a wheelchair. You think so?'

Jack was taken aback. 'A wheelchair?'

'Yes. He's got limited mobility which is why after his fall he was admitted to the care home for respite. He'd been in and out of a wheelchair for years and only ever walked with a Zimmer frame following an accident in the mid-eighties up near Stannington when he stepped out in front of a car when drunk.'

'Did he have an address in Stannington?'

'He might have. I don't know. A year or so ago I heard from one of the staff that he'd been moved back into Northumberland Hills care home and was now a permanent resident.'

After leaving Susan Dodd, Slade and Armstrong sat in their car outside her house and Slade banged on the steering wheel in frustration.

Armstrong did not often see his friend lose his temper but had some empathy. 'He's not our man Jack, is he?'

'The DNA is a match. The car accident up near Stannington came after the girls went missing. He has to be still in the frame for the murders, but he obviously can't be the one dumping the body parts.'

'An accomplice then? Or maybe he's faking his injuries. You see it all the time with these phoney disability claims. Maybe the whole Zimmer frame and wheelchair thing is just a scam.'

Slade started up the car.

'Get Chris Tait on the radio. I want him to dig up whatever he can about this accident in Stannington that Reed was involved in. There should be an accident report somewhere.'

'I'm not even sure if it will be on the computer Jack.'

'If it was so serious that it left Reed in a wheelchair then I've no doubt that it was reported in the papers.'

'Without an actual date it might take some time.'

'So he'd better get straight on to it.'

'I'll get him to make a start.'

'We also need to pay Edward Reed a visit. Wheelchair or no wheelchair we'll get him down to the nick and see what he's got to say.'

'Cramlington's only ten minutes away.'

'Ring Northumberland Hills. Tell them we have an enquiry but don't mention Reed. We've got him in our sights. The last thing we want to do is spook him into doing a flit.'

Chapter 60

Slade and Armstrong made their way to Northumberland Hills care home in the sprawling town of Cramlington.

The modern building was surrounded by neat lawns and well-kept flower beds. Armstrong had telephoned ahead so that they were expected but on arrival at the front entrance the door was locked. Jack pressed an intercom and a few seconds later a young woman dressed in a blue tunic appeared and let them in.

'It stops any of our residents from going walkabout,' she explained.

Inside the care home was very clean and bright with large windows allowing the daylight to pour in.

They were led down a short corridor to a door marked "Manager".

Behind a large desk sat Ellen Lowther. Middle aged with short dark hair she was dressed in casual clothes, which differentiated her from all the other uniformed staff. As the detectives were ushered into her office, they identified themselves and Lowther indicated to some chairs.

'Please take a seat. What can I do for you Inspector?'

When she spoke, her voice was clipped and she clearly felt she had gone to some lengths to suppress her north east accent.

She needn't have bothered. She spoke in what Slade's father used to call "posh Geordie".

Slade explained that they were making enquiries into one of their former residents who had been staying for respite some time ago.

'His name is Edward Reed.'

Lowther gave an involuntary frown.

'I see that the name rings a bell with you.'

'Yes. There was a very unfortunate incident some time ago that involved Edward.'

'We need to speak to him rather urgently concerning an ongoing enquiry.'

Ellen Lowther's face dropped even further.

'That's going to be very difficult. When you telephoned you should have said that it was to do with Edward Reed. I could have saved you a wasted journey.'

'Why is that?'

'Edward died about six weeks ago.'

'He's dead?'

234

'I'm afraid so.'

'Do you have any details of relatives?'

'He only ever had one visitor. It was towards the end. I believe it was his brother. I think he said his name was George.'

'Do you have his contact details?'

'I believe that he had been living abroad but when Edward became very ill he returned to the UK. He did visit several times. There was a mobile number… but when I tried to ring it the phone appeared to be disconnected.'

'And you don't have any address for him?'

'I'm afraid not.'

'Well can you give me Edward's address and we will see if we can make some enquiries there.'

'Certainly. Just give me a moment.'

Lowther went to a large metal filing cabinet and, taking a bunch of keys from her pocket, opened it.

After rummaging through some files, she withdrew a buff-coloured folder and returned to the desk.

'Right. Let me see now,' she said, opening the file and glancing through.

'Yes. Here we are. Dune Side Cottage… it's in Cambois.'

Slade's face fell. 'I've already got a couple of Detectives making enquiries there… but our initial information is that Edward hasn't lived there since the nineteen eighties.'

'Are you sure? I'm afraid that was the only address we were given. Why on earth would he have given an old address? I suppose he was suffering early dementia… perhaps he was confused.'

Jack wasn't convinced.

Perhaps he didn't want anyone knowing where he lived because he had a secret that he didn't want uncovered.

Chapter 61

The drive up to Cambois took almost half an hour in unusually busy traffic and when Gavin Oates and Mike Henderson arrived at the village it did not live up to the pretty coastal village they were expecting. Several boarded-up houses gave the impression that it was a little run down.

Dune Side Cottage was set back off the main road. They were hoping that the current owners would be able to give them some background information on Reed.

When they arrived at the address their heart sank.

The old cottage was clearly no longer a privately owned house. It had undergone major refurbishment and with a large dormer attic extension was now divided into two holiday apartments owned by a North East holiday lettings company.

'That's not going to go down well with the boss,' muttered Oates, glancing across at Mike.

'Who the hell wants to holiday here? The wind off the North Sea gets a bit chilly at the Costa del Cambois.'

'Looks like it's plan B. Let's ask around the village and see if anyone knows what happened to Reed.'

'Where do you want to start?'

Henderson glanced down the road at an imposing Victorian looking pub and smiled.

Following his gaze Oates took a coin out of his pocket. 'Spin for it. Heads!'

He flipped the coin.

Henderson smiled. 'Tails! Looks like you're driving bonny lad.'

'In that case, you're bloody buying.'

It was still afternoon as they entered the pub and there were just a handful of customers sitting at tables or propping up the bar.

Mike had always felt at home in bars. A regular haunt of many informants that he had cultivated over the years, pubs and drink had gone a long way to solving many of his cases. To Mike they were a grand repository of information and gossip.

This pub was no exception and after a couple of questions to the barman, the detectives were given directions to the person who was the closest thing that the area had to a local historian.

They didn't have far to go. Gladys Charlton was sitting at a table in the far corner of the bar looking every day of her seventy-eight years.

A mop of grey hair framed a face with so many lines that it looked as if someone had been chopping firewood on it. Her arms had the colour and texture of ancient parchment and ended in liver spotted hands and nicotine-coloured fingers. Those fingers were now wrapped tightly around a half pint glass of stout.

Gladys had lived in the village all her life and embodied everyone's idea of the stereotypical northern working-class woman of her time. She could have come straight out of an episode of "When The Boat Comes In".

If she could get her mind around computers and social media, she would be what is known as an internet troll. She was a treasure trove of all the scandal and gossip about everyone in the village going back decades… and she was clearly in her element passing it on to anyone who would listen.

This suited Henderson as much as the thought of a decent pint, so providing a half of stout to oil the old crone's vocal cords, he set about quizzing Gladys on her knowledge of village history.

'My Albert worked in the pit all his life 'til they closed it in 1968. He tried to get work in the smelter works but there were hundreds chasing the jobs. At the time there were rumours the plant would pollute the area with the aluminium waste so the company bought up all the land hereabouts. They still own it to this day. Anyway, Albert never got another job. His lungs were buggered from the coal dust ye kna!'

'What I'm interested in is the Reed family that lived in Dune Side Cottage.'

'Oh Aye! Now there was a right odd lot if ever I saw them. The old man… Frank, they called him was a funny looking bloke. Worked the pit… I suppose everyone did in those days. Very dark he was. Didn't look much different when he came up from the shaft as he did before he went down. They said his real name was Franco and his father had been Italian but I always said there was a touch of the tar brush about him… if you kna what I mean son.'

Oates decided he had to ignore the dated racial slur if he was going to get Gladys to open up further.

'What about the rest of the family?'

'Grace the mother, whey man, never was someone so inappropriately named. She had as much refinement as a cart load of horse shite.'

237

Unlike you Gladys thought Henderson but kept silent.

'She already had one kid Eddy who was fourteen but about a year after her husband passed, she had another little bairn, a laddie called George.'

Gladys leant forward conspiratorially. 'George the miracle bairn I used to call him seeing as he popped out at least a year after his dad went to his grave.'

She began chuckling to herself which brought about a coughing fit.

'Now I've heard about long labour but that's stretching it canny far, bonny lad. There were a few of the married blokes in the village had fingers pointed at them but no-one would put their hands up to it. Grace kept schtum about who the bairn's father was… though I had my own suspicions.' She gave a theatrical wink.

'We're interested in the older boy… Edward.'

'Aye! Young Eddy Reed. Now there's another one you wouldn't get thanks for taking home to yer mam and dad. You're the polis so ye'll kna all about him. When he was about twenty there was a bit of bother involving two of the little lassies in the village. That sort of thing didn't go down well in those days.'

'It's not too popular these days, Gladys.'

'Aye well pet, after that some of the blokes got together one night after a few down the pub and paid young Eddy a visit. He ended up getting a bit of a hiding and there was some damage to the house. After that he took the gypsy's warning and buggered off to Newcastle. I read in the papers he was up at the Crown and got three years for interfering with the young lassies.'

'Did he ever come back?'

'Nah lad! There were a few folk who wouldn't let summit like that lie. Prison was not enough for them. They wanted blood. His mam stopped in the house for a while. She kept 'hersel to hersel' but when Eddy got sent to clink, she sold up. I heard she got a canny bit for the cottage being right next to the beach and all that. It's now a holiday place they let out to "townies".'

'Where did Grace go?' asked Henderson.

'You hear things… not that I gossip ye kna!'

'Of course not Gladys,' Mike said, trying to keep any trace of sarcasm from his voice.

'I heard that she bought an old run-down farmhouse down past Stannington for her and young George but just a few years later she got the big 'C' and died. Her youngest George was about sixteen by then. His mam wasn't cold in her grave before he packed his bags and buggered off. I heard he joined the army. It took him away abroad.'

'But what about the older lad Eddy?'

'I'm not sure if Eddy took the house over when his mam died. I read something in the paper about him. Late-eighties I think it was. He had a canny nasty accident crossing a road in Stannington. He'd been drinking in a local pub and he stepped out in front of a car pissed… least ways that's what they said at the time.'

'You're not convinced?'

'It was a hit and run you kna. He spent weeks in hospital with both legs smashed and problems with his back. I heard he ended up in a wheelchair. They never found the driver. The car turned out to be pinched and ended up on fire.'

'Are you thinking that someone deliberately ran him down?' asked Oates.

She leant forward. 'Not for me to say… but the car was nicked from just down the road from here… and word in the village was that one of the lassies' fathers did for him.'

Gladys rattled her now empty glass and taking the hint Henderson stood up.

'Here bonny lad! You couldn't get a whisky chaser as well for an old pensioner could you son?'

Henderson went to the bar. This was proving costly and he was wondering whether he could claim it back on expenses.

Oates pressed Gladys. 'Did you ever hear what happened to young George?'

'After his stint in the army he must have got a taste for foreign places. Last I heard he was away living in France… or was it Spain?'

A couple of minutes later Henderson returned with a beer for himself and a coke for Oates. He placed a half pint of stout and a whisky in front of Gladys.

Gladys looked at the whisky as if weighing it up and frowned.

'They don't pay the polis enough these days to stretch to a double?'

After another twenty minutes Henderson and Oates believed that they had everything they were going to get out of Gladys and got up to leave.

'Here bonny lad,' said Gladys to Henderson, her speech now a little slurred. 'There's not everyone blamed the blokes in the village for Grace's miracle bairn you know.'

The whisky was kicking in, and with it Gladys the troll was coming into her own.

She beckoned Henderson closer and lowered her voice.

'Some reckon Grace got a bit lonely and young Eddy was a big lad for fourteen… if you get my drift. Thought himself the man of the house after his dad passed on.'

She gave a little smirked and winked. 'Maybe he was!'

Returning to the car Henderson looked across at Oates. 'She's a bit of a character is our Gladys'.

'You're not kidding. I wouldn't like to get on the wrong side of her. I've met serial killers less scary'.

Chapter 62

For the second time that day Donna pulled up on the driveway of Stannington Grange. The impressive name belied the state that the building had been reduced to.

The old detached stone-built house looked just as neglected as it had been on her previous visit and glancing up every window appeared covered in a thick film of dust. The steady drizzle of rain soaking the grounds merely added to the gloom.

She glanced down again at her notes and hoped that this time she could cross Stannington Grange off the list.

Getting out Donna walked up the overgrown dirt track that served as a drive, trying as best as possible to avoid the muddy tyre tracks and keep her shoes clean.

She approached the door and gave a knock but there was no reply.

Donna was about to turn and leave when she was seized by a thought.

Raising the letter box, she peered into the gloomy interior.

A man was standing alone at the far end of the hallway looking in her direction.

Donna knocked loudly and again looked inside.

The figure had gone.

She called through the letterbox. 'Police! Can you please answer the door? I know that you're in there.'

After a few moments the man re-appeared and walked slowly towards the door. Reaching out he opened the door by only a couple of inches and it remained secured by a metal chain.

From behind the door he peered through the gap.

'What do you want?'

'Mister Smith. I'm DC Shaw from Northumbria Police. It's just a routine enquiry concerning a Ford Transit vehicle registered to you. Do you still own the vehicle?'

There was a slight hesitation. 'No. I've sold it.'

'Look. Can I come in? It's nothing to be concerned about.'

After a few seconds the figure reluctantly stepped back. There was the rattle of the chain being released and the door creaked open.

George Smith was in his mid-fifties but looked older. His once black hair was now thinning and flecked with grey. His fingers were stained a dirty yellow and the nails were down to the quick. Beady eyes stared out from a sallow face and flickered from Donna to her parked car and back.

He moved to one side allowing Donna to step into a hallway. There was a feisty damp air about the place which reeked of stale cigarette smoke. Smith ushered Donna towards a room off the hallway containing a threadbare three-seater and two equally worn armchairs. Donna sat reluctantly on one of the armchairs and glanced around at the squalid room.

The whole place was in need of a good clean. The carpet felt sticky, the dust on a small set of drawers was thick and the curtains were closed shutting out any daylight. She suspected opening them would have made little difference as the windows were so filthy.

'Mister George Smith?'

The man nodded silently.

'It's just an enquiry about your Ford Transit. You say that you sold it. Can you tell me when you transferred ownership?'

Again, there was hesitation.

'A couple of months ago. Why? Is there a problem?'

'No. Just routine. Do you have details of the new owner? Maybe you have documentation with the transfer date on.'

'I'm not sure where the paperwork is. I can see if I can find it and if I do, I'll get back to you.'

'If you don't mind, that would be a help.'

'Well… if that's all I have some work I need to get on with.'

Donna wondered what work he had to do from home that was so urgent. It obviously didn't include any cleaning. However, the signals he was giving out were clear. He was making her feel as welcome as a turd in a swimming pool.

'If you find the paperwork please give me a call. This is my card.'

Smith's response was little more than a grunt.

Gathering up her file Donna headed for the door, happy to make her escape into the fresh air outside.

Starting up the car before reversing off the driveway Donna cast a casual glance around at the grounds of the house. It looked as scruffy close up as the occupant did.

She didn't notice the curtain twitch or spot the occupant peering out.

She was still there sitting in her car.

What was she doing?

The unexpected arrival of the Police had really spooked him.

Was it really just routine?

Why doesn't she just leave?

There was something about the place that was troubling Donna. The occupant clearly didn't want her hanging around that was for sure. But there was something else and she just couldn't quite put her finger on it.

Starting up the car she selected reverse and began slowly moving back trying to avoid the deep channels burrowed into the dirt track by previous vehicles.

She stopped abruptly.

That was it! The tyre ruts.

As well as those from her car there were clearly other fresh tyre marks imprinted on the driveway.

A vehicle had recently driven up through the mud.

Could it have been the postman… maybe a visitor?

No. The tracks went along the side of the building and around the back.

She got back out of her car and followed the tracks past the side of the house. They were leading up to the front of the ramshackle wooden garage.

George Smith let the dirty curtain fall back into place.

What was she doing now?

Why doesn't she just clear off?

This is private property.

She has no right to be snooping around.

Where has she gone?

Donna tried the garage door but it was locked with a large padlock. The window that she had previously glanced in was still obstructed by curtains and boxes. Cautiously she began negotiating her way through the thick nettles and weeds until she could access the rear of the garage.

There was another filthy window caked in dust and dirt. It wasn't much better than the first one but, as she peered through the almost opaque glass, she could just make out a shape.

It wasn't easy to see but it was definitely there.

A late model blue Ford Transit.

The one that George Smith claimed to have sold.

'Is there a problem?'

The voice made her jump and turning around Smith was standing only a few feet away from her.

'No everything is alright. I'm just leaving. If you think of anything, just give me a call.'

'Actually, there is something. I think I've found that paperwork you wanted. Do you want to come back inside?'

'I've had a call on my radio. I need to get back to the office. I'll telephone you later.'

'I don't think you asked for my number.'

Donna's heart was racing. She weighed up whether she could get back to her car before Smith could prevent her.

There was an opportunity. She took it. Shoving Smith to the side she made a run for the car. She was fast. Despite his age he was faster.

He managed to grab at her sleeve and pull her back.

She lashed out and tried to strike him on the side of his head but he pulled away and the blow struck his shoulder.

Donna went for his eyes with her fingers but again he managed to avoid her. She lashed out with her fist aiming for his head but once again he jerked back and she didn't connect.

As she went for his eyes a second time Donna felt a heavy blow to her face and could taste blood.

There was a second blow to the side of her head and then... blackness.

Chapter 63

In the Incident Room it was nearing the time for the regular afternoon debrief. Everyone was gathering around in front of the murder wall where Slade was attaching the most recent photograph of Edward Reed.

He turned and looked around at the gathered officers. 'Where's Donna?'

'Still out and about Boss. Working through her list of transit vans. It was longer than she had hoped but she should be back shortly,' said Tait.

'Well, we'd better get on and Chris, you can get her up to speed later.'

'Will do.'

'Right. We have established that the DNA recovered from the body of Elizabeth Mortimer is a positive match to our suspect Edward Reed. Unfortunately Reed died six weeks ago so he clearly isn't the person who has been dumping the body parts.'

'So where do we go from here?' asked Simon Walters.

'Before he died Reed was visited several times by a man who we believe may have been his brother George Reed.'

'Who may or may not be his son,' added Henderson.

'Brother… son… whichever, it's pretty clear that we have a new suspect. George Reed needs to be the new focus of our attention.'

'Do we have a last known address for either him or his dead brother?'

Henderson glanced down at his notes. 'According to my new drinking buddy Gladys, George was living abroad. France or Spain. The only address I had for Edward is the one at Dune Side Cottage and that's a non-starter.'

'That's the only address the care home had as well. Whether as the result of dementia on Edward's part or whether intended to be deliberately misleading by George Reed, we don't know.'

Chris raised his hand. 'What if, when his brother died in the nursing home and George started emptying the house. Possibly with the intention of selling it. Maybe as he was clearing it out, he came across Edwards trophies from the murders.'

'I suppose dismembered corpses in the freezer wouldn't be an ideal selling point,' muttered Henderson.

'Exactly. So he started disposing of them.'

Jack nodded. 'That's as good a theory as any.'

'So, assuming he is the one who snatched Theresa Harvey, how does George go from house clearance to kidnapping?' asked Oates.

Chris continued, 'From his communication with the press he clearly enjoys the attention. Maybe in disposing of the body parts he's been lapping up all the press coverage. He's getting a thrill from reading about himself in the local rag...'

'Harmon's got a lot to answer for,' growled Armstrong.

'...and our killer certainly gets his rocks off by taunting the Police.'

'It's not just Harmon's articles,' added Slade. 'It's on the news every night. He's being built up as some kind of cult killer. Meanwhile he's got us running around in circles chasing our tails. He's got to be getting some kind of buzz from that.'

'OK. Say you're right,' said Armstrong. 'Abducting another victim would still be one hell of an escalation.'

Chris was undaunted, 'It's become like a drug. Many kids start off on weed and end up on heroin. Dumping the bodies was his 'gateway' drug and gave him an initial high. Now he's lapping up the media attention and wants to feed his habit.'

Slade looked thoughtful. 'I think that Chris has a valid theory. George has had a taste of what it's been like clearing up after Edward... how much of a high would he get from taking over from him.'

Chris was nodding. 'Yes. And maybe Edward really was his father and it's a case of like father like son. What was it that Professor McNaughton told us in his briefing? Didn't he say that the biological relatives of sociopaths were five times more likely than the average person to also be sociopathic?'

'And now we have a possible fourth victim who may, or may not, be still alive. That makes it even more urgent that we track down George.'

Dave Armstrong spoke up. 'On that score we keep drawing a blank. So far we can find no trace of a George Reed anywhere in our files.'

'So is he still living abroad?'

'We know he was in the UK when his brother died.'

'So how come he hasn't shown up on any of our checks?'

'Maybe he's using a different name!' suggested Tait.

Jack began nodding. 'It's a logical thing to do if you want to distance yourself from such a dysfunctional family. George is most likely the product of incest by a hated sex offender. If Edward had been deliberately crippled by someone after revenge then George

246

might be worried that he might get the same treatment. Guilt by association.'

'It's a theory but it just makes it more difficult to trace him,' said Armstrong.

'And tracing George Reed has just become the focus of the investigation', said Jack. 'So let's get to it!'

Slade left the incident room and made his way to his office. He glanced down at his watch as he passed Armstrong.

'Where the hell has Donna got to. See if you can find out!'

Chapter 64

Donna felt something tapping away at her foot. She tried to open her eyes and allow them to adjust to the gloom. One eye felt swollen and remained closed. With the other she saw that she was in some kind of storeroom with a concrete floor. The room was dark with the only light coming from a very dirty transom window high up the wall.

Where was she? How did she get here?

She could recall struggling with the house owner George Smith but after that everything was a blank.

Her face really hurt and she could taste something metallic in her mouth.

She realised that it was blood.

There was that tapping at her foot again and she pulled her foot away to stop it.

As she did so she realised that her legs were bound together with some kind of strong adhesive tape.

She tried to get up but her hands were secured behind her back with what felt like plastic cable ties.

Squinting with her one good eye she looked around. In a corner partially covered by an old tarpaulin was a large chest freezer.

Donna's heart began beating fast as she came to a sickening realisation.

That might be for me!

Something tapped her foot again and she heard a muffled whimpering coming from the shadows.

Looking around she saw a young girl was sitting upright off to one side.

Although her legs were free her hands were bound together with tape and cable ties secured her to a heavy metal workbench.

There was a gag around her mouth and her eyes were wide with fear.

Donna immediately recognised her.

It was the missing girl, Theresa Harvey.

Chapter 65

Jack stood in his office in front of Dave Armstrong. His face betraying his concern. 'Dave, it's just not like Donna to go somewhere and not let us know what she's doing. What have you found out?'

'Control room have been unable to get a location for her radio which is not normal. They should be able to track it. They also can't open it to listen in to it. There's something not right Jack.'

'What about her mobile phone?'

'Likewise.'

'What about any tracker on her vehicle?'

'Henderson took the unmarked car to Cambois. Donna was using her own vehicle.'

'Have we got anything else?'

Dave shook his head. 'Nothing that we didn't already know. She was cracking on with the list of Transit vehicles that might fit the bill of the one we're looking for. Visiting each owner in turn. It was a longer list than we thought so she and Mike Henderson had divided it up by rough areas. They each took half.'

'You've got a copy of her half?'

'Yes, Mike gave it to me.' Dave handed over several pages of printed A4. Now she's gone missing, he's a bit pissed off that they divided it up. He's blaming himself that they didn't stick together. He's getting really concerned.'

'Aren't we all. Hindsight is a wonderful thing.' Jack started scrolling down the list. 'This is a long list.'

'You can see why they decided to divvy it up.'

'Any way of further reducing it?'

'Not without speaking to Donna. I don't know which ones she has or hasn't visited.'

As they spoke Jack ran his finger down the sheets of papers. 'There must be dozens.'

'We can probably cross some off the list if Donna has already updated the HOLMES receiver with any 'returned actions' so far.'

'Good thinking. That might slash several off the list.'

'It will still leave a lot left to work through.'

Jack was staring at the list deep in thought. 'Dave, I want you to ask the HOLMES analyst to run a cross check.'

'Using what search parameters?'

'We should already have logged into the system everyone who has been visited or actioned so far during the course of the enquiry. I want an analyst to cross check that with the list of Transit owners. Let's see if it throws up any matches.'

'Got it!' said Armstrong, already heading for the door.

Slade looked down at the list and felt very anxious.

Donna. What trouble have you got yourself into?

Chapter 66

George Smith yanked the cellar door open and switched on the harsh fluorescent light. The girl was tied to the heavy wooden table and the police woman was still lying on the floor, her wrists and hands bound tightly.

Both were awake and staring up at him with fear in their eyes.

How had everything gone wrong so quickly?

What clue had he left that had led the Police to his door?

None of it made any sense. He had been so careful.

What was clear was that he had to sort this mess out. And quickly.

He would have liked to have kept the young girl longer but it had all become too dangerous. The cops couldn't have a lot on him otherwise it wouldn't have been one lone police woman. They would have descended like locusts.

Once they realised that one of their own was missing they would be back. The next time they would be mob handed. He had to get rid of the evidence... and do it fast.

He had to get rid of the girl... and the Police officer.

Chapter 67

Jack was sitting at his desk when the phone began to ring. It was Ged Kirkby from the C.S.I. Department.

'I'm just calling to see if you've heard the good news from Berwick C.I.D.'

'I could do with some good news just at the minute.'

'The DNA has come back from their rapes. It's a positive match with your former suspect Alan Hall. Berwick are preparing a file and are going to be asking for him to be produced from prison. He's got a lot of difficult questions to answer.'

'Great news Ged. Sounds like he's dead to rights.'

'I'd say he's well and truly screwed Jack.'

'Thanks for passing on some good news for a change.'

Jack had hardly put down the phone when there was a knock on his door and Henderson hurried in.

'I'm sorry to disturb you Boss but it's getting to me. I shouldn't have let Donna visit the Transit owners alone.'

'Donna's a very capable cop. She would have been straight in contact if she had any inkling that something wasn't right. I can see from the list that it's extensive.'

'I know but…'

At that moment Chris Tait appeared clutching a piece of paper.

'Boss, I managed to locate newspaper reports of the accident in Stannington. It's true that Edward Reed was seriously injured. For a while he wasn't expected to recover.'

'Whoever hit him might have done the world a favour if he'd finished the job,' growled Henderson.

'The thing is… the newspaper article gave an address for Reed… Stannington Grange up in the Stannington area.'

'That's good work. Raise an 'action' and have someone visit and see if we can get any more information about our dead suspect.'

Chris was just about to leave when Jack suddenly stopped him.

'Hang on a minute. That address sounds familiar. I remember thinking it sounded a bit upmarket.'

He snatched up several sheets of paper from his desk and began scanning through them.

'I thought so. It's on the list as one of the addresses of the transit owners… a George Smith.' He frowned, 'It's on Donna's half of the list.'

Chris Tait looked shocked. 'You don't think that George Smith could really be…'

'George Reed!' said Jack finishing his sentence.

'Boss, I'll bet you a pound to a piece of shit he's our man. It looks like our luck might be finally changing,' said Henderson.

'It's not luck, it's been a lot of bloody hard graft!'

Jack was already out of his seat and snatching up his car keys.

Hurrying through the door he called back to Chris Tait, 'Get on the radio and inform the rest of the team. Give them Smith's address. Then shout up to the control room for some urgent backup in case any units are closer.'

As he hurtled down the corridor he saw Dave Armstrong coming out of the H.MET office. 'Dave, come with me!'

Slade took the steps down to the rear yard two at a time, closely followed by Armstrong.

Running across to his BMW Jack jumped in and started it up.

Armstrong didn't even have time to close the passenger door before Slade was pulling forward and out of the station yard.

Please God… let us be in time.

Chapter 68

As he was driving down into Morpeth, Mike Robson heard Jack's request over the radio for back up. Cutting through the town centre he crossed the old stone bridge by the castle and headed South towards the main A1.

His partner Steve Black shouted in to control that they were attending, but were still State Zero and available for any firearms incidents.

Taking the slip road onto the A1, Mike put his foot down, watching the needle of the speedometer swing sharply to the right as he accelerated up to one hundred and twenty. In the passenger seat Steve Black clicked down the switch setting off the blues and twos giving other motorists advance warning of their approach.

Mike shot past a long stream of traffic.

Stannington was only a few miles away.

Slade was heading for the same location except from the South. With great difficulty he tried to keep his mind fully focused on the road as he threw his BMW around the bends. Conscious that his private vehicle was not fitted with blues and twos he was well aware that if he had an accident there would be hell to pay. He doubted that the insurance would be happy paying out for any damage to his car.

In the passenger seat Dave Armstrong was clutching the sides of his seat as if his life depended on it.

At this speed he hoped that it didn't.

Slade gripped the wheel tightly, concentrating on the road ahead but his thoughts kept returning to Donna.

Was it his fault that the workload had caused her to split the actions and travel to the house alone?

Was he already too late to save her?

What about the missing girl Theresa Harvey?

Was she even still alive?

His mind wandered to the school photograph of the smiling blue-eyed teenager with the flowing blond hair and his heart sank.

Like many young abductees had she been murdered within hours of being taken?

Was she already dead, packaged in bin bags and frozen for disposal?

He tried to shut his mind to the thought of having to break the worst possible news to yet another grieving family.

Clenching his jaw he accelerated around a bend and felt the back end of the car starting to slide. Coming out of the bend he countered the slide, put on a slight acceleration and felt the car get back in line.

It was a long straight stretch and he stamped his foot hard down on the pedal and felt himself being forced back into his seat.

Chapter 69

Hurrying to the freezer George Smith gathered up the remaining body parts. They were still covered in the heavy-duty plastic that his brother had used to wrap them almost forty years before.

Throwing them into a large bin bag he struggled back up the stairs and outside to the drive where he heaved them in through the open side door into the cargo hold.

George stood panting by the van and looked up at the old semi derelict farmhouse. It crossed his mind that if it meant destroying evidence, he could set fire to the place. The land was the only thing of real value.

He had always hated the place as it held such bad memories of his childhood. When his mother died and left it to him, he had thought seriously about selling it, but just wanted to get away and start a new life. At least it gave somewhere for his brother to live.

Once Edward had died he was happy to empty it and stick it on the market for a quick sale.

Or so he had thought.

It was whilst clearing the cellar that he had come across the two freezers containing his brother's handiwork from the mid-eighties. After the car accident Edward had clearly not been in a position to dispose of the bodies himself, and could hardly ask anyone for help. They had remained there frozen for almost forty years.

Yet another of his brother's dirty secrets.

Revealing the contents of the cellar to the Police and the ensuing gruesome media coverage was hardly conducive to a quick sale… if any sale at all.

Who would want to buy a house where murdered corpses had been stored in the basement? Easier and better financially to get rid of the bodies and say nothing.

Leaving the van side door open he hurried back inside and, grabbing a large knife from the kitchen, hurried back down the steps to the basement.

The Police officer was lying on the floor staring silently up at him. Cops weren't stupid. She would know that having seen his face he was not going to allow her to live.

He contemplated killing both his captives where they lay, but dragging two dead weights up the cellar steps would be almost impossible. Best to take them away from the farmhouse and kill them wherever he decided to dump their bodies.

Looking down at the young girl sitting on the cold floor and sobbing, he took his knife and quickly sliced through the cable ties securing her to the workbench. Grabbing her arm he dragged her roughly to her feet.

As he tried to move her to the van, she kept stumbling. She was clearly finding difficulty walking having been cramped and tied securely for so long.

He placed the knife against her neck. 'Try to get away and I'll slit your throat. Understand?'

The girl nodded as tears streamed down her face.

He half guided, half dragged her up the stairs and outside towards the parked van when he heard the noise. It was very faint but definitely the distant wailing of a police siren.

His heart was beating fast and his breath became shallow.

The sound was some distance away but getting nearer. Tugging the girl in the direction of the parked Transit he heard a much closer sound.

That of a car sliding to a halt on the driveway.

He knew his time had run out.

Chapter 70

At first glance the farmhouse looked derelict and deserted as Slade skidded to a halt on the overgrown driveway. Then looking up the side of the house he saw the dark blue Transit.

'He's here. Shout for assistance!' Jack yelled out as he leaped from the car.

In the distance Slade could already hear the two tones of a police patrol car getting closer.

As Armstrong called the control room requesting urgent assistance, Slade ran across to the van. The side door was open and a quick glance revealed a few damp packages lying inside. They were wrapped in plastic and covered with a thin coating of frost.

He turned around. That was when he saw George Smith standing by the rear door of the farmhouse. He was not alone.

Smith was dragging a young girl who was stumbling and unsteady as if drugged. In one hand he held a long-bladed kitchen knife against the girl's neck. Despite her unkempt hair and dirt covering her face and legs Slade immediately recognised Theresa Harvey from her photograph.

She was alive!

On seeing Jack, Smith came to an abrupt stop.

He glared at Slade as Dave Armstrong appeared at his friend's side.

Jack was conscious that the two-tone siren had stopped, and only seconds later he heard the unmistakable sound of tyres sliding to a halt on the road in front of the house.

Slade and Armstrong's eyes never left Smith, Theresa… or the knife.

Smith looked like a trapped animal, and pulling the girl closer to him raised his right hand. Jack took a step forward and saw the long blade of the kitchen knife glint in the sun.

'Keep back!'

Slade and Armstrong stopped instantly.

'Put the knife down George. Let her go,' pleaded Slade raising his hands. 'Just put the knife down please.'

Instead, Smith placed the blade against Theresa's throat and her eyes widened in terror.

'Come any closer and I'll slit the bitch's throat!'

Steve Black had knocked off the two tones and blue lights about a quarter of a mile from the old farmhouse. As Mike Robson pulled their BMW in front of the derelict house, he saw that on the muddy drive was another car. He immediately recognised it as Jack Slade's BMW.

Both patrol officers jumped out with Mike in the lead, and started towards where they could see Slade and Armstrong standing beside a Transit van at the side of the house.

Mike saw Jack Slade who was standing in front raise his hands. He couldn't see around the corner but heard Slade call to someone to put the knife down.

Mike stopped in his tracks and silently held a hand in the air, an indication to his partner Steve Black to hold back. Backing away from where the two detectives were standing, the two armed response officers stealthily made their way past the front of the house and down the far side where they could get a clear view of the rear.

A quick peek along the back of the house and in a split-second Mike Robson had processed everything he needed to know about the unfolding drama.

He saw a man with his back towards them. His arm was restraining a young girl, holding her close as a barrier between him and the two detectives.

The man was brandishing a large kitchen knife which he was pressing against the terrified girl's neck.

Mike Robson had applied for the ARV department with eight years' service. There had been several psychological evaluations, regular firearms qualifying on the range, and constant training for various scenarios.

This was what all that training had led up to.

Mike weighed up his options and silently eased around the corner.

The correct procedure in such a life-threatening scenario was to request authorisation from the Force Operations Manager. This was a Chief Inspector based at Control Room who monitored all on-going serious incidents where Taser or firearms could be required and it was up to the F.O.M. to authorise any such deployment.

However, it always remained an option for any firearms officer to self-deploy if they felt the need was urgent in any dynamic unfolding situations.

Situations such as this!

Mike became emotionally detached, automatically switching into training mode.

Any form of empathy for the man in front of him could only hinder him and put lives in danger.

With the knifeman's attention fully focused on the two detectives confronting him, Robson cautiously eased around the corner.

Raising his Glock 17 nine millimetre semi-automatic, he began stealthily moving forward.

Throughout he remained impassive, detached, almost robotic, having practiced this so many times before in training scenarios.

Except this time, it was for real.

His grip remained steady. His gaze never wavering from the knifeman who was now shouting.

'Back off… or I'll kill her!'

Slade and Armstrong slowly retreated backwards.

Smith was dragging the terrified girl towards the open side door of the Transit van.

The two detectives saw Robson and moved to one side.

It gave him a clear line of fire.

Mike's glance flickered to Jack and their eyes met for a fraction of a second.

It is always the decision of the armed officer whether or not to fire.

Nobody else can ever make that irreversible decision to take a life, but in that glance, both knew what the other was thinking.

In the same instant some sixth sense seemed to alert Smith to the officer's presence.

He turned sharply to face Mike who was pointing his weapon rock steady in a two-handed combat grip.

'Armed police! Drop your…'

He never got to finish the sentence.

Everything happened so fast… but in Mike's brain it seemed as if in slow motion.

The terrified girl tried to pull free as her abductor struggled to restrain her.

Smith raised his arm and a flash of sunlight glinted off the blade.

Before he could bring it down on the girl there was a split second of opportunity.

Robson took it.

He squeezed the trigger.

There was a loud sharp crack and a spit of flame.

Smith's eyes opened wide, uncomprehending as the nine millimetre round travelling at 1104 feet per second struck him just to the left of his nose. Instantly bone fragments, hair and brain matter exploded from the back of Smith's skull, splattering both him and his intended victim in a cloud of red mist.

The girl pulled free just as Robson instinctively pulled the trigger for a second time, in what firearms officers refer to as a 'double tap'.

The second bullet struck Smith mid chest just below his throat.

It made no difference.

Smith was already history the instant that the first bullet struck.

He was dead long before his body hit the ground.

No flying backwards through the air arms outstretched as Jack had seen countless times in the movies and on television.

There was just a sharp jerk of the head from the first round, and he dropped to the ground, as if he had been a marionette and the puppeteer had cut his strings ending the performance.

Theresa Harvey, released from her captor's hold, ran to the detectives flinging her arms around Jack and crushing him to her.

She turned to glance over her shoulder at her abductor.

George Smith lay motionless on the ground, a large dark red void where the back of his head had been.

As if not understanding what had happened, Theresa looked down at her clothes, now soiled with blood and grey matter.

That's when the screaming began.

The two armed officers knelt down beside the prone figure of George Smith checking for signs of life.

Steve Black was already on the radio requesting an ambulance but everyone knew it would only be for Theresa.

George Smith, blood and brain matter spread out across the rear garden path, was way beyond any first aid.

His next journey would be in a body bag.

Jack looked across and saw Mike Robson step away from the corpse and holster his weapon.

As the firearms officer headed towards his patrol car, Jack caught his eye. Robson nonchalantly shrugged his shoulders as he passed and Jack was sure he heard him whisper under his breath.

'Oops,'

Ignoring the fact that the house was a crime scene Dave Armstrong entered and much to Jack's relief emerged a few minutes later with Donna Shaw.

She was bedraggled, head swollen and one eye shut. She walked unsteadily on her feet and was supported by Armstrong.

But she was alive.

Slade looked down at Smith lying on the path.

261

Any loss of life was a tragedy but Jack could feel no pity.

He was pleased that it was George Smith's lifeless body on the ground and not that of Theresa Harvey ... or Donna Shaw.

Chapter 71

Forth banks police station was a maelstrom of activity. The telephones in the reception area were ringing incessantly and the front office besieged by media hoping to put their own individual slant on the story. They would already be framing their questions in such a way as to grab a headline.

As Jack passed through the front office one of them shouted across at him. 'Is it right that the deceased was unarmed when shot and killed by the police.'

Jack frowned and didn't reply.

He might not have had a firearm, but how many of the press vultures would be complaining if it was their daughter's neck that Reed was about to slice through?

Mike Robson had managed to slip into the nick from the rear yard before the press arrived. That suited him. He didn't want any newspaper photographs published showing him dressed in body armour and carrying his Glock.

Robson was well aware that his sidearm would have to be seized as part of the investigation and that there would be the obligatory referral to the Independent Police Complaints Commission.

His every action would be scrutinised for any deviation from policy and procedure. What had taken seconds would be pored over for months in minute detail.

Mike actually felt fairly relaxed despite the storm he would soon face.

He knew that he had saved at least one young girl's life and quite probably that of a Police Officer.

He also knew that one very evil man was now no longer a danger to anyone.

For Mike Robson it was a job well done.

Superintendent Parker was updated and informed that the murders of the missing girls were solved pending a Coroner's decision and more importantly that the hostage had been recovered alive.

Armstrong claimed to have seen the Superintendent smile but Slade said that it was just his head beginning to crack open under the pressure.

As predicted Parker was no longer keeping the enquiry at arm's length and was now more than willing to accept the glory for his team's success.

Jack was equally happy to leave him to it and slip away to the calm of his office.

The enquiry had taken a heavy toll and he was exhausted. Tonight, there would be a lot of paperwork to complete but tomorrow he could take a step back and start delegating to Dave and the team.

A trip to Belford was on the cards. There was an eleven-year-old boy who was wanting to spend some quality birthday time with his dad… and vice versa.

On the stairs Slade spotted Chris Tait. 'Well Chris. You were right about it being George. You were also right about the name change.'

'A lucky guess.'

'Yeah. Well, my team knows my motto about how you get lucky… and you've definitely worked hard on this one.'

'It's been a great experience. The word is out that the additional team members brought in from other Commands are already being given the dates that they have to return. They're saying that everything will be wound up in a couple of weeks and cops sent back to their stations.'

'There's still plenty of work to do before that.'

'I hope you'll bear me in mind if you're ever seconding staff for any future enquiries.'

'Actually, I think the West can probably manage without you.'

Chris Tait looked back quizzically.

'I'm going to ask that you be permanently assigned to the squad… if you want to be.'

Tait looked shocked and for one second Jack thought he was about to give him a hug.

Now that would be a good one for the serious rumour squad.

FIN

David Jewell is a North East-based award-winning writer, a producer and director. His six-part television series "Write On" showcased various international writers from the North East and his feature length documentary film "From Pit To Parliament" concerning the life of Labour politician Ronnie Campbell was nominated for a Royal Television Society Award.

With 31 Years police experience, rising to the rank of inspector, David has worked at the sharp end of some of the toughest areas in the north east receiving several commendations during his service.

His writing captures, the voices and attitudes of a tough, working-class northern city, and often the black humour of those characters that inhabit it.

"Death Chill" is the second novel to feature his character Detective Inspector Jack Slade and is a very dark and gritty murder mystery set in the city of Newcastle upon Tyne.

Printed in Great Britain
by Amazon

44617871R00155